Let it
it
Glow

Let it Glow

Marissa Meyer and Joanne Levy

FEIWEL AND FRIENDS
NEW YORK

A Feiwel and Friends Book
An imprint of Macmillan Publishing Group, LLC
120 Broadway, New York, NY 10271 • mackids.com

Our books may be purchased in bulk for promotional, educational, or business use.
Please contact your local bookseller or the Macmillan Corporate and Premium
Sales Department at (800) 221-7945 ext. 5442 or by email at
MacmillanSpecialMarkets@macmillan.com.

Library of Congress Cataloging-in-Publication Data is available.

First edition, 2024
Book design by Maria W. Jenson
Feiwel and Friends logo designed by Filomena Tuosto
All emojis designed by OpenMoji—the open-source emoji and icon project.
License: CC BY-SA 4.0
Printed in the United States of America by Lakeside Book Company,
Harrisonburg, Virginia

ISBN 978-1-250-36067-0 (hardcover)
1 3 5 7 9 10 8 6 4 2

ISBN 978-1-250-36081-6 (paperback)
1 3 5 7 9 10 8 6 4 2

For Sloane and Delaney, who arrived on Christmas Eve and will always be the most incredible gifts that Santa ever brought me
—M

For all the parents, including mine, who ever opened their hearts and homes to adopt a child —J

CHAPTER 1
Aviva

"YOU'RE GETTING TO BE SUCH A PRO WITH THOSE CHOP-sticks," my grandmother said. We were at our favorite Chinese restaurant in the middle of the dim sum rush on a Sunday. It was our special day together—one I looked forward to every week, and not only because we stuffed ourselves with dumplings and then hung out at the mall, either. (Though that was a major perk.)

Some kids think their grandmothers are boring or too old to be fun, but my bubbe is the Best. She's smart, sassy, and loves being the center of attention—just like me.

When I looked up to agree with her about the chopsticks, the slippery dumpling slid out of them onto the tablecloth with a plop.

"Whoops!" I exclaimed, grinning at her. "Maybe not as good as you think!"

She leaned closer conspiratorially. "I guess we'll just have to come back next week. After all, practice makes perfect!"

We both laughed. She'd been saying this for years. But really, who needed an excuse to go out for dim sum?

"Speaking of practice," Bubbe said, "I have great news."

I stabbed the dumpling with a chopstick and lifted it up carefully so it wouldn't slide off. "Oh?" I said before I shoved the entire doughy package of deliciousness into my mouth.

"The holiday pageant at Rowena Village is coming up later this month."

I was still chewing, but said, "Okay," as I reached for the steamer basket of sticky rice. "Sounds fun."

Bubbe lived at a senior center—not because she was old, but because she hated to cook for herself, all her friends lived there or were close by, and there were fun programs almost every night. I knew part of it was also that her eyesight had gotten pretty bad and she couldn't drive anymore, but that hadn't slowed her down yet.

Still, the way she talked about Rowena Village made it sound really good. Like a year-round summer camp. More than once I'd asked her when I could move in. (She always laughed, even though I wasn't totally joking.)

"You should be in it," said Bubbe.

Sticky rice instantly forgotten, I looked up at her. "Really?"

"Of course. You're a born performer!"

"You are not wrong!" I sang, shimmying in my seat.

She winked as if to say, *Of course I'm not wrong!* and picked up a har gow dumpling with her chopsticks. "The best part? I made sure they're including a Hanukkah number this year." She took a bite of the dumpling, not dropping the rest. She was such a pro.

Once she was done chewing, she pointed the half-eaten dumpling at me. "You'll be in the Hanukkah number and will shine like the star you are, my bubbeleh."

See? This was one of the reasons I loved my grandmother. She knew I was meant to be a star. In movies or on Broadway. Wherever.

Except . . .

"Of course I want to be in the pageant, Bubbe," I said. "I want to sing and dance and perform. You know I do. But . . ." I reached again for the sticky rice, dropping my eyes to the steamer basket, not sure how to finish the sentence.

"But what, Vivvy?"

I grabbed one of the packets of rice wrapped in a lotus leaf and plunked it on my plate. Then I gently pulled at the corner to open it. Yes, I was stalling.

"Vivvy?"

"Fine," I muttered through a sigh. "I'm just not that Jewish."

"Speak up, bubbeleh."

"I said"—I looked up at her—"I'm not very Jewish."

Her eyes narrowed a little. "What do you mean? You're Jewish. There is no 'very.'"

"I just don't *feel* very Jewish." I shrugged. "We don't celebrate anything. Dad's not even Jewish. And, well, you know, there's that whole I'm-adopted thing. I just don't feel very Jewish. How can I do a Hanukkah number?"

Bubbe put down her chopsticks slowly and reached for her small cup of jasmine tea. She took a drink before returning it to the table. Now *she* was stalling, her eyebrows knitted together like she was thinking hard about what she should say.

Finally, she looked straight at me with the kind of serious face that made me want to fidget and squirm. "That you are adopted has nothing to do with it. You were wanted and instantly loved by your family the second they brought you home. As a baby, you were taken to the mikveh and given a Hebrew name and became as Jewish as if you'd had a Jewish birth mother. You will have a bat mitzvah next year like your brother had a bar mitzvah. And your father not being Jewish does not make *you* less Jewish. Aviva Libby Davis. You. Are. Jewish."

She stared at me until I nodded in agreement. Then she reached for the teapot. "But as for your family's lack of observance, well, I wish that was different. Your parents had agreed you kids would be raised Jewish, and I'd hoped that when it came time for Benny to study for his bar mitzvah, your family would have taken it more seriously and not just done the bare minimum. Though I do think your brother was glad he did it in the end."

She sighed and shook her head before she met my eyes again and said, "But, Vivvy, you can always celebrate with me. I would love to take you to synagogue for the High Holidays next year. Or to the Jewish community center for dances or programs. If you want to enroll in Jewish Sunday school or go to Saturday morning services, we can do that, too."

"Really?" I said, not sure I wanted to go to synagogue for regular services. But it was the first time she'd ever suggested that, and I believed she would take me, even though she didn't normally go every week. And Jewish Sunday school? I hadn't even known that was an option. Benny's bar mitzvah lessons had been mostly online, but going to a place with other Jewish kids might be fun.

"Of course"—Bubbe nodded—"you just need to say the word. But it has to come from you so your mother doesn't think I'm pressuring you. It's up to you how observant you want to be. But no matter what you decide, you are nonetheless one hundred percent Jewish."

She seemed really sure, even though I still had my doubts. "Seriously, you think I'm Jewish enough to be in a Hanukkah number in the pageant?" I asked. "Even though I don't really celebrate Hanukkah?"

She nodded. "Yes, of course."

I gave her the side-eye. "Will I get to sing?"

She grinned as she filled my teacup. "I'm counting on it."

"And dance?"

"I don't know if there will be dancing, but if there is, I fully expect you to dance. Sign-up is tomorrow evening at the center. Ask your mother to bring you."

I couldn't help it. I jumped up out of my seat and threw my arms around my grandmother. "Oh, Bubbe, this really is the best news. I'm going to make you so proud."

"Of course you will." She laughed as she hugged me back with one arm and put the teapot down with the other, a little spilling out of the spout. "You always make me proud, bubbeleh. Always. But I think this is going to be your moment. I can't wait."

Neither could I.

CHAPTER 2

Holly

THE ELF IS A TRAITOR!

This thought had popped into my head one hour before the bell rang to let us out of school Friday afternoon, and I hadn't been able to concentrate on anything else since.

Instead of completing the worksheet on local governments I was supposed to be focusing on, I'd spent that hour bent over my notebook, jotting down all my new thoughts. I liked to think Ms. Chang would understand. She was my favorite teacher because she always assigned the most interesting writing prompts—things like *What mythical creature would you want to keep as a pet?* (Dragon, obviously.) Or *If archaeologists discovered the lost city of Atlantis, what sort of technology would they find?* (Magical headsets that let you communicate with mermaids!)

Ms. Chang even once said my stories were really good and that I had the "potential to be a published writer someday." When I heard those words, my whole body lit up inside like a Christmas tree. I mean, my grandpa had been telling me this for years, but he was family, so I wasn't sure it counted. Coming from a teacher, it felt extra special.

Usually Ms. Chang reserved the last thirty minutes of class for reading or freewriting, but we'd been behind on Friday, so we were stuck doing social studies instead. It was hard enough to pay attention to social studies on a normal day, but when my fingers were itching to work on a story, it was impossible.

Then on Friday evening there were chores to do, and I had to make dinner for me and Gramps because Mom had worked late at the bank again. After we ate, Gramps asked if I wanted to watch the newest spy movie on demand, and I couldn't pass up an invitation like that. Besides, I'd thought that I would have all Saturday to work on my elf-traitor idea, but *no*. Mom finally had a day off, and instead of getting our Christmas tree like we were supposed to, the whole day had turned into one long, tedious slog of errands and housework. Grocery shopping, the pharmacy, the hardware store for new strands of Christmas lights for the so-far-nonexistent tree, followed by laundry, dishes, vacuuming . . . It was never-ending.

So when I woke up Sunday morning, I didn't give anyone a chance to derail me. Mom had gone for a run and Gramps was sleeping, so I left a note on the counter, bundled up in my coat and boots, and hightailed it to the public library a couple of blocks away. I ran the whole way through the slush, my backpack bouncing on my shoulders. I waved to Ms. Clark at the front desk as I hurried past, heading straight for my favorite spot.

The library was like a second home to me, and all the librarians knew me by name. Mr. Merino, the youth librarian, would even set aside new books for me when they came in, especially anything with a dragon on the cover.

My reading nook was waiting—a bright-yellow beanbag chair that lived in the bay window behind the graphic novel section. I dropped my backpack on the floor and slumped into the squishy beanbag, exhaling in the same way Gramps did when he finished the long, slow walk from his bedroom at the end of the hall to his favorite recliner in the living room.

I fished my notebook from my bag and flipped to the pages I'd started working on in class. My brilliant epiphany was written in the margin at the top, underlined twice.

The elf is a traitor!

For Christmas this year, I'd decided to write an original story as a gift for Gramps. I wanted it to have a holiday theme, and had started writing about Santa Claus and a sidekick elf on the Polar Express. They were trying to take all the toys from the workshop at the North Pole to train stations around the world, so that the helper mall Santas could distribute them to the kids on the Nice list. But things kept going wrong. The train would break down, or part of the track was missing and they had to find a different route, and even the toys had begun to mysteriously disappear!

Except, halfway through writing the story, I still didn't know *why* these things were happening. It had been bothering me for days.

But not anymore. Santa was being sabotaged . . . by Barnabus, the traitorous elf!

It felt like a perfect twist, and Gramps was always telling me that a good story needed a great twist. He would know. He was a writer, too, and had written dozens of novels. (Mostly murder mysteries, which I wasn't old enough to read yet.) He had retired a few years ago because his arthritis made it difficult for him to type, though he still dabbled in the occasional short story.

No one would have suspected Santa's cheerful little helper to be the villain, so I knew I was onto something. But it also opened up a whole bunch of new problems that I needed to figure out.

Most importantly—*why* did Barnabus want to sabotage the train and ruin Christmas? Maybe he had been on the Naughty list when he was a kid, and now he wanted the toys to go to the naughty kids? Or maybe he wanted all the toys for himself? Or maybe he was the long-lost son of the Grinch, wanting to finish the job his dad had started years ago?

The next few hours flew by as I brainstormed new ideas and wrote out the next part of the story. It was different from the things I usually liked to write—more reindeer, fewer fairies—but it was turning into a fun story that I knew Gramps would love. I couldn't wait to give it to him on Christmas morning.

Once my stomach started to growl, I packed up my things again and waved goodbye to the librarians on my way out. The air was crisp and smelled like fresh snow was on its way, and now that I wasn't in a hurry, I could enjoy all the lights strung on the eaves and the wreaths hung in doorways. Our town felt so enchanted this time of year, like the whole world was celebrating together.

When I got back to the apartment, I skipped the elevator and took the stairs to the second floor. I opened the door quietly in case Gramps was resting.

As soon as I entered the apartment, though, I could hear the TV on in the back bedroom. Sherlock, our gray tabby cat, meowed from his favorite perch on top of the kitchen cabinets. He stood and gave a long feline stretch before jumping down to the counter and then to the floor. He meowed again and brushed past my ankles as he pranced over to his empty food bowl.

"Hey, Sherlock," I said, giving him a quick scratch on his neck as I set my backpack down. "Did Gramps forget to feed you?"

I filled his bowl before making my way down the hall.

"I'm home!" I called, knocking softly on Gramps's door, which was partly open. "Can I get you any—"

My gaze landed on a form sprawled across the floor. I gasped. "Gramps!"

He groaned as I dropped to my knees beside him.

"Gramps, are you okay?"

"Yes, yes," he said with a grunt. "I'm fine, Holly. Can you help me up?"

But he didn't sound fine, or look fine. He was lying on his side, his walking cane on the floor a few feet away.

"What happened?" I asked, taking his arm.

"I just lost my balance," he said, accepting my help. "I'm not hurt. It happened just before you got home."

I frowned, shaking a little as I helped him up onto the bed. He sat down and exhaled, resting his elbows on his legs. I grabbed his cane and leaned it against the mattress. I couldn't help looking around at the furniture in the room. The sharp corners of the dresser and his nightstand. Mom had told me that falling was dangerous for older people. It wasn't like they could just bounce back up, or heal from a bad bruise practically overnight, like I could. If he hit his head or broke a bone, it could put him in the hospital . . . or worse.

"It's all right," Gramps said, and I knew he was trying to reassure me, but I was worried. No, more than worried. I was *scared*.

Neither of us wanted to say it, but this was the third time he'd fallen in the last couple of months. His balance was getting worse.

"I'm sorry," I said, sitting next to him. "I was at the library. I shouldn't have been gone for so long. I should have been—"

"Now, now, enough of that." He put an arm around my shoulders. "It's not your job to take care of me. Were you working on a new story at the library?"

"Um . . . yeah," I said. "But I can't tell you about it, because it's a surprise."

"I'm sure it will be fantastic. After all, storytelling runs in our blood." He smiled at me, like he always did when he reminded me that we had storytelling in common. But this time I thought he looked tired beneath that smile, and I couldn't help but feel like he was just trying to distract me from the real issue.

He said it wasn't my job to take care of him, but Mom worked so much, and there was no one else.

If I couldn't take care of him, who would?

CHAPTER 3
Aviva

HOURS AFTER MY WEEKEND DATE WITH BUBBE, I WAS AT the dinner table with my family, working up the courage to tell them I wanted to be in the holiday pageant at the senior center.

Why was I so nervous? My parents and brothers knew how much I loved to sing and dance and perform, but somehow it still felt weird. Like, were they going to think it was strange that I wanted to be in a Hanukkah number? Were they going to think I wanted to become religious? *Did* I want to become religious? What did it all mean?

All of this whirled around in my head while we ate and talked about . . . I don't even know because I was too busy thinking. And worrying. And trying to figure out how to tell them.

"Vivvy!" Dad barked loudly.

Startled, I nearly tossed my chicken wing across the table. "Gah! What?"

Dad chuckled and shook his head before saying, "I asked you if something's wrong. You've been so quiet tonight."

"Aw, Dad, why'd you ruin it?" teased Benny, my fourteen-year-old brother. "She's never quiet."

I gave him a look. "Dork."

He opened his mouth to show me his half-chewed dinner.

"Ew," I moaned, at the same time my seven-year-old brother, Aaron, whined, "*Mom!* Benny is being gross again!"

"Kids," Mom warned.

"Anyway," Dad said, drawing out the word. "Something on your mind?"

"I'm going to be in a holiday pageant!" I blurted out before turning toward Mom. "And I need you to take me tomorrow at five for the sign-ups at the senior center." Then, adding a smile, "Please and thank you."

Dad blinked. "Okay . . ."

"I mean," I said. "Can I?"

"Of course you can," Mom said. "That would be great for you. I know you were disappointed that your school didn't put on a play this year."

Disappointed? More like *devastated*.

"And Bubbe said I'm Jewish enough to be in the Hanukkah number," I added, even though I still wasn't so sure.

Mom and Dad exchanged a weird look.

"Of course you're Jewish enough," Mom said with a frown. "What would make you say that?"

I stabbed a carrot and swirled it around in the sauce on my plate. "I don't know."

"Vivvy?" Dad said, sounding concerned. "What's going on? Did some kids say something? Did someone say you're not Jewish? Or . . ." He blew out a loud breath. "Does this have something to do with me or your brothers?"

I looked up at him and could tell he was worried that someone had said racist things because he's Black and my brothers are biracial and I don't look like any of them. "No," I assured him, glancing at my brothers, too. "It's not that."

There was a long silence.

Aaron broke it. "Well, then? What is it?"

Benny snorted.

Dad shot the boys a glare before he said, "Vivvy, what's going on? Should we be concerned?"

"No. It's just . . ." I sighed, "It's just that we don't *act* very Jewish, so I guess I don't *feel* very Jewish. We don't celebrate anything or go to synagogue. I don't have any Jewish friends, and the only bar mitzvah I've ever been to was Benny's. I don't know . . . It would feel weird to be in a Hanukkah number when we don't even celebrate Hanukkah."

The room was quiet, other than the sound of Benny scooping more food onto his plate.

"That makes sense," Dad finally said. He looked at Mom. "She does have a point, Dee. Other than bar mitzvah lessons for Benny, it's not like we've ever actively practiced. Maybe we've been falling short there."

Mom turned to me and said, "As you know, your dad was raised in a Christian home. Conversion to Judaism was something we talked about before we got married, and as you can imagine, my mother petitioned for it. But we didn't feel it was necessary since neither of us was religious. As for not celebrating Hanukkah, we didn't want to buy into the commercialism of the season. Still, you kids are all Jewish—you know that. We may not go to synagogue very often, but being Jewish is about our culture and traditions, too."

I shrugged, not exactly sure what that even meant. *What* culture and traditions? I didn't celebrate Christmas or Easter, and we never went to church . . . but was being Jewish only about the things we *didn't* do?

Mom tilted her head. "You're going to have your bat mitzvah—assuming you want to—although that's awhile away yet."

"I do want one," I assured her. But I wasn't sure if I wanted one for myself or because I knew it was important to Bubbe. Of course, I loved any opportunity to perform, but did I really want the Jewish part of it? I wasn't a hundred percent sure.

"For now, what would make you feel Jewish, Vivvy?"

"Wait," Benny said. "Do we have to start going to synagogue on Saturdays? Because I have hockey."

"No one is asking anyone to make any changes," Dad said, and then turned to me, waiting for my answer.

What would make me feel Jewish enough to be in the Hanukkah number?

It was suddenly obvious. "I think we should have a real Hanukkah," I announced. "The whole thing—latkes, menorah, dreidels, all eight nights of it." After I said it, I held my breath and looked at Mom, worried that it was going to be too much.

"A real Hanukkah," she said. And then she smiled. "Okay. We can do that. Let's have a real Hanukkah."

I HAD JUST FINISHED TEXTING WITH BUBBE TO TELL HER the great news when Benny appeared in my bedroom doorway. I put my phone down on my nightstand and looked at him. "What's up?"

"Can I come in?"

I narrowed my eyes suspiciously—my big brother and I didn't

have many heart-to-hearts—but I could see on his face that something was bothering him.

"Sure." I scootched over, making room on my bed for him.

He sat down, scratching the back of his head. "I just wanted to say that I know what you meant when you said you didn't feel very Jewish."

Huh. Okay, so that was not what I was expecting. "Really? But you had a bar mitzvah and everything."

He nodded. "Yeah, and having my bar mitzvah was cool. But"—he glanced at the door and lowered his voice—"there are some kids at school who don't even believe we're Jewish. Like Black kids can't be Jewish?" He shook his head. "They think we just don't like Christmas or something. I don't have anything against Christmas, but that's not who we are. I wish people would get that. It's like . . . Sometimes it feels like we don't fit anywhere, you know?"

I did know. I'd seen how some people looked at our family. I could tell there were whispers about us. But Mom and Dad had always told us that no matter what anyone said, our family was held together with love, and *that* glue was stronger than other people's judgments about what a family should be and look like. But it still made me sad.

"I'm sorry, Benny," I said, leaning into him. I hated that some people were jerks. My family was awesome. "Do you ever wish you weren't Jewish? Like, would it be easier if you weren't?"

He shook his head. "No, it's not that. I'm glad I had my bar mitzvah. I'm proud of that. And all of us—our family, I mean." He sighed. "But people can be so clueless. I usually don't even mention it anymore. It's just easier if no one knows and everyone assumes I'm Christian . . . or nothing, like Dad."

"That's sad," I said. "That you feel you have to hide it."

"I don't hide it as much as I just don't deny being Christian."

Which is the same as hiding it, I thought but didn't say.

He shrugged. "I wish other people were cooler about it, you know?"

I wished people were cooler about a lot of things. It was stupid that people could not like someone because of their skin color or their religion—things that didn't even affect them. It didn't make any sense.

"Yeah." I nodded, not bothering to tell him that he should ignore other people and what they thought, like Mom always said, because sometimes that was impossible. "But hey, at least we'll get a real Hanukkah this year. Eight nights of presents!"

His serious expression shifted into a big grin. "And latkes," he said. "Don't forget the latkes!"

CHAPTER 4
Holly

"I'M TELLING YOU, THIS ROWENA VILLAGE LOOKS REALLY nice," said my mom. We were sitting at the dining table, sharing a pepperoni pizza from Lorenzo's. I was still picking at my first piece—I wasn't feeling so hungry—but all that was left of Mom's and Gramps's pieces were grease stains on their paper plates.

Lorenzo's pizza and paper plates were a Sunday night tradition for us. Mom often said that after a full week of working at the bank and getting me off to school and putting up with Gramps's ranting about how his arthritis made it hard to work his blasted smartphone (even though he managed just fine when it came to playing *Words with Friends*), she couldn't be expected to cook and do one more load of dishes, too.

Honestly, though? I think she just really liked pizza.

"Look at these pictures," said Mom, turning her laptop so we could both see. Normally screens weren't allowed at the table, but she was making an exception tonight, trying to do research on nearby senior centers. She scrolled through the website for Rowena Village, which was less than a mile away. It showed people around Gramps's age playing Scrabble, doing yoga, and even having birthday parties. Mom was right—everyone looked like they were enjoying themselves.

But it was a brochure. Of course they'd take pictures of people living their best lives there. But were they really?

I glanced at Gramps, who hadn't said anything but was frowning, his forehead creased.

"I know change is scary," said Mom hopefully, "but I really think this could be good for you. It would be nice to have a social life again. Make some friends." She lowered her voice and raised a suggestive eyebrow at my grandpa. "Maybe a lady friend?"

Gramps scoffed. "Not interested," he muttered.

I didn't know if that was true—the idea of him dating was too weird to contemplate—but I did know that Gramps always referred to my grandma as the love of his life. She'd passed away when I was little, and I was sad that the only real memory I had of her was sitting on her lap at Christmas and sharing one of her famous cinnamon rolls, the icing sticky on my fingers. If it wasn't for our photo albums, I wouldn't even have remembered what she looked like. Still, it felt special that every year Mom baked cinnamon rolls from her recipe.

Mom sighed. "Or . . . I don't know. Maybe we're rushing into things." She frowned at the computer screen. "We could look into having someone come in to help you when Holly's at school. And install some grab bars in the bathroom. Maybe it's time to replace your cane with a walker? I wonder how hard it would be to navigate the hallway . . ." She sighed again. "I don't know, Dad, I'm just worried."

Gramps tore his gaze from the photos and peered at my mom. For a second I thought he would declare, *Yep, that's that! I'm staying here, then!*

But instead, he looked from Mom to me and then, after a long moment, cleared his throat. "It won't hurt to go look at the place," he said, "But I'm not committing to anything."

Mom bit her lower lip. "You know I love having you here, and it's been so good for Holly and you—"

"Charlie," he said firmly. "I said we'd go take a look." He nodded at the screen. "Besides, it says here they have a library."

"Ooh!" I said. "I want to see the library!"

Gramps grunted in agreement. "You're my granddaughter, all right."

I grinned at him and took another bite of pizza, though it had gone cold. I could practically feel the relief emanating off my mom. This wasn't the first time she'd brought up the possibility of Gramps moving into an assisted living center, but it was the first time he hadn't seemed completely opposed. Maybe the last couple of falls had worried him, too.

The bite of pizza sat heavy in my stomach after I swallowed it down. "You won't move out before Christmas, will you?"

I tried to picture Christmas morning without my grandpa sitting in his recliner, watching me open my stocking. Eating cinnamon rolls and breakfast sausages while Mom put on a Christmas music playlist. Or opening all the books he'd bought for me, because Gramps was the only person who understood how much I really only wanted books for Christmas—not new clothes or another craft kit or anything else, just books. So every year, he would buy me a bunch from the local secondhand bookstore, picking them out himself and painstakingly wrapping each one, even though it was so hard for him to do with his arthritis. Maybe this year I'd tell Mom to get him some gift bags to put the books in instead.

"No, no," my mom said, shaking her head. "Even if we like Rowena Village, they said the earliest he could move in would be January."

"January!" exclaimed Gramps. "That's next month! I just said I'm not committing to anything, and you're telling me to go pack my bags. No, I said I'd look. For down the road. *Way* down the road."

"Yes, of course," said Mom, shutting her laptop. "This is simply an exploratory mission. We'll go in and take the tour when I get home from work tomorrow."

"Tomorrow?" I said. "But we were supposed to get our tree tomorrow night."

Mom winced. "That's right, I forgot. But that's the only night that works to visit this center." She looked at me apologetically. "We'll go for the tree soon. All right?"

I frowned, doing the math in my head. Christmas was only two weeks away.

But what could I say? Clearly, Mom had already made up her mind.

"Okay," I grumbled.

Mom reached across the table and took my hand. "Thanks, Holly." Then she took my grandpa's hand, too. "You know I worry when you're home by yourself all day, but we don't need to rush into making any decisions. I only want what's best for you."

"I know," he said, his swollen fingers squeezing hers.

If this Rowena Village was even half as nice as they made it seem on their website, then someday Gramps was going to live there, and he wouldn't be here anymore, with me.

Who would I talk to about my stories? Who would help me when I got stuck on a tricky plot point or needed help making a character more interesting? Who would read my writing and give me just the right amount of feedback? Ms. Chang was great at encouraging me, but Gramps was a real published author who knew all the best writing tips.

I swallowed hard. "I'm going to miss you," I said, tears pooling in my eyes.

"Oh, my little Holly Tree." Gramps tugged me close. I stood and gave him a hug.

"I'm not going anywhere," he said softly into my ear. "We'll check it out to make your mother happy. I'm staying right here with you."

CHAPTER 5
Aviva

I UNBUCKLED AND JUMPED OUT OF THE CAR ALMOST before it came to a stop. Mom hollered my name.

"Sorry!" I yelled over my shoulder, already on my way to the door of the senior center, eager for my audition. To say I was pumped was the understatement of the century.

I was going to be onstage!

"Vivvy!" Aaron called out. "Wait up!"

With a sigh, I stopped and turned, waiting for my little brother. "Are you auditioning, too?"

His eyes widened in horror. "What? No! I'm here to watch you sing."

I grinned at him. He was so adorkable. "I'm going to crush it."

He nodded like there wasn't a doubt in his mind.

"All right, kids," Mom said as she caught up to us. "Do you know where you're going, Vivvy?"

"Yeah. Bubbe said it was in the social hall. The same place where we came to play bingo that time."

Mom grabbed the door and pulled it open. "Good. You kids go ahead while I check on your grandmother. I'll see you shortly."

Passing the front desk, Mom headed toward the residents' apartments, and I led Aaron to the social hall. "I bet there's going to be lots of Jewish kids there," I said, excited that maybe I'd get to make a new friend or two. "For the Hanukkah number."

"That would be cool," Aaron said.

"You sure you don't want to be in the show? Maybe there's a part that isn't singing or dancing."

Aaron cringed. "No way! I would die of stage fright."

"You wouldn't die," I assured him, hoping he'd change his mind when he saw all the other kids there to try out.

Voices drifted out of the social hall as we approached, making me even more excited to get in there. Once we stepped inside, a big whiteboard on an easel told us we were in the right place:

HOLIDAY PAGEANT—SIGN-UPS TODAY

I couldn't help it—I squealed in anticipation. There were voices coming from backstage and a few kids on the stage talking, too. But there was no microphone or spotlight set up. Weird.

"If you're here for the sign-ups, come on over."

I turned toward the voice to see a woman—about my grandmother's age—looking at us from the other side of the large room. She was holding a clipboard and had glasses pushed up on the top of her head, holding back wisps of silver hair that were escaping her thick braid. I didn't recognize her as one of Bubbe's friends, but she probably lived at the center.

"Hi," I said, skipping over. "I'm Aviva Davis. Sylvia Cohen's granddaughter. This is my brother, Aaron. We're here to try out for the pageant."

"Not *we!*" Aaron interjected, poking a finger into my arm. "Just her. I'm here to watch."

"I'm Doris, the show's director and talent wrangler," she said with a laugh. "My partner, Clara, is backstage with some of the other kids working on costumes—we only have a couple of weeks to get this pageant ready, so we need to hit the ground running."

"I can't wait!" I exclaimed. "It's going to be the best pageant ever! I've got my audition piece all ready. I'm going to do 'Memory' from *Cats*. I hope no one else has done that yet." I pointed up at the empty stage. "I guess I'm next?"

Doris smiled at me kindly. "Oh, we're not doing tryouts, hon. I'll just add your name to the list."

"But," I began, my heart sinking, "I'm ready to audition for the Hanukkah number. How will you know who should be the lead?"

Doris's smile turned into a frown. "Lead?"

I resisted the urge to roll my eyes. "Every production needs a lead: Grizabella in *Cats*, Elphaba in *Wicked*, Annie in . . . well, *Annie* . . ."

Doris glanced down at her clipboard and then back up to me. "In that case, so far you're it. No one else has signed up for the Hanukkah number." She turned toward Aaron. "Unless you want to be in it, too?"

Aaron shook his head. "Oh, uh, no, thanks."

Shut the front door. "No one else wants to be in the Hanukkah number? Like . . . no one?"

"Sorry, no." Doris shrugged. "We don't normally have a Hanukkah number."

Figured. Hanukkah never got any attention. I was used to it, mostly, but it felt like no one cared about Hanukkah. Everything was Christmas this and Santa Claus that. Yuletide Cheer and the Most Wonderful Time of the Year, blah, blah, blah. Last year when I'd gone to the gift store to get Bubbe a Hanukkah card, there had been exactly one—and it had been the same one I'd given her the year before.

Sigh.

"You can join the other kids," Doris said with a hopeful smile. "We're going to do a nativity play. You can be in that."

"But . . . I'm Jewish," I explained, even though it felt like it should have gone without saying.

She shrugged. "I'm sorry, I don't know what to tell you."

"My bubbe said there was going to be a Hanukkah number."

"There still can be." Doris tilted her head. "We can wait to see if anyone else signs up, or . . . oh! You could do the dreidel song in a solo number. How about that?"

Seriously? "Dreidel, Dreidel, Dreidel" was the worst. I didn't want to sing a song that even kids Aaron's age thought was silly and boring. I crossed my arms tightly over my chest, considering my options. I still really wanted to perform. Should I just go along with the nativity play? Or do a Christmas song? I knew the words to most of them already, and I did like the sound of doing my own solo number . . .

Plus, if I was being honest, I'd always secretly longed to go caroling, like they do in all those Hallmark movies. How different would this be? I just wanted to sing!

Doris lifted her eyebrows. "Well?"

I felt myself deflating because no, I couldn't do a Christmas number. I couldn't be in a nativity play. Christmas might be the star of the holiday show, but *this* star was Jewish, and she would be doing a Hanukkah number.

"What if I write and perform my own song about Hanukkah?" I asked. "Something original. Would that be okay?"

Just then, loud voices erupted behind us. Doris looked over my shoulder, her eyes widening. "Oh, the Scout groups are here. I'll need to sign them all in and give them their roles, then send them

backstage for costumes. Thanks for signing up, uh . . . Amanda?"
She started turning away.

"Wait," I said. "It's Aviva, and you didn't answer my question.
Can I sing my own song?"

"Do you have it ready?" she asked.

"Well, um, not yet, but I will, and it will be awesome!"

She waved her hand. "For now I'm putting you down for the
dreidel song. You let me know if that changes."

And then she was gone, rushing over to the busload of kids
that had arrived.

I stared after her, horrified. I so did not want to do the dreidel
song!

"If anyone can make the dreidel song amazing, it's you," Aaron
said.

He said it so sweetly that I almost smiled, even though I was
seething inside. I knew I could do better, and I wasn't about to
give up that easily.

"Forget that," I said. I'd come here to audition today, and no one
was going to keep me off that stage. I needed to show that Doris
lady that I was capable of so much more than the dreidel song!

I marched onto the stage and took my position right up front.
There was no mic, but I didn't need one. I'd learned in drama
class and by watching YouTube singing lessons how to project my
voice. I took a couple of deep breaths to prepare my diaphragm
and then I began to sing "Memory"—the most famous song from
the musical *Cats*.

At first, my only audience was Aaron. But by the time I got to
the end of the first line, people started to notice.

The talking stopped. Heads turned. And then all eyes were

on me. Watching me, awe on their faces as I sang my heart out. Because I was good. Really good.

And then when I got to the hard part and hit *that* note, belting it out, channeling my sad and lonely Grizabella, people even clapped! I kept singing, not wanting to break the spell over my audience.

This. *This* was why I wanted to perform.

I got to the very last note, holding the final word as long as I could while people applauded.

And then it was over.

I took a bow and blew a kiss to the crowd.

As I was thinking about what to sing next, Doris called up to the stage. "Yes, yes, fine, Aviva, you got the part!" I could tell from the way she nodded at me that she'd been impressed by my performance. "Sing any song you like, just make sure you show up for rehearsals and let us know what music you need to accompany you."

I bounced on my toes. "I will! Thank you! You won't regret this!"

She waved me off. "Now that you've had your moment, get backstage and see if you can find a costume that fits. I have the rest of this pageant to cast."

CHAPTER 6

Holly

"THIS LOOKS OKAY," I SAID, STANDING IN THE CLEAN AND bright lobby of Rowena Village, holding my grandpa's hand to help steady him as we took in the place. "I guess."

There were a bunch of couches and potted plants, and a table in the corner with a huge, unfinished jigsaw puzzle on it. Lots of elderly people were hanging around, reading books and chatting with each other.

The lady at the front desk had been nice when she handed us visitor tags and a brochure that detailed all the amenities and events the center offered, which mostly repeated what we'd already read on their website.

It wasn't terrible, but it was hard to imagine Gramps living there when I knew he'd be more comfortable at home.

"The lighting in here is atrocious," he grumbled, his thick eyebrows bunched in a familiar expression. He called it his "detective frown," but Mom said he only looked that way when he was "trying to find fault with something."

"And is that what they're calling a library?" He gestured toward a small bookshelf against one wall that held only a few dozen books. Mostly tattered romances, judging from the spines.

"Oh, no, sir," said the front desk worker, smiling amiably. "We have a full library on the second floor, with a much more robust collection of books. You'll see it on your tour. This is just our quick reads section for our drop-in day programs."

Mom shot Gramps a *See? Don't be so critical!* look.

To which he said, "I'm only here to humor you. Don't get excited."

Mom sighed in annoyance. Gramps shot me a wink as soon as she turned away.

A man in a polo shirt and khakis approached us, grinning brightly. "Hello! You must be the Martin family. I'm Gregory, one of the resident ambassadors here. I'm going to be showing you around today."

"Ed," said Gramps, shaking Gregory's hand. "This is my daughter, Charlie, and my granddaughter, Holly. You should know, I'm here rather against my will."

Gregory seemed to take this comment in stride. Maybe he was used to meeting potential residents who had reservations about moving in. "Even so, Ed, I'm glad to meet you. Are we ready to take a look around? I thought we'd start on the first floor with our various community spaces, then I can take you to see the residences, and we'll finish up with the dining room. You can even have dinner with us if you're hungry. Everyone always wants to know about the food, right?"

"That sounds perfect," said Mom. She was looking a little smug, because Grandpa had, in fact, spent most of the drive over complaining about the tasteless cafeteria food they tended to serve at these sorts of places. When she'd asked him how he knew, he'd just muttered something about how he'd "heard things."

I was feeling torn about the whole situation. Even though he wouldn't admit it, I knew that Grandpa needed more assistance than Mom and I could give him, and that it would be good for him to make some friends. But he'd said himself he wasn't going anywhere right away, so it didn't matter how nice this place was.

Gregory led us past a small gym with mirrored walls, where men and women were moving their bodies through a series of poses that Gregory called tai chi. "Really helps with balance!" he said, earning another pleased look from Mom, like *balance* was a magic word.

And yeah, maybe Gramps could use some help with that, and maybe these classes would be good for him. But did he really have to move out just to take a few fitness lessons? Couldn't he join a local gym or something instead? Gramps kept saying that Mom was overreacting about the falls, and I really wanted to believe him. He wasn't *that* old. He was fine.

Totally fine.

"Up here is our social hall," said Gregory, pointing to a set of double doors. "This is where we have a lot of our entertainment and different social functions. We often have live music on the weekends, and occasionally host a swing or ballroom dance party. Bingo and game show nights, too. It's always a lot of fun."

As we got closer, we could hear a cacophony of voices and laughter coming from the hall. It sounded like a school playground at recess.

"What's happening in there now?" Mom said.

"Right now we're taking sign-ups for our annual holiday pageant," said Gregory, opening one of the large doors. "One of the highlights of the year for our residents."

I had expected to see lots of old people today, but not this. The room was packed with kids, a lot of them wearing matching Scout uniforms.

"What's this holiday pageant all about?" asked Gramps.

"Oh, it's a blast," said Gregory with a big smile. "Kids from the community, and a lot of family members of our residents, all put on a show. There's singing and dancing, and they usually do the nativity story. Last year, one kid did a Christmas-themed magic show. Everyone always gets a kick out of it." He looked at me, beaming. "You're more than welcome to participate! Doris, the director, is right over there. The woman in purple, with the clipboard? I'm sure she'd love to have you. The more the merrier!"

"Oh! No. No, thank you," I said, backing slowly out of the door. "I'm not much of an actress."

I thought about mentioning the time I puked during the opening scene of my third-grade class's performance of *Charlotte's Web*, but some things are better left unsaid.

Gramps put his arm around me, squeezing me against his side. "Holly here has a bit of stage fright. But she is a fantastic writer."

"Oh, great!" said Gregory. "Maybe you could work backstage? Help with the scripts, or work with other kids to memorize their parts? I'm sure Doris could find something that makes sense for you."

"Umm." I looked from him to my grandpa to Mom. "I don't know . . ."

"Why don't you go say hi?" said Mom, nudging me into the room. "We're just going to check out the residences and then talk about financials and move-in details—boring stuff. We can meet up again in half an hour for dinner?"

I glanced at Gramps, who rolled his eyes. He was going through the motions with Mom, but I could tell he thought this was all a waste of time.

I looked back into the mass of kids. The woman in purple—Doris?—seemed frazzled as she called off names and attempted to organize kids into various groups.

"There's no pressure to be in the show," said Mom, "but if your grandpa does end up moving in, it would be nice to make friends with some of the other residents' grandkids, wouldn't it?"

"I'm not moving in," said Gramps.

Mom ignored him. "Just go say hi. What could it hurt?"

"I guess," I said, but really I was wondering what she expected me to do. Walk into a room full of strangers and be all, *Hi, I'm Holly! Want to be friends with me?*

How awkward was that?

But Mom was looking at me hopefully, and even Gramps shrugged as if to say, *The sooner we get this over with, the sooner we can go out for peppermint ice cream.*

"Okay," I said. "I'll see you in half an hour."

I wanted to add, *But I'm not joining any pageant!* As Gregory led Mom and Gramps away, I slinked into the social hall. There was a stage where half a dozen kids were trying to build a human pyramid while singing "O Tannenbaum." Key word: *trying.* I weaved my way through the crowd. No one was paying any attention to me as they read scripts and sang carols and argued over roles.

I waited for Doris to finish shouting at a little boy who was licking a candy cane decoration before I tapped her on the shoulder.

She spun around so fast she nearly hit me on the head with her clipboard. I jumped back.

She took one look at me and gave an exasperated eye roll. "You again," she said. "Yes, write a song, whatever. Just please. Go talk to Clara about costuming!"

"W-wait," I stammered. "I don't think—"

But before I could say anything, Doris grabbed me by both shoulders and shoved me toward the stage wings. "I don't have time to answer any questions right now. Go talk to Clara. Tell her you're doing the Hanukkah number."

"Hanukkah number?"

"Go! Go!"

Doris turned away from me, surveying the crowd and muttering something about Mother Mary. I couldn't tell if she was looking for a kid who was supposed to be *playing* Mother Mary, or if it was more of a *Mother Mary, help me survive this.*

"Okay, then," I said. Clearly, Doris had me confused with someone else and wasn't too interested in giving *me* a part. No problems there. I started to tiptoe away, glancing over my shoulder to check that Doris wasn't paying me any attention. This gave me a full half hour all to myself. I'd just go check out that library on the second floor until—

My back collided with someone else. "Oof!"

I spun around. "I'm sorry! I didn't . . ."

I trailed off. My jaw dropped.

Oh.

My.

Doppelgänger.

CHAPTER 7

Aviva

WHOA.

I was looking at . . . myself?

At least how I'd looked before my last haircut when I decided to get bangs. So, basically me without bangs. But with wide eyes and a mouth open in shock.

No, wait. Because as I stood there, *I* had wide eyes and a mouth open in shock.

So yeah, me without bangs. And not in costume, because I was currently wearing the very sparkly, very rainbowy coat Clara had let me try on backstage. She'd said it was from the residents' production of *Joseph and the Amazing Technicolor Dreamcoat*, and it had been the most colorful and flashiest thing I could find. It was so me.

"Who are you?" fell out of me, but it came out as a whisper.

"H-Holly," the girl said. "Holly Martin. Who are you?"

"Aviva Davis. You . . . look like me."

"You look like *me*."

I glanced around the social hall. There were a million kids milling around. Doris was yelling for everyone to shush and get back into their assigned groups, but no one seemed to be listening to her. It suddenly felt too loud and too close. I needed some quiet. I needed to think. I needed to figure out what was going on.

"Come with me," I said, grabbing Holly's hand and tugging her toward the ladies' room.

I pushed open the door and peeked under the stall doors: empty. I turned back to Holly, studying her features. Unbelievable.

She was doing the same to me, her eyes darting around my face. "It's like . . ."

"I know," I said. "We look exactly alike."

We leaned into the big mirror, our eyes sliding back and forth between our faces.

"You have bangs," she said, leaning closer to the mirror. Then she turned and looked at me straight on. She pointed at the spot on my cheek on the right side of my nose. "And a freckle."

"But that's it," I said, looking in the mirror again. "Eyes? Same hazel. Hair color?"

"Same brown, with bits of red," she said, turning back toward the mirror, too.

"Height?" I asked.

We both stood up straight. I leveled my hand across our heads, but I already knew.

"Same," Holly repeated. "Shoe size?"

"Seven. Yours?"

Holly nodded. "Same! We could be twins."

"What if . . ." I shook my head. "No, that's ridiculous. Never mind."

"What?"

I took a breath, feeling my face heat up because this was all so strange. "What if . . . Do you think . . . *Could* we be twins?"

Holly's eyes widened, growing even bigger than they had before. "That's . . . impossible."

"You're right," I said. "We couldn't be. Even though I'm adopted."

"Aviva!" Holly blurted out. "*I* am adopted!"

My heart tripped over itself. "Seriously?"

She nodded.

As one, we looked in the mirror again.

Same hair color. Same eyes. Same mouth. Nose. Ears.

"Could we really be twins who were separated at birth?" I whispered. "Does that even happen?"

"I don't know. Maybe? When's your birthday?"

"December fourth. I just turned twelve."

"You've got to be kidding me. Mine's December fourth! *I* just turned twelve!"

"This is unbelievable," I blurted out as I reached for her hand. "Holly Martin! I think ... No, I'm sure—at least I'm pretty sure ... Could we really be *twins*?"

"We must be! Twin sisters!" Holly said. "Or maybe we're aliens that got planted on Earth! Maybe there's more of us. Maybe there's a million of us! How do we know we're even human? Maybe we're clones! Or robots!"

Was this girl for real? I let go of her hand and crossed my arms. "Robots?"

"Okay, maybe not robots." She cringed, her cheeks turning pink (exactly like mine did when I got embarrassed). "Sorry. I have a vivid imagination."

I laughed. But then it really sank in. Was this girl with the vivid imagination my sister?

Did I seriously have a sister?

OMG I HAD A SISTER!

CHAPTER 8
Holly

"A SECRET IDENTICAL TWIN!" I SAID, MY GAZE STILL darting between our reflections in the mirror. "This is like a plot twist from my grandpa's books. Except, if it was, then one of us would be dead. Or a murderer. Or both."

Nerves were making me ramble, and it took me a minute to realize that Aviva was giving me a strange look. "What kind of books does your grandpa read?"

"Mysteries," I said. "He writes them, actually." I gasped. "And I think he did have a book about an impostor who killed their twin and tried to take their inheritance! Evidently people are always being killed for their inheritance." I shook my head. "That doesn't matter. Come on! Let's go find him and my mom. They are going to flip out when they meet you!"

I turned toward the bathroom door, but Aviva grabbed my arm. "Wait! You just gave me an amazing idea!"

I froze, eyeing her suspiciously. "For the record, I'm not entirely sure what an inheritance is, but I'm pretty sure I don't have one."

Aviva let out a big, boisterous laugh. Even having just met her, I could tell that she was the sort of girl who didn't mind being the center of attention. The sort of girl who would never be afraid to walk into a room full of strangers and ask—or demand—that someone be friends with her. I mean, look at what she was wearing—the most colorful coat I'd ever seen in my life. That was confidence!

I liked her already. My sister. *My twin!*

"I'm not going to kill you!" said Aviva. "But picture this: What if we told our families about each other in a really dramatic way? Like, what if we showed up together and were like, 'SURPRISE!' Or . . . Oh, wait a minute. I've got it. What if we do a flashy number at the pageant and that's our big reveal? Just imagine their expressions! Two Avivas! Or . . . two Hollys. Or . . . you know what I mean."

I smiled, a little weakly. "Yeah, that would be hilarious. Except, I'm not doing the pageant."

Aviva reeled back, letting go of my arm. "What? But you're here. At pageant sign-ups."

"My mom said I should check it out, but I wasn't planning on being in the show. I'm not much of a performer."

"But you have to sign up! We'd be in it together! It would be our big moment! It would be amazing!"

I recoiled, my stomach already churning with the very mention of going up on that stage. "I really don't think . . ."

"Please?" Aviva stuck out her lip and gave me big puppy eyes.

"I just don't want to—"

"Pleasepleaseplease?" Aviva clasped her hands together. "Just think of how epic it would be!"

"Aviva. You don't get it. My third-grade school play was a disaster, and I swore I would never—"

Aviva dropped to her knees, her coat pooling on the floor, and grabbed my hands, literally begging. "It's a once-in-a-lifetime opportunity to do this huge twin reveal. Seriously! Please?"

She wasn't wrong that doing a big reveal would be epic. I couldn't even imagine how my family would react, but Gramps always said he loved a good plot twist. Had he ever written a better one than me revealing I had an identical twin?

Except there was no way I was going to perform. On a stage. In front of people.

I looked at Aviva, her eyes hopeful as she gripped my hands.

"I'm sorry, but I just can't. Although . . ." I thought about what Gregory had said and how there were nonperforming jobs to do. "I guess I could sign up for a backstage job so we could at least hang out."

Aviva's expression turned sour as she stood up. "Backstage? Boring. Are you sure you don't want to be in the show?"

"*Positive.*"

She huffed, but finally conceded. "All right. I guess having you on stage crew is better than nothing and will give us time to be together. I can't believe my identical twin has stage fright. That's so bizarre!"

"It's not as bizarre as finding out you *have* an identical twin."

"Good point." Aviva laughed. "Anyway, the pageant is going to be so much fun. I'm doing the Hanukkah number, obviously."

I frowned, tilting my head to one side. "The Hanukkah number?"

She tilted her head, too—mirroring my expression exactly. "Of course. Because we're Jewish."

I blinked at her.

"Wait . . . Aren't you Jewish?"

"Oh. Um, no. I'm not really anything." I paused, before adding, "I mean, I was baptized Episcopalian, because that's what my grandma was. And we do celebrate Christmas and Easter."

"Oh. Okay, cool." Aviva nodded.

"Is that okay?" I asked.

"Yeah, of course!" Aviva beamed, right back to her bubbly self. She grabbed my arm, and together we looked at our reflections again. "We're sisters. Even better than sisters—we're twins! The best kind of sisters! We should still keep it a secret and then totally do a huge, awesome twinsies reveal!"

I frowned. "I don't know. What would that look like?"

"I'm not sure yet," Aviva said. "But if you won't be in the pageant with me, at least you have to agree to surprising our families. Also," she added, her face getting serious, "shouldn't we find out why they never told us in the first place?"

She had a point. I wasn't sure how I felt about a big, splashy reveal, but keeping it between us for now, while we solved this secret twins mystery, probably wasn't a bad idea.

"You're right," I agreed.

And then, to prove it to myself later, when I was going to doubt that any of this had even happened, I pulled out my phone and took a selfie of us, memorializing this moment forever.

Secret twins. No one would ever see it coming!

CHAPTER 9
Aviva

I COULD HAVE STOOD THERE IN THE BATHROOM STARING at my sister—my twin—all day.

It was so unreal to be standing in front of someone who looked so much like me but who *wasn't* me.

At first, looking at her was like looking in a mirror, but then I started to see the differences in the ways we talked and acted. It made me want to know everything about her—her favorite food, color, musical—everything! But before I could start asking, my phone buzzed in my pants pocket.

Shoot. I reached under the dreamcoat, which smelled musty and gross, honestly, and pulled out my phone.

A text from Mom: **Where are you?**

Uh-oh. I tapped out a quick **OMW** and then turned toward Holly and offered her my phone. "I have to go. Give me your number?"

We traded phones to put in our info. Of course, we had the exact same type of phone! But where my home screen was a selfie of me and Bubbe smushed together during one of our lunch dates, Holly's was of her sitting on a couch with an older man who had his arm around her, a friendly-looking gray tabby cat spread out across both their laps.

"Is that your grandpa?" I asked. "The mystery writer?"

She glanced up from where she was creating a new contact on my phone. "Yes. Is this your grandmother on yours?"

"My bubbe," I said, adding, "Not *boobies* like . . ." I pointed at my chest. "But rhymes with *hoodie*. It means 'grandmother' in Yiddish."

"Cool," she said.

"Anyway," I went on, "it's so funny that we both have pictures with a grandparent." I leaned over and pressed my forehead into hers, our eyes only inches apart so she was blurry. "Like we share a brain or are in sync or something. Twinsies."

Holly started at the sudden closeness, and I cringed—my parents were always reminding me to stay out of other people's personal bubbles—but then she began to laugh and pressed her forehead back against mine. "Twinsies. Or, you know, robots." She pulled back to look at me. "This is all very strange."

"Right?" I agreed. "Anyway, I'd better go. I'll leave first. Just wait a couple of minutes before you go out. We shouldn't let anyone see us together."

"Yes, of course," she said with a nod. "We can't ruin the secret twins mystery before we solve it."

Before I knew what I was doing, I threw my arms around her, pulling her into the huge sisterly hug I never knew I needed until that very moment. "This is so weird, but I'm glad I met you, Holly," I said into her ear.

"Me too," she said. "Although that coat smells kind of gross."

"I know." I pulled away and made a face. "I'm not wearing this for the pageant, don't worry. It just looked cool, so I thought I'd try it on." My phone buzzed again, and it was like I could feel my mother's annoyance in the vibration.

"Text me!" I called over my shoulder as I rushed out of the bathroom. "Bye!"

I was halfway back to the social hall when I stopped in my tracks. Tears pricked my eyes, and my heart raced like I'd just run the track at school.

I had a sister. A *twin* sister. It was suddenly so overwhelming. How had I not known this? How had my parents not told me? Did they know about Holly? My parents were pretty big on honesty, so I had to think they didn't know. But how? I wouldn't get any answers until I could talk to them about it. But how was I going to ask them about Holly without spoiling our big we-found-each-other surprise?

"Aviva! There you are!" I looked up to see my mother standing in the hallway, her hands on her hips, wearing her upset-Mom face. "What are you doing? Your brother said you disappeared—he thought you left him in the social hall. And what on earth are you wearing?"

"You like it?" I did a twirl and then chasséd down the hall toward her. "It's Joseph's Technicolor dreamcoat. I was trying it on for the pageant."

"Well, it's certainly on-brand for you." Her nose wrinkled. "But it stinks like sweat and mothballs."

"I know," I said. "It's disgusting. And hot. I'll find something else to wear."

Something that will match my twin sister's outfit. I mean, she can still wear an epic costume even if she isn't onstage, right? Of course she can! This pageant is going to be ah-may-zing! I did another twirl.

"Good plan," Mom said, obviously having no idea what was going on in my head. "I don't think there's enough Febreze to make that thing less . . . funky. Come on. Your brother was pretty upset that you abandoned him."

"Sorry," I said as we walked into the social hall. But then I stopped in my tracks again. This time for a completely different reason.

Because there, out of the way of the group of kids that Doris was talking to, were my grandmother and my brother. And talking to them was the man I'd seen on Holly's phone. Her grandpa.

What the what?

Did he know my bubbe? Were they friends? Wait: Did they know about me and Holly? Were they talking about us right now? Was I the only one who didn't know?

I glanced over at my mom, but she looked clueless.

My heart lurched as I thought about my grandmother keeping such a big secret from me.

No. That didn't make any sense. I was sure of it: My grandmother would have told me if she knew I had a twin sister.

And Holly hadn't known. Did that mean her grandfather didn't know either?

But then I realized if he saw me now, the big pageant reveal that I'd already started planning in my head was going to be a bust.

What should I do?

There was only one thing I *could* do.

"I have to go return this coat!" I blurted out as I pulled the smelly thing over my head and ran toward the stage.

CHAPTER 10

Holly

I TRIED TO SEARCH THE SOCIAL HALL FOR AVIVA AFTER I left the bathroom, but it was so crowded, and she could have been anywhere. As I started toward the doors, I spied my mom and grandpa talking to a woman with finely coiffed white-blond hair, red-framed glasses, and a silky navy blouse with a scarf tied artfully around her neck. Very elegant, and strangely familiar . . .

Wait. Wasn't that Aviva's grandmother who was in the picture with her on her phone?

Before I could decide what to do, the pageant director spotted me and a look of relief flashed across her face.

"Oh, good!" she said, charging toward me through the crowd. "I thought you'd left already. Here, I wanted to make sure you had the rehearsal schedule. Give this to a guardian, okay?" She handed me a slip of paper, simultaneously scanning her clipboard. She looked even more harried than before—her hair falling from her thick braid and reading glasses slightly askew on top of her head. "There you are. It's Aviva, right?"

"Holly, actually," I said automatically. Then I froze. Would that give us away before we'd even figured out the mystery?

This secret-keeping thing was *hard*!

"I—I mean . . . Holly Aviva," I stammered. "Sometimes I go by Holly for short. Or Aviva. Depends on how I feel."

The director looked at me like she did not have the brain capacity for this. "I don't care if you want me to call you St. Nick," she said, making a mark on her clipboard. "Just be here for rehearsals at these times, and have something prepared for that Hanukkah number."

I swallowed hard. "Sure."

"Good," she said with a decisive nod before she hurried away.

"So much for signing up for the backstage crew," I said aloud to no one. Not that I was heartbroken about it.

My phone chirped from my pocket, and I thought maybe it was Aviva texting me already. But when I checked, it was Mom.

> Gramps and I are in the social hall, but it's so crowded! Can you meet us in the dining room?

I looked up to see Mom and Gramps bidding goodbye to the woman in the blue blouse and walking to the door.

Yes, I typed back. **I'll see you there.**

I was just about to put the phone back in my pocket when it pinged again. Aviva!

> Hey, sis!!! miss U already!

A grin split across my face.

> Can't wait to see you next weekend!

MOM AND GRAMPS WERE ALREADY SEATED WHEN I GOT TO the dining hall. The room was spacious, with lots of round tables and a buffet against one wall where all the delicious smells must have been coming from. It reminded me of my school cafeteria, but way swankier, with white tablecloths, and brass chandeliers hanging from the ceiling. There was even a big red amaryllis flower blooming on each table.

"Holly! There you are!" Mom said as I sat down. A dish of fettuccine was in front of me, along with a chocolate chip cookie on a small dessert plate.

"Our tour guide just left, and Grandpa and I were talking about what we think of the place. What are your first impressions?"

"Oh," I said, twirling my fork into my noodles. I was bursting to talk about Aviva, and it took me a second to think of all the other things I'd seen today. "I mean . . . it seems okay. For an old folks' home, I guess."

Gramps harrumphed. "A lukewarm review, and one that I completely agree with. Speaking of lukewarm, the food could be hotter, too." He sounded sulky—but I noticed that his pasta was already half gone.

"Did you make any friends?" Mom asked me, ignoring him.

My body tensed, and I shoved the noodles into my mouth to give myself time to respond. "Mm-hmm," I said through tight lips, nodding.

"Oh, good!" said Mom. Then she shot Gramps a sly look. "Your grandpa may have made a friend, too. A very nice lady, wasn't she, Dad?"

Gramps narrowed his eyes at my mom. "What are you insinuating, Charlie?"

"Nothing, nothing," Mom said in a singsong voice. "You just seemed to like her. It would be nice to have friends here, is all."

"She was very polite," said Gramps. Which was a boring description, I thought, especially for such an elegant lady. And yet . . . was I imagining the pink in his cheeks? I couldn't remember ever seeing my grandpa blush before.

"Her name was Sylvia, right?" my mom continued. "She has a granddaughter your age, Holly. Maybe the two of you could meet sometime."

My memory flashed back to seeing them talking with Aviva's bubbe, and I almost choked. I took a drink of water. "Okay. Great."

"What do you have there?" asked Gramps, gesturing at the table.

I'd forgotten all about the rehearsal schedule. It was a little crumpled from being squeezed in my fist, so I smoothed out the paper before handing it to him. "It's the schedule for pageant rehearsals."

My mom gasped. "You signed up? Oh, that's great, Holly. I'm so proud of you!"

"Well, not the pageant proper. I'll be doing backstage stuff." And by "backstage stuff," I meant spending time with my twin sister.

Twin sister. My heart skipped every time I thought about it.

I was trying to think of some sly way to ask about my adoption and figure out if either of them knew about Aviva. Mom had always been open with me about my adoption story. She liked to tell me how she'd always wanted to be a mom, and even though it was harder for a single parent to adopt a kid, she said the challenges were infinitely worthwhile. She loved to talk about the first time she held me, and how she fell in love with me, her baby girl, from the very first moment.

Until now, I'd never been all that curious about where I came from. Until now, I'd never given a whole lot of thought to my biological relatives.

Surely, *surely*, Mom would have told me if she'd known I had a twin.

I had almost worked up the nerve to ask when Mom picked up a folder and opened it on the table. "Now, I know we don't want to rush into any decisions," she said, pulling out some paperwork, "but Gregory did say there was a waiting list . . ."

"Charlie," Gramps said in a stern voice. "I said I would come for this tour, but I will not have you pressuring me into this."

"Dad, please," Mom huffed. "I'm not trying to pressure you into anything. I'm just trying to do what is best for you, for everyone!"

I slumped back into my seat while they started to argue about . . . er, *discuss* whether or not Gramps should move into an assisted living facility. A discussion that seemed to be more heated each time it came up.

There would be plenty of time to bring up the twin thing later.

CHAPTER 11
Aviva

BUBBE HAD INVITED US TO STAY AND HAVE DINNER WITH her and her friends at Rowena Village. It was fettuccine night, which was my favorite because it usually meant the fudgiest chocolate chip cookies. Technically, the cookies were for dessert, but I always ate mine first.

Anyway, I'd already had a close call with Holly's grandpa, and while my grandmother's eyes weren't the best, I didn't want to risk getting found out.

So, reluctantly, I told Mom I had homework to do and should get home.

She'd looked at me funny because I wasn't one to turn down rich, creamy fettuccine and extremely delicious fudgy cookies, *especially* so I could be responsible about homework. But I reminded her that our resident foodie—Dad—was making his famous Buddha bowls and he'd be hurt if we didn't show up to eat them. It was true. But mostly it was about that whole close call thing.

We said goodbye to Bubbe, and when I gave her a big hug, I reminded her I'd see her soon for our regular Sunday date and then she'd come home with me so we could celebrate the first night of Hanukkah. She said she couldn't wait. I couldn't, either.

Back at home, during dinner, I told everyone about my amazing audition, how I'd nailed "Memory" and impressed everyone there. I glossed over the part where I was the only kid who signed up to do the Hanukkah number, but I did mention that I wanted to write my own song rather than be stuck singing "Dreidel, Dreidel, Dreidel." Mom and Dad said that was ambitious, but I wasn't sure why. How hard could it be to write a song about Hanukkah?

I only left out one tiny detail about the pageant sign-ups. That one tiny detail of *Hello, I have an identical twin sister and did you know about her and if so how could you not have told me?*

After I finished my story, Benny started on about hockey (blah, blah, blah) so I stared at my Buddha bowl, barely tasting it because my brain was too busy whirling to think about what I was stuffing into my mouth. That tiny detail started to get bigger. And bigger. Until it felt like one of those giant saguaro cacti that we'd seen on our vacation to Arizona. Huge and prickly and something you couldn't ignore. Not that Holly was a cactus, just this whole situation.

The more I thought about her and how unbelievable it was that I had a sister, the more I realized I had to find out if my parents had known about her. Why would they have kept this from me? Why would they have kept *her* from me? They weren't normally super-secret people, but it just didn't seem possible that they couldn't have known. There was only one thing I could do; I was going to have to ask. But carefully. Because if they didn't know, I didn't want to spoil the big reveal at the pageant.

After we'd tidied up from dinner, when Benny had disappeared to what Dad called his dungeon in the basement and Aaron had been excused to go play video games, Mom wiped off the kitchen table. Then she and Dad sat down to go over their paperwork from their dental office. They were preparing for an audit, which had something to do with taxes. I wasn't really sure what it meant other than they were stressed about it. They'd opened their dental office a couple years ago, after we moved here, back to my mom's hometown, to be closer to Bubbe. They'd both worked a lot trying to get the practice up and running since then, and this audit thing meant they were working even more than usual.

As I stood there, trying to figure out what to say, Mom looked up. "I thought you had homework to do?"

I took a breath and sat down at the table across from them.

"Vivvy?" Dad said, sounding concerned. "What's up?"

Oh, you know, just the regular: What can you tell me about my identical twin?

I looked down at my hands in my lap. My parents waited patiently as I tried to figure out what to say. How to ask.

"Um," I began, because I had to say *something*. I felt them staring at me so hard, I couldn't help but fidget. "Can you tell me again about my adoption?"

I looked up to see them exchange a glance.

"Of course. Why do you ask?" Mom said in a strange voice, like she was trying to sound normal, but . . . didn't.

I shrugged. "I just . . . I'm just curious about where I came from, that's all."

They exchanged another glance before Dad looked straight at me. "You know you are loved. You know we wanted you very much."

"I know," I said automatically. Because they'd told me a million times over the years that I was loved and wanted. I'd always known I was adopted. But now there was more to the story. How could they know they wanted *me*? What if they'd wanted Holly? What if they'd picked the wrong twin?

"After Benny," Mom said, "we had a lot more love to give and wanted more children. We—*I* . . ." She sighed as she looked at Dad.

"*We* had trouble having another baby, and so we decided adoption was the best way to add to our family."

I knew all this. I also knew that Aaron was their bonus surprise kid that they hadn't expected. *But please don't tell me the details, because I learned all that in health class, thank you very much.* I shook my head. "What I want to know is about my family. Like, not you guys but my biological family."

"It's understandable that you've been questioning your identity," Mom said. "Your grandmother told me about the conversation you had yesterday, and then you brought it up last night at dinner, and well, you are Jewish, Vivvy. You are one hundred percent Jewish. And you are definitely Jewish enough to be in the pageant."

"I know," I said again. They weren't getting it, but I couldn't ask about Holly. I'd told her that I didn't want to tell anyone, so we could do a mind-blowing reveal at the pageant, but the bigger reason was that I needed to figure out what it even meant that I had a sister. Did it mean I had a whole other family? Was I going to have to meet them and visit them? Was I half Episcopalian now? What did Episcopalian mean?

Pushing all that aside, and returning to the conversation in front of me, I obviously wasn't getting anywhere with my parents. *Sigh.* I was just going to have to ask, straight up.

"What I mean is, do I have any siblings?"

Dad's face went blank while Mom took in a deep breath.

"We don't know," she said. "The agency didn't divulge that information. But it's conceivable that you do have some siblings somewhere, or half siblings. It is possible."

Siblings. Or half siblings. Not *full-on identical twin* siblings.

Mom and Dad exchanged a knowing look that felt like they were having a telepathic conversation. After a long moment, Mom nodded and Dad turned back toward me.

He took a deep breath. "There is a letter from your birth mother," he said.

It took a moment for that to sink in. When it finally did, I gasped and jumped up from my chair. *"What?"*

"Vivvy." Dad held up his hand and motioned for me to sit back down, staring at me until I did. "Before you get upset, you should know that it's sealed, and your birth mother wanted it to remain so until your thirteenth birthday. Since she gave us the greatest gift—you—we felt it was important to respect her wishes."

"Whoa," I said. "So you don't know what it says?"

Both of my parents shook their heads. "We never met her," Mom said. "The letter came to us through the lawyer."

"Can I see it?"

"I'm afraid not," Dad said. "It's in a safe-deposit box with the legal papers."

"Locked up?" I asked.

"Yes," Mom said. "But at the bank."

I huffed. There was no way I was going to be able to get to that letter if it was at the bank.

"When you're older," Dad went on, "after you've read the letter and decide you want to, there are ways to find out more about your birth family. It's your choice to seek that information out. Or not—that's your choice, too. We understand that you may be curious, and we'll support you however we can. It's natural to want to know where you came from and where you fit into the world."

But what about where I fit into *my family*? And who even *is* my family? What exactly did *family* even mean?

"Okay" was all I said.

They looked at me expectantly for a long, awkward moment. They were clearly waiting for something.

"Um, so . . . thanks."

"That's it?" Mom said. "Nothing else?"

"No. Not if I can't read that letter."

"We're sorry, Vivvy," Dad said. "We hope you understand. And why we didn't tell you—we figured that would just make it harder to wait."

They were right. But for now, I'd learned everything I needed to know: They had no idea about Holly. They hadn't been lying or keeping anything from me—other than the letter, of course, but it wasn't like they knew what was in it.

I wondered if the letter was about Holly. Then I wondered if she had one, too, and if her letter was about *me*. If so, then she obviously hadn't opened it, either, or she wouldn't have been so surprised to meet me.

I pushed back from the table and got up. "I'd better get to that homework." And by "homework," I meant texting my sister.

Dad stood up, too. "Not before I get a hug."

I stepped into his arms, and he pulled me in for one of his big Papa Bear hugs, squishing me a little but in a way that I didn't mind. "Don't ever doubt that you are loved and wanted," he said into the top of my head. "Okay, Vivvy?"

"I won't," I promised, my voice muffled into his chest. "I love you, too."

Aviva! Are you there? I still can't believe I have a sister! I feel like I dreamed it all up!

Holly!!! IKR? BTW, I stealth asked my parents bout adoption-they have NO IDEA about u.

I don't think my mom does, either, but I'll try to find out tomorrow.

Do u have a letter?

What kind of letter?

From our birth mom. My parents just told me about it.

What?!!

😲 That's what I said!

What does it say?

??? NO IDEA. In a safe @ the bank. They won't let me open til I'm 13!

Maybe u have 1?

Mom never said. I'll see if I can find out.

Q: What's your fav food?

Oh my gosh, I really love food! It's hard to choose.

But probably tacos?

You?

Mac and cheese! Fav color?

Aquamarine! You?

Rainbow! With sparkles.

HAHA of course it is! Favorite hobby?

BEING FABULOUS.

jk. Performing, obvs. You?

Writing and reading! Fav book is A Wrinkle in Time.
Yours?

Drama = amazing graphic novel! Fav musical theater?

Holly?

You there?

???

Monday, 8:19 P.M.

Sorry! Gramps asked me to help with the dishes.
I've never seen a musical. Does Frozen the movie
count?

Frozen = good. Cats = best musical. You'd prob like
Wicked

Oh! That's about the Wicked Witch of the West, right?
I love the Wizard of Oz books!

Ugh. Time to floss & brush. Dad's a dentist so oral
health is a VBD. BRB

Monday 9:15 P.M.

You there, sis?

Yes. In bed. Reading.

I like having a sister.

Me too.

Good night, Holly.

Good night, Aviva.

Tuesday 7:02 A.M.

Good morning, sister!

Too early!

I'm a mrning person!

I am not!!

Sorry not sorry! Fav breakfast?

More sleep. Go away.

FiNE! 😜 Later!

I was kidding!! It's cinnamon rolls!

Aviva, come back!

Ugh, fine, I'm awake, I'm awake.

You're welcome!

CHAPTER 12
Holly

I HEARD SHUFFLING AROUND IN THE KITCHEN, TELLING ME Gramps was awake from his nap. I looked down at my phone and scrolled through my text messages, reading the last couple that Aviva had sent. I kept opening up our thread because I still couldn't quite believe she was real, and reading through all her notes, with her abundance of emojis and exclamation points, made me smile every time.

Except that one where she said her parents had no idea about me.

It didn't seem possible that our parents wouldn't know their own child had a twin, but I also felt like Mom and Gramps would have told me if they did know. There was no way they'd have kept this a secret, right? And what was this about a letter?

If our birth mom had written Aviva a letter, did that mean she'd written me one, too? If so, where was it? Why hadn't Mom told me about it?

I'd spent my whole school day trying to figure out how to broach the subject. Sighing, I tossed my phone on top of my pillow and headed out to the kitchen, where Gramps was pouring steaming water into a mug.

"There's my Holly Tree," he said. "I just got off the phone with your mom. She's working late and won't be home until after dinner."

I froze in the doorway. "Again? I'd hoped we were getting our tree tonight."

He shot me a sympathetic look. "She mentioned that. I know she feels awful about it. But we'll get the tree soon. Things have been hectic for her."

I pouted and sat down, folding my arms on the table. We usually got our tree during the first week of December, sometimes as a part of my birthday celebration, but this year it felt like Mom always had an excuse. We were too busy, there was just too much going on . . . At this rate, by the time we finally got our tree up and decorated, it would be time to tear it right back down again.

"Can I make you some tea?" asked Gramps. "Ginger maple?"

"Sure. Thanks," I said, heaving a sigh.

Gramps was able to make his way around the kitchen pretty well, but since his fall a couple of days ago, I was on edge, ready to jump up and help him if he looked unsteady. Still, it wasn't like he couldn't move around at all. If Mom got more grab bars and Gramps used his cane more consistently, he'd be fine.

Totally fine.

He plunked a second tea bag into another mug and filled it with ease, but it wasn't until he'd sat down at the table across from me that I let out a relieved breath.

Pushing my annoyance about our Christmas tree out of my head, I wrapped my hands around the warm mug. "So . . . I was actually hoping you could help me with a difficult plot device I've been working on."

His eyes lit up. My grandpa loved to talk about writing. "With pleasure," he said. "Talk me through it."

I bit my lower lip. Even though I'd gone over this conversation in my head when I should have been working on my holiday story during freewriting time, I still wasn't entirely sure how to approach the subject without giving everything away.

"So . . . the story is about this girl," I started. "And she's adopted."

Grandpa's mouth twitched knowingly.

"She's not me!" I said hastily.

His smile only broadened. "Of course not. Go on."

"Okay. Well." I cleared my throat. "She discovers one day that she has . . . a sister." I watched him closely, waiting for a spark of understanding or recognition. But he just kept his eyes focused on me, nodding slowly. "A *twin* sister," I added.

My grandpa's eyes widened, and for a second I thought, *I have him! He does know about Aviva!*

But then he sat back in his chair with a satisfied nod. "There's a lot you can do with twins. All sorts of fun reveals and surprises for your readers. In fact, in one of my early books, I had a twin murder his brother and then impersonate him for the inheritance." He stared off into the distance. "That was a fun one to write. One of my bestsellers."

I frowned. That was not what I expected him to say. Maybe he didn't know about Aviva after all?

"So," said Gramps, blowing on his tea before taking a sip, "what has you stuck?"

I drummed my fingers against my own cup. "I'm just not sure how to make it believable. I mean . . . how do identical twins get separated like that?"

"Ah." He nodded as comprehension filled his gaze. "Well, it's rare, but you do hear stories about this sort of thing happening. You could make it an international adoption, where perhaps some of the paperwork got lost, or there was some mistranslation, or something along those lines?"

I shook my head. "It happened here. In the States."

Gramps furrowed his brow, and I busied my hands by adding some honey to my cup. I didn't usually shoot down his ideas so quickly.

"All right," he said. "Well, could you add a sci-fi twist? Maybe one of the twins was temporarily abducted by aliens and has just been returned to Earth? Or if it's fantasy, you could have a changeling subplot?"

Aliens? Changelings? "I said I wanted it to be *believable*."

"Oh, right. I forgot about that part," he said.

I peered at him suspiciously. "But you said this does happen in real life sometimes?"

He shrugged. "Certainly. I'm no expert on the matter, but I've read an article here or there. Truth is often stranger than fiction."

"And the families that adopted the twins . . . they had no idea, either?"

He shrugged. "Apparently not."

"But how is that possible?"

"Well . . ." Gramps stared up at the ceiling, deep in thought. "I suppose maybe it could have something to do with the birth mother. Maybe she . . ." He swirled one hand through the air. "Had an adoption arranged with one family, and didn't realize she was carrying twins until after she gave birth, and then for one reason or another decided to keep it a secret from them and find another family for the second child . . ." Suddenly his eyes brightened and he snapped his fingers. "Now, if it's a mystery you're working on, you could work in some sort of revenge plot . . . or blackmail!" He started to go off on a tangent about financial greed and red herrings and mistaken identities, but I was only half listening. It was clear that, in my grandpa's mind, we were talking about purely make-believe characters. Not me. Not my twin sister. Not my real life.

He didn't know anything about Aviva, and if *he* didn't know, then I was sure my mom didn't, either.

"Does that help at all?" Gramps asked after a minute. "Give you some new ideas to work with?"

"Yeah. Yeah, yeah. It helps a lot. Thanks," I lied.

"I'm glad." He took another sip of tea. "*Is* it a mystery that you're working on?"

"Yep," I said, faking a smile. "It's definitely a mystery." I leaned over my mug and inhaled the sweet, spicy steam from the tea.

Although . . . Aviva had mentioned a letter. I wondered if there was one for me. There had to be, didn't there? Would it tell us everything about our birth mom? About each other? If so, why hadn't Mom told me about it? And where was it now?

"What are you thinking so hard about, Holly Tree?" Gramps asked, interrupting my thoughts.

"Nothing," I said. "Just a really great plot twist."

Aviva?

Hey, sis! (I luv saying that!)

Me too!

What's up?

My family has no idea about us.
No mention of a letter, either.

So bizarre. We could totally swap places.
No 1 would know!

Ha! That would be hilarious!

Q: Fav flower?

Gerbera daisy. You?

Those are so pretty! I like dandelions.

Like, the WEED?

Underappreciated, edible, and
resilient.

Don't tell my dad. He hates them!

I won't!

Fav movie?

Elf. Ever seen it?

Nope. Mine's The Princess Diaries.

I love that one too!

Someday we'll watch it together! 🎥 🤍

CHAPTER 13

Aviva

Light the candles
one by one.
Spin the dreidel,
We'll have some fun!

SERIOUSLY? THIS WAS THE BEST I COULD COME UP WITH?
Ugh. I might as well perform "Dreidel, Dreidel, Dreidel."

I was sitting on my bed with my phone open to the Notes app, staring at the horrible song I'd written. Actually, it wasn't even a song but just the beginning of a song that would be deleted immediately.

So, okay. Maybe writing a song was harder than I thought. What had I been thinking when I told Doris I'd create something original for the pageant? This was definitely not my thing, and I was hating every second of it. I was a performer, not a writer!

Wait a minute . . .

I opened up the text thread with Holly.

HI, sis. Ever write songs?

I waited. And waited. No response. No three dots. Maybe she was eating dinner. She'd told me last night when I texted her that she's not allowed to have her phone at the dinner table.

I scrolled up through our thread where we'd compared our lives since we'd first discovered each other. All the things that we'd been too shocked to think to ask each other on Monday when we'd been face-to-face. I couldn't help but smile as I saw our back-and-forth. Favorite foods, colors, hobbies. We were so different, but I already felt so connected and close to her. Which made sense. We'd spent at least nine months together and had the same DNA. (We'd looked it up, and yes, identical twins share the same DNA. So far, the only physical difference we could see was the freckle by my nose. So weird.)

I couldn't wait to see her again on Monday for the next rehearsal.

"Where are you?" I said out loud to my phone. "Holly? I need you, Holly!"

Nothing.

"Look at your phone! Please! I'm sending you twin telepathy! Text me now. NOW. PLEASE, NOW!"

Nada. So much for twin telepathy being a thing.

I scooted off my bed and shoved the phone into the back pocket of my jeans. Following the sound of the TV, I found my mom in the living room, watching *Jeopardy* with Aaron. Dad had taken Benny to hockey practice, so it was just the three of us at home.

Mom patted the couch next to her. "Watch with us?"

"No, thanks," I said. *Jeopardy* was not my kind of show. No singing or dancing. Just trivia. Yawn. "Did you find the menorah?"

"Sorry, I forgot, but . . ." Mom snapped her fingers. "I think it's in the crawlspace."

She was not wrong to call it the *crawl*space. "You mean spider central?"

Mom shivered and made a face. "The same."

Aaron stayed behind on the couch (I could hardly blame him) as Mom and I went down the stairs to the basement, around the corner from the finished part that was Benny's dungeon, and past the laundry area to the nasty old door that I could easily imagine led to the kind of world where monsters stole and ate little kids.

In fact . . . I pulled out my phone and took a picture of it to send to Holly later. Maybe she'd be inspired to write a story about what was behind the door.

Mom pulled it open, swiping away some cobwebs and reaching in to yank the chain to turn on the light. The tiny room was lined with shelves that held old boxes, each labeled with what was inside: DVDS, PHOTO ALBUMS, BABY CLOTHES, JUNK.

"I'm pretty sure it's in here with some of your grandmother's dishes and platters," she said as she opened up a box labeled SYLVIA—HUTCH CONTENTS. "She had to downsize so much when she moved into Rowena Village, and they don't allow open flames there, so she had to get herself a menorah with electric candles."

I noticed a box labeled SYLVIA—COSTUMES. "Costumes? Why would Bubbe need costumes?" I opened up the flaps to peek inside.

"Oh, you know your grandmother," Mom said with a laugh. "Some days I swear you get your flair for the dramatic from her. When your zayde was still alive, they used to hold big costume parties. Halloween, Purim, sometimes a masquerade fundraiser— any excuse to dress up."

One more reason to love my grandmother. I grinned as I looked into the box. "Can I have this?" I asked, suddenly sure I was going to find the perfect Hanukkah outfit inside.

Mom shrugged. "I can't see why she would mind. It's basically forgotten down here. Ah, here it is." She pulled the menorah out of the box she was digging around in. "Oh. It's a bit . . . worse for wear." She held up the silver menorah, and as the light hit it, I could see it was tarnished.

"We can still use it, though," I said.

"We'll clean it up," she said. "We'll need some Hanukkah candles. I'll pick some up when I'm out tomorrow."

"And we'll do latkes and play dreidels for gelt?" Because while I didn't want to sing the awful dreidel song at the pageant, I still wanted to play. Especially for gelt—gold-foil-wrapped chocolate coins.

Mom smiled. "Sure. I'll drop by the synagogue's gift shop and get everything we need." She tilted her head. "You're looking forward to it, aren't you?"

"Yeah," I said with a nod. "I want to do Jewish stuff. Everyone else gets fun Christmas—I want *super*-fun and totally amazing Hanukkah."

Mom closed up the box and wiped her hands on her jeans. "I understand. It's hard to escape Christmas this time of year. And as for celebrating our own holidays, I'm sorry we haven't done a better job with that."

I was about to tell her it was okay when my phone buzzed in my pocket. *Holly.*

"Okay, well, looks like we're good to go," I said, grabbing the costume box and turning toward the door.

"Oh sure, leave me alone with all the spiders," Mom said, but she was laughing.

WHEN I GOT UP TO MY ROOM, I WAS ABOUT TO PUT THE box on my bed but realized there could be spiders in it. And it was definitely dusty, so I put it down on the floor so I could go through it.

Then I got out my phone and saw the text from Holly:

No! I've never written a song. Only stories. Why?

I sat down on my bed and typed back.

Maybe you could write my pageant song? And, you know, if you changed your mind and wanted to perform it with me, that would be pretty cool too!

. . .

. . .

. . .

She sure was taking a long time to respond. Maybe she thought I meant she should write the song *now*.

I put down my phone and opened up the box. "Please no spiders, please no spiders, please no spiders," I chanted.

Most of the things in the box were clothes—fun stuff, but nothing that would fit me properly. It all smelled a bit musty, too, reminding me of the Technicolor dreamcoat, which had been cool at first but was heavy and hot, and after a while, the smell started to give me a headache.

As I rooted around some more, I discovered some bright-pink satin drawstring bags. I was about to open the first one when my phone buzzed.

I am definitely NOT doing the pageant! I know you'll be great though!

Oh. My heart sank. I wanted her to be onstage with me! And not just to do the big epic reveal, although that would be amazing.

The most important thing was that she was my sister, and we should do the number together. Aviva and Holly together at last!

But it wasn't like I could force her.

> **Okay, but can you write ME a song?**

> **Me? Write a song about Hanukkah? I don't know anything about Hanukkah!**

> **I'll teach you!**

I texted back, figuring I'd just google it and tell her all the details.

> **Just please help me? Please, please? 🙏**

> **. . .**

> **. . .**

> **OK, but it may not be very good . . .**

Yes! I did a fist pump in the air.

> **I'm sure it will be awesome!**

I was beaming as I set aside my phone and yanked open the first drawstring bag. My heart flipped excitedly when I saw what was inside.

Perfect.

CHAPTER 14
Holly

FINALLY. THE LAST DAY OF SCHOOL BEFORE WINTER BREAK arrived. This entire week had been beyond tedious as I counted down the days until the next pageant rehearsal, when I could see Aviva again. Sure, we'd been talking almost nonstop via text message, but it was nearly impossible to FaceTime, because one or both of us was almost always surrounded by family. Gramps kept asking me who I was talking to and why I kept smiling so much. He'd even dared to ask if I was texting with a *crush*, and despite my face turning holly-berry-red, I didn't deny it. Better he assume I had a crush than know the truth.

Besides, the pageant itself was on Christmas Eve, barely more than a week away. It wouldn't be long before the cat was out of the bag and I could shout to the heavens that I had a twin sister!

"I'm not going to give you a whole lot of homework for over the break," said Ms. Chang, scrawling on the whiteboard. My class cheered at this declaration. "But I do have one writing assignment that will be due when we get back." The cheers turned to groans, which Ms. Chang ignored.

"We've been talking a lot about how the protagonists in our favorite books always show some sort of initiative," she said. "They take action. The plot doesn't just happen to them, even if they have to overcome obstacles and things that scare them, right? So this assignment is your chance to cast yourself as the protagonist of your own story and tell me about one time in your life when *you* took action."

I pulled out my notebook. My pencil hovered over the top margin as Ms. Chang wrote out the prompt.

> *Write about a time when you faced a personal fear.*
> *How did you overcome it? What happened?*

I started copying down the assignment, but paused halfway through.

Wait. *What?*

I looked back up at Ms. Chang.

"There is room for interpretation here," she said, capping the marker and setting it on the whiteboard's tray. "What's frightening is very subjective and means different things to different people. But I want you to focus on a time when you faced a fear and acted brave. What that fear is, is up to you." She looked at the clock. "We've just got a few minutes left, so go ahead and use this as free time until the bell rings."

The classroom immediately filled with the slamming of books and shuffling of backpacks as my classmates put their things away and prepared to make a hasty exit the moment the school day was over. But I was stuck staring at the prompt on the board, dumbfounded.

This wasn't like one of Ms. Chang's usual prompts. Our writing assignments were always based around imagination and creativity. She encouraged us to follow our inspiration wherever it led us. Vampires, unicorns, talking rubber chickens? It was all fair game in Ms. Chang's class, and the wackier, the better.

But this was different.

She was asking us to write about . . . real life. My real life. The things that scared me.

The words swirled in my head. If the prompt had been *What is the most surprising thing that's ever happened to you?* that would have been easy. I literally just discovered a secret identical twin! What could be more surprising than that?

But Ms. Chang had been clever in the wording of the assignment, making it a time when we had to be brave. When we faced a fear and actively dealt with it. And she was right—a protagonist didn't just have things happen *to* them. Heroes took charge. They made decisions. They did things that scared them, no matter the consequences.

I could write about how I was supposed to create this original holiday song for my recently discovered twin sister, but while writing a song sounded challenging, it didn't feel *scary*.

There was the time I'd thrown up in the *Charlotte's Web* play, but after that humiliating first scene, I'd run offstage and cried in the hallway until my mom found me. I'd hardly call that facing a fear or being brave.

I looked back down at my notebook and finished writing out the prompt, but my stomach was in knots as a painful realization hit me.

If I was supposed to be the protagonist of my own story, then I was in danger of writing the most boring story of all time.

CHAPTER 15
Aviva

"BARUCH ATAH ADONAI, ELOHEINU MELECH HA'OLAM, asher kid'shanu b'mitzvotav v'tsivanu l'hadlik ner shel Hanukkah."

"Perfect, bubbeleh, perfect," Bubbe said proudly. "It's as if you've been saying the blessing over the candles your entire life!"

We were in the back of the Uber on the way home after our regular Sunday together. It had been so busy at the mall: thousands of shoppers darting into store after decorated store, while Christmas carols played in the background in every shop and throughout the entire mall.

Even though it was the first night of Hanukkah, and Christmas was still days away, there was not one Hanukkah decoration to be seen.

I did my best to be positive and say, "Same to you!" when people wished me a Merry Christmas, because they were just being nice. But it kind of hurt that my holiday didn't seem to count.

Bubbe didn't say anything, but I wondered if it bothered her, too. I didn't want to upset her, so I kept it all to myself as we did our shopping. I only had some allowance and birthday money I'd saved, but I got her and Mom bath bombs, the boys some of their favorite truffles, and Dad a hilarious silicone egg separator that looked like a fish. I didn't have a lot to spend, but since Hanukkah had been my idea, I had to get them *something*.

I'd gotten Holly a gift, too. Something I already knew she'd love, even though we'd only met a week ago.

But now that we were on our way home for the first night of Hanukkah, I was focused on the lighting of the candles and the amazing meal that would come after. I'd been practicing the blessing over the candles, thanks to YouTube videos, determined to get it right.

"I can't wait," I said. "A real Hanukkah."

"Do you know what your parents are serving?" Bubbe asked. "Your mother's been so busy this week with the audit at the office and Benny's hockey tournament today, I haven't even talked to her."

"Latkes, I'm sure," I said. Although, I *wasn't* sure. I'd been so focused on practicing the blessing and texting with Holly and then figuring out the perfect gifts for everyone, that it hadn't occurred to me to find out. Maybe I also felt a little guilty for not offering to help. "Probably a roast or something. Dad mentioned a brisket when we first talked about it, but I don't know."

"Whatever it is, I'm sure it will be wonderful," Bubbe assured me with a nudge of her elbow. "Your mother's not much of a cook, but your dad is. Thank goodness for him!"

The car pulled into our driveway, and after I thanked the driver and jumped out with my bags, I came around to Bubbe's side of the car to help her out. She gave me a loud "Pfft, I'm fine!" and waved me off.

I started toward the front door, sure that the second I opened it we'd be treated to the aromas of a delicious Hanukkah dinner: chicken soup, fried latkes, braised brisket, maybe even jelly donuts for dessert. My mouth was already watering as I waited for Bubbe so we could go in together and make a grand entrance.

Only to be met with the smell of . . . nothing.

No. *Not* nothing.

One step inside the front hall, and the foul stench of Benny's hockey bag met us.

"Uchhh!" Bubbe said. "What is that smell?"

"Benny's hockey stuff," I said as I kicked off my shoes.

I looked around the corner to the landing for the basement stairs, and sure enough, there was the offending bag. So gross. I could hear Benny's shower running downstairs and used my foot to push the bag down the steps.

"Hello?" I called out, putting my bags on the hall table and starting toward the kitchen.

Dad was standing there, phone to his ear and the Lorenzo's take-out menu in his hand. The oven wasn't on. The table wasn't set.

Dad nodded at me and then ducked out the other side of the kitchen. I heard him say, "Hello, I'd like to place an order for delivery."

Pizza. On what was supposed to be our epic first night of Hanukkah. Tears sprung to my eyes. So much for the Jewish holiday. So much for feeling legit enough to do the Hanukkah number at the pageant. I bet real Jewish families didn't eat pizza on Hanukkah.

I sighed and turned back toward my grandmother. "Apparently Hanukkah isn't happening."

Bubbe frowned and looked over my shoulder. "Deanna?" she said. "What is going on? What's the matter?"

I spun around to see my mother coming into the kitchen. She looked . . . not great. Her hair was a mess, and her eyes had purple smudges under them.

Still . . . "I thought we were having Hanukkah. A real Hanukkah with latkes. Not pizza!"

Mom dropped down into one of the kitchen chairs, letting out a big sigh. "Aviva, please don't start. We've had a day. We only just got back from Benny's game. The team lost. Then Aaron got carsick and vomited all over Benny in the van on the way home. Which is why *both* boys are showering right now. And I'm sorry, I know you had your heart set on Hanukkah, but between the audit at the office, this being our busy time of year, and the tournament, well, it's been a week. We're just going to have to wait and start celebrating Hanukkah tomorrow. We've got eight nights, after all."

Eight nights? Didn't she get it? We were supposed to have eight nights to celebrate, but now we were already losing one, and it was like no one cared at all!

"But you promised!" I said, disappointed tears escaping my eyes.

"Vivvy," Mom said, her lips pursed. "Please have a little grace. It's been a tough week. We'll start tomorrow, and we'll call it a do-over. Okay?"

"Tomorrow is the pageant rehearsal," I said. "And what about presents?"

"We'll light the menorah and eat after the rehearsal. And as for presents," Mom said, her voice stern, "if you want a real traditional Hanukkah, well, it's not even about gifts. It's only in response to Christmas that giving presents at Hanukkah is even a thing."

I harrumphed but didn't say anything, because I was the one

who'd said I wanted a real Hanukkah. If real Hanukkah wasn't about presents, could I argue?

"Still," Mom said, "your father and I have decided that this year each of you kids will get one gift—on the final night."

Okay, so at least there was that.

"Vivvy. It'll be fine," Mom said.

Fine. I didn't want a holiday that was *fine.* And a day late. I wanted a real holiday that everyone cared about enough not to forget.

"Pizza's on its way," Dad said as he came back into the kitchen, sliding his phone onto the counter. He smiled at Bubbe. "Hi, Sylvia. Hope you're hungry."

"Pizza for Hanukkah. That's a first!" Bubbe said with a laugh that sounded more like a snort.

Dad leaned against the counter and crossed his arms. "We're sorry about Hanukkah. We'll start celebrating tomorrow. I don't have any clients after four, so I'll come home early and start on the latkes and the rest of dinner."

"And I'll finish up early, too," Mom said. "I'll stop at the synagogue and get some candles and we can—"

"Wait," I said. "We don't even have candles for the menorah?" *The most basic thing?*

Dad turned and pulled open the kitchen junk drawer. "We probably have some birthday candles in here somewhere."

Birthday candles. No latkes. No celebration.

"Never mind," I said and took myself and my bags to my bedroom.

HANUKKAH IS OFF, I TEXTED TO HOLLY. ALONG WITH A bunch of sobbing emojis.

> **What? Why?**

> **My parents dont care. 2 bsy, 2 stressed. DISASTER!**

> **That's the worst. I'm so sorry!**

Three dots instantly followed. Another text came in a second later.

> **If it makes you feel better, we still don't have our Christmas tree. Mom keeps saying we'll get it soon but soon is never!**

> **UGH. PARENTS!**

I sent more emojis, then reached for a tissue because the emojis weren't the only things that were sobbing.

> **I'm bailing on pageant. Don't bother with song.**

Suddenly my phone rang. It was Holly. I mopped up the rest of my tears and tossed the tissue onto my nightstand before pressing the green button.

"Aviva," Holly said, sounding concerned. Way more concerned than my parents had been that they'd postponed Hanukkah. "What happened?"

I sighed. "'Oh, we got busy, and Benny's hockey and Aaron puked and . . .' I don't know. Drama."

There was a long silence.

"Hello? Holly?"

"You should still do it."

"But . . ."

"No," she said in a strong voice. "You should do it. I've been working on the song, and . . . Well, it's not perfect yet, and I'm going to need your help with some of the details, but we can work on it tomorrow."

"Are you sure?" I asked. "Why do you care if I quit?"

"Because I know this means a lot to you, and you'd regret it if you didn't do it."

She wasn't wrong about how much I wanted to do it. I took a deep breath and then let it out. Was it possible to love a sibling you never even knew you had just days after you met her? Seemed so.

"All right, sis. All right. I'll do it."

I may not have had the real Hanukkah I wanted, but at least now I had Holly on my side.

CHAPTER 16

Holly

I STOOD ON MY TIPTOES WHILE I SURVEYED THE MASSIVE crowd, searching for Aviva. I was waiting for her near the stage in the social hall, because if there was one thing I'd learned about Aviva since we met last week, it was that if there was a stage nearby, that was where she would end up.

Gramps had driven me—even though his balance wasn't great, he was still a good driver—but had disappeared to the cafeteria for a cup of tea as soon as we arrived. He'd said that once we left here, we would go straight to the tree lot to finally pick out our Christmas tree.

Yeah, right. I'd believe it when I saw it.

I bounced from foot to foot, feeling anxious as I searched for Aviva, worried that at any moment someone could yell at me to go up onstage and start practicing some song or skit. I shuddered at the thought.

Although I had to admit that the kids currently trying to harmonize to "Frosty the Snowman" did look like they were having a blast, pretending that one of the boys was Frosty while they all sang and danced around. None of them seemed nervous to be performing in front of a crowd.

I felt a pang in my chest, and at first I thought it was just my stage fright kicking up. But was it actually . . . jealousy? Did I wish I could be like them?

"Holly Aviva!"

I spun around to see Doris, the pageant director, marching toward me. Her face was flushed, and locks of hair were falling out of her thick braid into her face.

"Um. Yes?"

She looked down at her ever-present clipboard. "I'm putting you near the end of the lineup. Do you have your song figured out yet? I've already talked to the sound guy. I need to have a backing track set up and ready to go."

"Oh. Okay. Um. It's . . . coming along?"

Her frown deepened, and the look she gave me could have melted a snowman. "What does that mean?"

I shrank back a little. "N-nothing," I stammered. "It's going to be great. I promise."

After a long, tense moment, she heaved a sigh and cast her gaze to the ceiling. "I'm sure it will be. But what I need to know is whether or not it will be accompanied by music."

I considered her question. "To be determined?"

She huffed through her nostrils. "Fine. But if you are going to have music, then I need it by our dress rehearsal on Thursday. If you're not ready by then, we're going with the dreidel song. Got it?"

"Got it," I squeaked.

The woman marked something on her board, looked around, and stomped off.

"Aviva!"

At the sound of my sister's name, I gasped and spun around, searching for her in the crowd. But I didn't see Aviva. Instead, I saw a little boy, maybe six or seven years old, marching right toward me with a grumpy face and arms tightly crossed. With brown skin, curly black hair, robes that were three sizes too big, and a crooked golden crown on his head, he was adorable, despite his pouting. Maybe in part *because* of his pouting.

"She's making me stand in for one of the wise men!" he said.

I blinked.

Looked around.

Realized—nope, he was definitely talking to me.

I faced him again. "What?"

He gestured angrily toward Doris. "Some kid is sick, and they needed a standby. I told her I didn't want to be in the pageant, but she said if I was hanging around, I could do it dressed as a wise man." His nose crinkled petulantly, but then softened. "Can I hide out here with you?"

"Uh . . ." I looked around, panicking. Who *was* this kid? And how did he know Aviva? And what did he want from me?

The boy tilted his head to one side, inspecting me, his expression growing curious. "Your hair looks different today. What did you—"

"Sorry, I have to go!" I said, backing away. "Just tell the director to find someone else. Okay? Bye!"

I hurried away. I could hear him calling after me. "Aviva!" But I didn't stop until I'd rushed up the stage stairs and behind the curtains. I leaned against the wall of a small manger—the nativity play set, I guessed—and exhaled, pressing a hand to my stomach.

Wow! Someone actually mistook me for Aviva. This was surreal!

I hadn't even caught my breath when a hand grabbed me. I yelped as I was pulled back into the shadows of the manger.

I turned and came face-to-face with a pair of dark, oversize sunglasses and a head of bubblegum-pink hair. "Hey, sis!"

I gaped at her. "What are you wearing?"

"Found it in some of my bubbe's old stuff," she said, flipping her pink hair off one shoulder. "What do you think?"

"You look great," I said, laughing. The wig actually did look great on her—funny, because I was sure I could never pull it off myself. But the glasses were conspicuous, especially in the darkness of backstage.

"I'm incognito," she explained. "I was worried your family would see me and our big surprise would be over before it even began!"

"Oh, yeah, speaking of that . . ." I turned and peeled back one of the curtains. "Someone thought I was you." It only took me a second to find the boy in the crowd, since he was now standing with two other "wise men" in cloaks and matching golden crowns. I guessed he hadn't found the courage to tell the director to find someone else after all. "See the three kings? The little one thought I was you!"

Aviva peered over my shoulder, lowering her sunglasses to the tip of her nose. "That's my brother Aaron!"

"Really?" I said, unable to keep the surprise from my voice.

"I know, we don't look anything alike," said Aviva. "Because, you know, *adopted*."

I grinned at her. "It's the opposite for me. Strangers are always saying, *Wow, you have your mom's nose!* and things like that. Except, I obviously don't. We always laugh about it afterward."

"I don't look like anyone in my family," said Aviva, before grabbing my shoulders and giving me a shake. "Except you!" We'd had a week to come to grips with being twins, but it was still hard to believe. "Wow, Aaron really thought you were me? Once we clue everyone in, I am never going to let him forget that he didn't even recognize his own sister. Just imagine! We could trick our whole families!"

I tried to picture it. What if Aviva walked up to Mom and Gramps and pretended to be me? How long would it take for them to figure it out? I wanted to believe that they'd know right away, but . . . maybe not. I mean, no one would ever expect you to secretly swap places with a surprise identical twin, right? I almost laughed when I thought about how Gramps, with his imagination, would probably assume I was an alien clone before he'd believe Aviva was my twin.

"Come on, I found a greenroom back here," said Aviva. "I can't wait to hear what you have for the song so far." She tugged me further backstage. The greenroom wasn't green at all (so disappointing), and it really wasn't even a room, just a little alcove backstage with a mirror surrounded by big light bulbs and a desk that was strewn with old costumes and props. Aviva shoved aside a pile of sequined fabrics and an ancient-looking makeup kit and hopped up onto the desk, her legs swinging.

I joined her and pulled out my notebook, where I'd started working on the song.

"It's not very good so far," I said, feeling like it was important to set expectations. "I've never written a song before, and I don't really know very much about Hanukkah. Just that it's the Jewish

Christmas, right? So you get presents and sing songs and—" I glanced up and my words stuck in my throat. Aviva's eyes were widening, and I could immediately tell that I'd said something very wrong.

CHAPTER 17
Aviva

JEWISH CHRISTMAS? DID HOLLY SERIOUSLY THINK Hanukkah had anything to do with Christmas? I was about to blurt out that Hanukkah was not, never had been, never would be, Jewish Christmas. Everyone was so Christmas-obsessed! Didn't they know it wasn't the only holiday?

But as I looked at her, staring back at me, biting her lip like she knew she'd said the wrong thing, it hit me that she hadn't *meant* it as a bad thing. She just didn't know. It was up to me— her Jewish sister—to tell her.

I slid off the desk and turned away from her, focusing on a row of light switches on the wall, thinking about what I knew of Hanukkah. Which, I realized, wasn't much.

"Aviva?"

I turned back toward her. "Hanukkah isn't Jewish Christmas," I began, with a smile so she knew I wasn't criticizing. "I think people call it that because the holidays happen around the same time of year. But they're totally different. It's like comparing Valentine's to Presidents' Day."

"Oh," Holly said with a nod. "Okay."

"Hanukkah is . . . It's about the Maccabees and how they fought . . . someone about . . . stuff . . . and in the end there was only enough oil in their destroyed temple for one night but it lasted for eight nights. That's why we celebrate for eight nights, and why we eat latkes. Because they're fried in oil."

"So they ate latkes for eight nights?" Holly frowned. "Also, why do you light candles? That seems important. If I'm writing a song about it, I feel like I should know."

Why did we light candles? "Um. Because of the oil?"

Holly tilted her head like it didn't make sense. Probably because it didn't make sense.

My face heated up. I looked away from her and slid my sunglasses down over my eyes. "Never mind."

"Aviva?" Holly asked softly, jumping off the desk to stand in front of me. "What's wrong?"

I lowered my head, fighting tears.

Holly grabbed my hand. "Please tell me. We're sisters, right?"

I swallowed the lump in my throat and turned back toward her. "I don't know."

"We *are* sisters," she said. "Maybe someday we'll do a DNA test, but we already know, don't we?"

"It's not that," I said. "I don't know about Hanukkah. I don't even know who the Maccabees are or what they did or why we light candles. Just that we do. Or, some Jewish people do. My family . . ." I shoved my hands up under my glasses to swipe at the tears. "My grandmother says I'm Jewish, but I don't feel Jewish."

"Do you feel . . . Christian?" Holly asked. "Or something else?"

I shook my head, looking down at my hands. "No. I mean, I feel Jewish, but just not Jewish *enough*. I should know more about it."

"Well . . ." Holly sniffed, making me glance up at her.

"What?"

She shrugged. "Can't we learn together? When I'm working on one of my stories and don't know something, I research it.

That's what my grandfather taught me—if you don't know something, go find out. We can learn about Hanukkah together. Not just for the song, but because we want to know."

"But shouldn't I already know?"

She made a face. "No one is born knowing stuff. Just look at us. We didn't know about each other, and we lived together for nine months!"

"Would we have found out about each other if we hadn't been at the pageant thing?" I asked.

She shrugged. "I don't know."

"I bet it's in that letter from our birth mom. Did you find out if you have one?"

"Not yet." She looked down toward her feet. "It would make sense, though. Mom keeps all sorts of paperwork in a filing cabinet, but I'd have to ask, and it's a hard thing to bring up, you know?"

"Just go find it," I suggested.

Holly looked up at me, her eyes wide with alarm. "That's . . . I can't do that without permission!"

Oh. So much for finding out about the letter.

I stared at her for a long time, studying her face. So like my own but totally different.

"What?" she said self-consciously.

"Do you think we were like this?" I stepped forward and put my arms around her and squished her to me. "In the womb, I mean."

"Or maybe one of us was upside down," Holly said, squeezing me back, chuckling a little. "I bet I had to face the other way because you were singing all the time. A baby can't get any rest with you around!"

I laughed. "Probably. But I bet you had smelly baby feet."

"Maybe. But, speaking of smelly . . ." She pulled back, her face wrinkled in thought. "Do you think babies fart? Like, are there little fart bubbles floating around in there?"

I grimaced. "That's gross. And awkward."

"Ha!" she said. "That's my superpower, you know. Asking awkward questions."

"No," I said. "Your superpower is that you're so smart and have a great imagination."

She reached out toward my face, pushing my sunglasses up onto my head so she could look straight into my eyes. "The real superpower is that our cells divided extra and now I have a twin sister."

I grinned at her until she beamed the same smile back at me.

"Or maybe," she said, "our superpower is procrastination. At this rate, we'll never get this song written in time for the pageant."

I laughed. "You're right. Let's see what you've got." I jumped back up onto the desk and patted the space beside me.

Holly sat on my right, opening her book and flipping past page after page of writing until she got to one near the end, pressing her palm to cover it up. "I found some instrumental music online to help me get in the songwriting mood, so maybe it will help if I play the music while you read?"

"Oh, that's a great idea!" I said. "We hardly have time to write both the lyrics *and* the music."

"That's what I thought," said Holly. "But remember, I only just started, and I've never—"

I was way too excited to hear her doubts. "I'm sure it's great. Be positive. Let me see."

She slowly moved her hand, revealing the song. "Don't look yet!"

It took all my willpower not to glance at the words on the page until after she'd grabbed her phone and found the music track.

Soft piano music began to play. When she nodded, I started to read the words, fitting them to the music that flowed around us, while Holly stood beside me. I could sense her holding her breath the whole time.

"Is it awful?" she asked when the music stopped. "I can start over. I can—"

"No!" I interrupted with a surprised laugh. "Holly, it's brilliant! I love it."

"Really?" Holly asked shyly. "You're not just saying that?"

"No," I shook my head. "I really, really like it. Except . . ."

"Except?"

I sighed. "Well, some of the lyrics sort of . . . make Hanukkah sound like Jewish Christmas."

She cringed. "Which it's not."

I shook my head.

"I wish I knew about Hanukkah. Maybe we really should swap homes." Holly laughed.

That's when it all clicked into place.

"What?" Holly's smile dissolved. "I barely know you, but that expression on your face looks like trouble."

"We *should* swap homes," I said, the idea sounding better with every second. "Just think—I'd get a crash course in Christmas to see what all the fuss is about, and you'd get one in Hanukkah." At least, a small crash course in Hanukkah, since I wasn't exactly convinced that my parents were going to manage that do-over. Even though they'd promised.

"You're kidding, right?" Holly said, leaning back to look at me straight on. "We can't do that. It's . . . No, it'll never work."

"Holly, think about it—my brother thought you were me. My own brother!"

"Aviva," Holly said, easing down from the desk. "I can't . . . *we* can't . . ."

I jumped down also and grabbed her hand, dragging her over toward the wings. I returned the sunglasses to my eyes, wishing they weren't so dark, but if we were identical enough to fool my brother, my disguise was necessary. I looked out beyond the stage where kids were being barked at by Doris to find their marks (including Aaron, who looked like he wanted the floor to swallow him up, poor kid), down to the regular part of the social hall.

"There, look, there's my bubbe sitting at that table. She'll take you to my house with her. But in an Uber, because she can't drive anymore."

"Hold on!" Holly said. "She's talking to my grandpa!"

We swiveled to look at each other. "Are they talking about us?" I asked.

"They don't know," Holly reminded me. "It must be a coincidence."

We looked back just in time to see Bubbe let out a peal of laughter and press her hand to Holly's grandfather's arm.

"Um," Holly said. "Is it just me, or are they *flirting*?"

"I have no idea," I said as I tugged her back behind the curtain. "But I think we should do this. It's the best way for us to experience each other's holidays. I've never had a Christmas tree or gone caroling or any of that."

And I can search for your letter, I didn't say.

"We *are* supposed to be getting our tree today," Holly said.

"Really? I've never decorated a Christmas tree! And tonight's the second night of Hanukkah. It's the perfect solution, and will definitely help you write this song. Plus, it'll be so much fun. What do you say, sis?"

CHAPTER 18
Holly

WHAT DO I SAY? *WHAT DO I SAY?*

I wanted to laugh at the absurdity of Aviva's suggestion. Switch places? Me, go to her house? With her parents and her brothers? Who I'd never even met? While Aviva went off with Gramps to my home? Pretend to be each other?

It would never work! It was ludicrous to even consider it!

But when I opened my mouth to say as much, something stopped me.

Because yes, I *was* curious about her Hanukkah traditions, and that would help me write her song. And yes, I wanted to make Aviva happy, and I could tell she was really keen on this idea.

But more than that, I couldn't help feeling like this was exactly the sort of thing that I would never, ever do. Holly Martin was too chicken to go that far out of her comfort zone. Impersonate her newfound sister and move in with total strangers? No way. That would be too bold. Too daring. Brave, even. Like . . . facing a fear.

Something to write a story about.

Me—awkward and nerdy Holly—trading places with my exuberant (secret!) twin sister. It sounded like a Hollywood movie. Ms. Chang probably wouldn't even believe that it was real until I showed her evidence. Evidence like . . . photos of me at Aviva's house, lighting the menorah and eating latkes. (Whatever those were.) And a video of Aviva performing my song at the pageant.

I swallowed hard. I almost couldn't believe I was even considering this.

But when I finally spoke, it wasn't to say no. It was to ask, "For how long?"

Aviva gave me a confused look. "For how long, what?"

"How long would we switch places for? I mean, everyone will probably catch on right away, and the jig will be up. But if they don't, then . . . do we confess the truth tomorrow morning and switch back? Or . . . when?"

Aviva's mouth bunched to one side as she thought about it. "Well," she said slowly, "today is Monday, and the dress rehearsal is on Thursday. If our families don't figure it out, we could switch back then. Imagine their surprise when we reveal the truth at the pageant!"

Switch back Thursday? I counted in my head. That would be three nights away from home. Three nights away from Mom and Gramps. Three nights away, right before Christmas!

But I would be back home *for* Christmas, I reasoned. And with how things had gone lately, it wasn't like we were going to be doing any fun traditions anyway. Maybe we'd finally get our tree, but I couldn't see us baking cookies or going ice-skating or any of the things that made this time of year special.

And even though I would miss Gramps while I was gone, it wasn't like I was abandoning him. Aviva would be there to help him, and in a way, she was his granddaughter, too. Right?

Besides, who was I kidding? I wasn't an actress. There was no way I could fool Aviva's family for that long. We'd be found out in hours!

But I could still say I'd done it. I could still write a story that proved I could be the protagonist of my own life, facing my fears and triumphing in the end.

"So?" Aviva said, nudging me with her shoulder. Her eyes were shining eagerly.

What did Gramps always say? *You have to take risks in your writing and your life.* He would never let fear get in his way.

I gave a decisive nod. "Okay. Let's do it."

Aviva squealed and threw her arms around me again. "Yes! This is going to be so much fun!"

I smiled, but my stomach was churning with nerves. I couldn't believe I was doing this! Going to a strange house with *strangers*! But I had to reason that they weren't complete strangers. They were Aviva's family, which made them my family, too.

Sort of.

"But if anything starts to go wrong," I said, "we'll text each other and call it off immediately. Deal?"

"Absolutely. Deal!" Aviva held out her hand and gave mine a firm shake. Then she pulled off her bright-pink wig and held it out to me. "But first—makeover time!"

That's when I remembered that we weren't completely identical.

"Bangs," I said, pointing at her forehead as she finger-combed her hair. "You have bangs."

"Oh, right."

I took a deep breath and mustered up all the risk-taking, fear-facing courage I could and said, "I'm going to need bangs, too, if this is going to work."

"Yeah?" she said, like she was skeptical.

"Yes. If we're going to do this, we have to do it right."

"YES!" Aviva turned around and rifled through the desk until she found a comb and a pair of scissors. "Are you doing the honors, or am I?"

"You'd better do it," I said. "And you'd better hurry before I change my mind."

I held perfectly still as Aviva brushed some hair in front of my face, blocking off my view. I didn't know if she'd ever cut hair before, and I was too scared to ask. Her movements were sure and precise, though, and before I knew it—

Schick.

She handed me the lock of hair she'd just cut. My eyes widened. Suddenly, this all felt very real. I looked around for a garbage can and, when I didn't see one, shoved the hair into my pocket.

"So, okay, you've seen my bubbe already," said Aviva as she worked with the scissors to tidy up the edges of my new bangs. "And my little brother, Aaron. My older brother is Benny, and then there's my mom, Deanna, and my dad, Steve. But you'll call them Mom and Dad. Obviously."

Mom and Dad. Bizarre.

"What else do you think you should know?"

I blew a puff of air to get rid of some stray bits of hair on my nose. What else should I know to be able to impersonate her? It seemed like I should be asking a zillion questions, but I couldn't think of a single one. So I just shrugged. "I guess I'll text you if something comes up."

"Ditto," said Aviva. "And you live with your mom and grandpa, right?"

"Yeah. Gramps is taking you out to pick up a tree tonight, but my mom works a lot, so you won't see her all that much, except in the evenings. Just keep an eye on Gramps, okay? He has bad arthritis and his balance isn't so great these days, so if you see him struggling, you can take his hand and help steady him."

Aviva gave me a solemn nod. "He won't fall on my watch, sis."

I appreciated her confidence, but it didn't do much to calm my nerves.

Aviva tilted her head, frowning slightly. "And your dad is . . . ?"

I could tell she was worried this might be a touchy subject, so I smiled. "No dad. My mom adopted me as a single parent."

"Ah. Okay. Got it."

"There's also Sherlock," I said. "He's our cat."

Aviva brightened. "Perfect. Cats *love* me—they must know *Cats* is my favorite musical. And now . . . for the finishing touch." She set down the comb and scissors and returned to the drawer, grabbing something. She turned to me and, before I knew what was happening, aimed a marker at me and pressed a dot to the right of my nose, giving me a freckle. "There," she said, beaming. "Now we really *are* identical!"

As one, we swiveled to look at ourselves in the mirror.

My heart stuttered.

She was absolutely right.

CHAPTER 19
Aviva

WE WERE DOING THIS! WE WERE SERIOUSLY GOING TO SWAP places! And homes. And families. Whole lives!

After I'd covered up my freckle with some of the gross old makeup we found backstage, I helped Holly straighten the pink wig on her head.

It was then that I started to have doubts. Did I really want to miss Hanukkah? The one that I'd made a big fuss about? Oh, who was I kidding? My parents weren't going to follow through.

Seriously, though, what were Holly and I doing? We'd never be able to pull this off!

But the thought of finding out what Christmas was all about had me pretty curious. Dad had told me a bit about the holiday and how his family celebrated when he was a kid. And there were movies, of course. But I wanted to live it. To smell the pine, to eat the treats and decorate the cool tree. And to go caroling! I wanted to see what all the fuss was about. Because if there was one thing I'd learned about Christmas, it was that there was a *lot* of fuss.

Plus, I was going to get a chance to look for the letter I knew Holly's mom must have tucked away somewhere. Holly obviously didn't want to go snooping for it, but Aviva was on the case!

"We need to trade clothes," Holly announced once the sunglasses were in place. "And ugh, how can you see through these?"

"It's not as dark out there," I said, pointing my thumb over my shoulder. "Meet me in the bathroom in two minutes, and we'll change. Try not to talk to anyone until our transformation is complete."

After we separately snuck into the bathroom, we locked ourselves in the big accessible stall and swapped outfits. It was so strange to see my colorful sweater and jeans on Holly. But it made it feel even more like I was looking into a mirror. Especially since I'd given her my freckle and bangs.

"You're me," I said.

She smiled. "And you're me, except . . ." Her smile faltered.

"What?" I looked down, but nope, everything was buttoned and tucked in.

"Just that my clothes are boring on you."

I shook my head, rubbing what was now my sleeve. "I don't think so. This flannel shirt is really soft. And your jeans are pretty comfy."

"Well, sure," she said with a smirk. "*My* jeans don't give wedgies. How do you wear these?" She did a little hip-wiggle.

I laughed and rolled my eyes. "Whatever. Just don't make my socks stinky with your smelly feet."

She was blowing a raspberry at me when the door squeaked.

Someone's coming, I mouthed to her. She nodded. I mimed that I was going to go out and she should give me time to make my escape and then leave.

Holly looked like she was about one second away from bailing on this whole plan, so I gave her a quick hug, grabbed her backpack, and, once I heard the clunk of the lock on the stall next to us, I hurried out.

Stopping at the big mirror to make sure I looked okay, I heard a sigh from the stall. Not our stall but the one next to it.

Wait. I knew that sigh. I bent down to look under the stall door, and sure enough, there were my bubbe's shiny gold sneakers.

This is it, I thought. *This is the moment we either bail or go all in.* I opened the accessible stall door to see Holly standing there, her eyes wide in shock and fear.

Okay? I mouthed to her.

She shook her head.

Good thing I had more faith in her than she did.

"Is that you, Bubbe?" I called out as I grinned at my sister.

"Vivvy?"

"Yes!" I said. "I'm just finishing up and then we can get an Uber to go home for our Hanukkah do-over. You excited?"

Holly shook her head, really fast now, her expression one of alarm. She was about to bail. I could feel it.

"I am!" Bubbe said. "Your mother promised tonight would be better. We're going to have a wonderful Hanukkah, bubbeleh!"

"I can't wait!" I said, even as I waved goodbye to Holly. Then, as she reached for me, I leaned out of her grasp, hitched her bag up on my shoulder, and ran out of the bathroom.

No turning back now.

WITH BUBBE OCCUPIED, I RUSHED TO FIND HOLLY'S grandpa so we could get out of the building. The less that Holly and I were in the same place at the same time, the better.

When I got back to the social hall, he was there, sitting at the table like he was waiting for something. Or some*one*. Like Holly. Or . . . maybe my grandmother?

Were they a thing?

But before I had a chance to think about that too much, he saw me and his eyes lit up.

Which almost made me stop in my tracks until . . . Oh yeah, he thought *I* was Holly!

Okay, so this will be the first real test, I told myself. I did my best to channel Holly as I walked over to him.

"Hey, Grandpa," I said. "We should probably get going, right? It's tree night!"

He frowned.

Oh no, was he already onto me? I hadn't even been impersonating Holly for two seconds!

"What did you do to your hair?" he asked, sounding surprisingly gruff. "And since when do you call me Grandpa?"

"Oh! I'm just trying something out. You know, with the name . . ." I struggled to think about what Holly called her grandfather. "Gramps!" I blurted out, making him lift a gray eyebrow. "And my hair? I don't know, I thought it would be cute if I had bangs for Christmas. Festive, don't you think?"

He made a face. "If you say so. It's your hair."

"Anyway," I said, glancing over my shoulder, worried Holly would come in with Bubbe and this would all be a bust. "We should go. Uh, you know. Now."

"There's no rush." He looked past me. "I was just talking to Sylvia. I'd love for you to meet her. Her granddaughter is somewhere around here, too . . ."

Uh-oh. Time to put my acting skills to good use. "Uuughhhhhh," I moaned as I doubled over. "I'm not feeling great, Gramps. We should probably go home. Immediately."

I glanced up, and he was looking at me like I'd sprouted a second head. "Holly? What's going on?"

"I'm not feeling well, that's all. Can we go? Please?"

He looked back but nodded as he rose slowly from his chair, putting a steadying hand on the table, and took hold of a walking cane.

"Can I help?" I asked, rushing to his side, remembering what Holly had said about him being unsteady.

"I'm fine," he said, although he didn't complain when I put my hand on his arm as we walked toward the door. "I didn't see you with the other kids. I'm so proud of you for signing up for something that is taking you outside of your comfort zone. Even if it's the backstage crew and not performing. Backstage is still very important. I can't wait to hear all about it."

"Thank you, Gramps," I said, my hands itching to get out my phone so I could text Holly and tell her that really sweet thing he'd said. "But I'm pretty burned-out on pageant stuff, and want to get that tree!"

"I thought you weren't feeling well and wanted to go home?" he asked suspiciously.

"Oh!" I exclaimed, straightening my shoulders. "I'm okay, I just . . . I guess I was nervous-excited to get the tree. I'm fine now. Can we go, though? Like, right now?"

"Sure, sure," he said, leading me down the hall and out to the parking lot. "It's been tough to wait this year, hasn't it?"

"You have no idea!" I said.

He laughed and swept his eyes around the parking lot. "Now, where is the car?"

I was no help since I had no idea what kind of car he drove.

Maybe Holly and I should have made notes. But it wasn't like we'd had a lot of time to prepare!

"Uh, why don't you hit the button on your key thingy?" I suggested. That's what Mom did when she forgot where she parked.

"Good thinking." Gramps hit the button and, of course, the car that was maybe two feet away from us beeped.

"Oh, ha ha," I said. "Here it was all along. Sun got in my eyes, I guess."

I got into the car and buckled in, practically bouncing in my seat at the adventure ahead. All right, Christmas, here I come!

CHAPTER 20
Holly

WELL. I GUESS WE'RE DOING THIS, I THOUGHT AS I EMERGED from the bathroom stall. I washed my hands and looked at myself in the mirror. My new self. My Avivified self.

It was so strange that we were identical—she was outgoing and vivacious, so much so that I wondered if her name *meant* vivacious. Could *I* be outgoing and vivacious?

Giving myself an exaggerated grin in the mirror, one that was so big, it almost hurt my face, I had my answer. Yes, I could absolutely be outgoing and vivacious.

Avivacious!

The stall door behind me swung open, and there was Aviva's grandmother. She was a little taller than me, with short, curled hair that looked like it wouldn't move if I touched it. She had thick glasses with red rims that were very stylish.

What had Aviva called her?

Bubbe. Rhymes with hoodie, got it.

"Hi, Bubbe," I said, trying it out.

She smiled at me in the mirror as she came up beside me at the sink. "I love that wig on you! You're like my own little Lady Gaga!"

"Thanks," I said with a laugh. I *felt* like a little Lady Gaga with the wig on. "So, ready for our Hanukkah party?"

She nodded, pumping some liquid soap into her hand. "Yes. I had a talk with your mother about that catastrophe last night, and she promised she and your father would make up for it. Don't you worry. Your dad is making all your favorites!"

"Okay, great," I said with as big a smile as I could muster, because what exactly had happened the night before? Aviva hadn't gone into the details, though she'd obviously been disappointed. But now I had to act like I knew and that of course I was excited about *all my favorites.* "I can't wait for all the latkes and the"—I waved my hand vaguely—"you know, everything."

Bubbe tugged a paper towel from the dispenser on the wall and dried her hands. "Good thing your father's such a great cook. Your mom was always more interested in her books than learning to cook. All right, bubbeleh, let's go to the front desk to wait for our Uber."

"Awesome," I said as I followed her out into the hall. Aviva hadn't mentioned her mom loved books. I wondered what kind.

As Bubbe talked to the receptionist at the front desk, I pulled out my phone and sent Aviva a text: **what is a lotka? And also, what does bubbela mean?**

I watched for the three dots that would tell me she was responding, but they didn't come. I hoped everything was going okay with Gramps. I was actually surprised I hadn't gotten a call yet telling me that we'd been found out and he was coming back to get me.

Aviva didn't respond until ten minutes later, when Bubbe and I were in the Uber on our way "home." And when she *did* text me back, it wasn't to answer either of my questions.

> **Don't forget to take Aaron home w you!**

What?! Oh no!

"Stop the car!" I barked at the driver. She slammed on the brakes, causing Aviva's grandma and me to lurch forward. Thank goodness we were on a quiet street with no one behind us, and that we were wearing our seat belts.

"Aviva!" Bubbe said sternly. "What are you doing?"

"We forgot Aaron." I looked up, catching the eyes of the driver in the rearview mirror. "I'm so sorry. My little brother. He's back at the center. I totally forgot he was with us. Can we go back and get him?"

"Of course!" the driver said, doing a one-eighty once the road was clear.

"Oy!" Bubbe said. "I had no idea he was with you today. I forgot you kids are out of school for the holidays."

"I'll text and let him know to be out front," I said as I hurriedly tapped out a message to Aviva: **Tell him the car will be out front in 5.**

After I hit send, I noticed she'd responded to my questions: **latkes = potato pancakes. Bubbeleh = sweetie.**

That made sense. **Thanks! How's Gramps?**

You mean grumps? she returned with a laughing emoji.

Oh boy. He was my grandpa and I loved him, but yes, he could be grumpy. Mostly from all the arthritis pain, I figured. He was a big teddy bear on the inside.

Be nice to him! I sent back, just as we pulled up to the senior center. A sullen-looking Aaron stood there, his hands shoved deep into the pockets of his jeans. I slipped my phone back into my pocket.

Bubbe pressed the button to roll down her window. "Hop in, bubbeleh."

Apparently, everyone was bubbeleh.

"I can't believe you forgot me!" Aaron whined as he climbed in, cramming himself into me until I moved over.

"Sorry?" I said meekly.

Bubbe reached across me and squeezed Aaron's arm. "We're here now."

He harrumphed and then frowned at me. "Your freckle looks . . . different, but that wig is hilarious."

"Um, okay," I said, not sure how else to respond. I turned away from him so he couldn't look at my "freckle."

"We are getting a real Hanukkah tonight, aren't we?" said Aaron.

"Of course," said Bubbe. "Your parents have been working very hard."

"They'd better," he grumbled.

I fidgeted uncomfortably in my seat. The car was suddenly feeling a little cramped, with me in the middle and my Huge Secret taking up all the extra breathing room. "So. Uh . . . Bubbe, what's *your* favorite part of Hanukkah?"

I dared to glance over at her in time to see her eyes light up. "Oh, all of it. The food is a big part—the latkes and the jelly donuts, of course. And lighting the candles makes me feel connected to our traditions. But being with family—that's always my favorite. I'm so glad we're doing Hanukkah this year." She leaned into me, smelling faintly like roses. It was nice. What a grandmother *should* smell like. It made me wish I still had a grandma. Well, if all went well, I'd get to borrow Aviva's for a few days.

If all went well. That was a humongous *if.*

GRAMPS ALWAYS SAID I SHOULD NOTICE SETTINGS SO I could write them well, so as we turned into the driveway, I did my best to memorize every detail of Aviva's house. It was a brick one-story on a winding street filled with other houses that looked similar, except Aviva's was the only one without Christmas lights twinkling in the dusk. Strange how a house without lights could stand out so much at this time of year.

I wondered if that made her feel left out or even sad.

A porch lamp lit the way to the front door. A dusting of snow covered the lawn, and there were two cars parked in the driveway.

I can't believe I'm doing this, I thought as we hopped out of the car. *Dinner with strangers. A whole evening pretending to be Aviva. If this isn't facing a fear, I don't know what is!*

While Aaron ran up to the front door, I hung back, rethinking all the life choices that had brought me to this moment. My palms were so sweaty I was probably leaving stains on Aviva's too-tight jeans.

"Come on, bubbeleh," Bubbe said, grabbing my arm, almost like she knew I was a flight risk. "Let's go in. I'm starving."

I was barely inside when I was hit with a cornucopia of aromas. Obviously home cooking, but different than the smells that came out of my kitchen. My mouth knew that good food was to come, and it started watering immediately.

Following Aaron's lead, I kicked off Aviva's sneakers in the front hall and toed them neatly together. I no longer needed the disguise, so I laid the pink hair and glasses on top of the shoes, glad to get that itchy wig off my head.

Aaron disappeared down a set of stairs, but Bubbe kept a hold of my arm and led me toward the source of those aromas.

"We're here!" she sang.

I took a deep breath and put on my best Avivacious smile as we got to the kitchen doorway. "It smells so good in here!" I proclaimed. That was something Aviva would say, wasn't it? Or would she say it smelled *amazing*, or even *stupendous*? I felt like every word out of my mouth could give me away by not being Avivacious enough. But to my relief, no one seemed to notice me standing there feeling awkward and thinking up a thesaurus's worth of words to describe the delicious smells wafting my way.

The kitchen was large, with elegant wood cabinets and silver appliances. There was a giant island in the center of the room, covered with platters and dishes—all empty except for serving utensils, ready for the feast to come.

On the other side of the kitchen was a big stove, each burner covered by a pot, the front two steaming away.

The man who had to be Aviva's dad was standing beside the kitchen island, a big smile on his face. He had dark-brown skin, short black hair, and kind eyes that were crinkled at the corners.

"Welcome, one and all," he said in a deep voice, sweeping an arm toward the stove. "You'll be delighted to know that all the traditional Jewish holiday food groups have been represented: gefilte fish, latkes, braised brisket, lokshen kugel, and, of course, for dessert, jelly donuts. And, because *someone* insisted on at least one vegetable, steamed broccoli." He made a cringey face on the last word.

I laughed, liking him already.

"Pfft, broccoli," Bubbe said with a dramatic wave. "There's potato *and* onion in the latkes—that's two vegetables."

"Ma," a woman said as she entered the kitchen, walking straight over to Bubbe and delivering a noisy kiss on her cheek. "A *green* vegetable that's not fried in oil." In a softer voice, she added, "I'm sorry about yesterday. Thanks for coming back." Then she turned toward me while I held my breath. "Well, Vivvy?"

Vivvy, short for Aviva. My heart pounded. "Yes?"

She rolled her eyes. "What do you think?"

"About . . . ?"

Now her eyes went wide, her eyebrows up high on her head. "All this. Hanukkah! The real Hanukkah that you wanted?"

"I think your exact words were," Aviva's dad began, looking up like he was trying to remember, "latkes, menorah, dreidels, all eight nights. All of it."

"Oh, right! Yes! This all seems incredible. Thank you!"

"Come on," Aviva's mom said. "Time to light the candles. I set up the menorah in the front window." She turned toward the hallway and yelled, "Benny! Aaron! Time to light the menorah."

Bubbe's arm came around my shoulders. "And Vivvy's been practicing her blessings over the candles, haven't you, Vivvy?"

Blessings over the candles? I didn't know any blessings, not over candles or . . . anything!

But before I could totally freak out, I told myself I could handle it. I was a writer, I'd just make something up. This was what Gramps would call a writing prompt—where you have to improvise on the spot.

Aaron appeared, along with a boy who looked like him and was a couple of years older than me. That had to be Benny. Together, we gathered around a silver candle holder—the famed menorah. It stood on a tray that was covered in tin foil on the windowsill. I'd seen one of them before, but now that it was right in front of me, I noticed it had nine spots for candles: four on each side and a taller one in the middle.

There were already three unlit candles set in it: the center one, plus two in the far right spots.

Now what?

"Vivvy?" Bubbe said, breaking into my frantic thoughts. "Go on."

Right. The blessings.

I swallowed hard. "Of course." I took in a long breath before I began. "Dear God, thank you for the . . . um, for Hanukkah. And the oil for the eight nights. And for the latkes, which smell amazing, and for everything else. Oh, and also for my family. So, you're pretty great, and thank you for everything. Amen."

I exhaled, pleased that I'd remembered about the oil and the latkes. But as I looked around, it was clear that something wasn't right. Everyone was staring at me like I'd just recited "The Night Before Christmas." In the awkward silence, dread started to roll around in my stomach, almost like that time right before the *Charlotte's Web* incident.

Uh-oh.

Suddenly, Bubbe laughed. "That was funny, Vivvy! Now do it in Hebrew like you practiced."

Hebrew? The blessings over the candles were in *Hebrew*?

But that was, like . . . a whole different *language*!

Clearly Aviva had left out a few important details. Now what was I supposed to do?

CHAPTER 21

Aviva

OKAY. NO OFFENSE TO HOLLY, BUT I DEFINITELY WON THE grandparent lottery. My bubbe was one of the funnest, most cheerful, and coolest people I knew. Whereas the guy at the wheel next to me had a dark shadow hanging over him. In Christmas terms, definitely more Scrooge than Santa.

I wouldn't have said that to Holly, though. I knew she loved her grandpa. Maybe by the end of this adventure, I would start to understand why.

Speaking of grandparents, I didn't think I was imagining the googly-eyed looks this man had been giving Bubbe at the center. What better time to get the scoop on that?

I swiveled in my seat. "*So . . .*" I said, drawing the word out and wiggling my eyebrows. "I saw you talking to that cool-looking grandma at the senior center. Do you *like* her?"

Gramps made a suspicious noise in his throat, and we pulled forward again. "I've met a few nice people at the center," he said after a brief silence, "including Sylvia."

I pressed my lips together, waiting for him to say more about my grandmother, but after a silence, he just grunted quietly to himself and added, "The people have been very friendly. It's a decent facility." His tone lowered threateningly. "But don't you dare tell your mother I said that or she'll have me moved in there before we know it!"

"Why *wouldn't* you want to live there?" I asked. "They cook for you, and the food's awesome. Plus they have games and concerts and bingo nights!"

He glanced over at me. "I thought you were on my side."

"Huh?"

He looked back at the road. "You're not trying to get rid of your old gramps, are you? You think I'm some sort of fuddy-duddy who can't hang around with you, my 'cool' granddaughter?"

Oh. Something was going on there with him not wanting to go live at the center. Time to change direction! "I'd never try to get rid of you, Gramps! I'm just saying, it seems like a nice place."

"Nice enough," he said a little unhappily. "But there's nothing like being in the comfort of my own home, with my family and my independence. Bingo nights couldn't replace that."

I frowned, thinking of Bubbe. Did she ever feel like she'd given up her independence to live at Rowena Village? It didn't seem that way. She talked about the center like it *was* her home. She still spent lots of time with me and the rest of our family. But Holly's grandpa made it sound like the place was a prison.

I needed to think of a way to respond that would still be Holly-appropriate, but after a few quiet minutes, he turned on the radio. Which—wow. I didn't know people even listened to the radio anymore! We always just connected to Bluetooth and listened to Spotify playlists in our car.

The radio dial was set to a station playing Christmas music, and a deep voice came out of the speakers crooning about *silver bells* . . . I recognized the song, of course. I recognized all the Christmas songs. You couldn't avoid them even if you wanted to. Sometimes this annoyed me. Like, why did Christmas have to infiltrate every single place we went—from the grocery store to the coffee shop?

But as Gramps started to hum along, the song sounded different to me now. I glanced over at Holly's grandpa, and his lips had turned up at the corners. Not a giant grin—this was Grumps, after all. But the music seemed to make him happy.

In that moment, a Christmas carol felt like something I didn't want to rebel against but something to embrace. This music clearly brought a lot of people joy at this time of year, and I was feeling a when-in-Rome vibe.

Finally, I would get to do all the Christmasy things I'd seen in holiday movies, special sitcom episodes, and in practically every commercial that played during December. This year, *I'd* be the one decking the halls, roasting chestnuts on an open fire, and walking from door to door in the snow serenading random strangers with Christmas carols!

And that's when I realized that even though I was Jewish, Christmas felt like the kind of holiday that was made just for me.

I KNEW HOLLY LIVED IN AN APARTMENT, SO I'D EXPECTED us to drive downtown, but soon I realized we were actually heading away from there, toward the suburbs.

"Um, where are we going?" I said. And even though I trusted Holly and, by extension, her family, I couldn't help thinking of all those things she'd said about murder and inheritances. What did I really know about this guy anyway? Was I going to become part of a real-life murder mystery?

"To the tree farm, goofball," said Gramps. "Your mom had to work late, but she said to pick out any tree you like, and she'll have the decorations out of storage and waiting for us when we get home."

I inhaled giddily, fighting the urge to clap my hands and let out a whoop. (I had a feeling Holly wasn't much of a whooper.) But seriously: *a real Christmas tree farm!* If that wasn't reason to whoop, I didn't know what was.

It wasn't long before we were on the outskirts of town. Gramps pulled off the freeway and turned into a parking lot with a big blow-up Santa in one corner beside a sign that read GINA'S TREE FARM. We got out of the car, the boots I had borrowed from Holly crunching on the gravel. I breathed in the smell of fresh pine. There were trees everywhere I looked, stretching for acres and acres as far as I could see.

How did anyone choose the perfect one?

I started for the main path but hadn't gotten very far before Holly's grandpa called me back. I paused and swiveled around.

"Forgetting something?" he said, leaning on his cane next to the small cashier hut that was the same size as the shed where Dad stored our lawn mower and gardening tools.

"Oh! Sorry, Grandpa—er, Gramps."

I hurried back and took his arm, but Gramps laughed and shooed me off. "I'm fine," he said. "But what are you planning on cutting down the tree with?" He gestured to a table boasting a collection of work gloves and handsaws. I blinked. Did he mean that *I* was going to have to cut it down? By myself?

I guessed that Gramps might not be strong enough, or able to get down close enough to the ground. But . . . I'd never even held a saw before!

Something told me that Holly wouldn't argue, so I didn't, either. I just took a pair of boring gray gloves (they could at least have had pink ones available) and a saw, figuring . . . how hard could it be?

I went slower this time so Gramps could keep up as we made our way deeper into the tree farm.

"What are you feeling like?" he said, carefully picking his way around a slushy mud puddle in the path. "White pine? Douglas fir? Oh, how about a Norway spruce this year?"

I stared at him. "Umm . . ."

"You know your mother always likes a noble fir, but it isn't my personal favorite."

OMG, he was talking about different kinds of trees. Who knew there were different kinds of Christmas trees? I thought it was just . . . you know . . . *the Christmas tree.*

I looked around and spotted a tall, bushy tree with dark green needles not far off the path. I pointed. "How about that one?"

"Ah, a Fraser fir. Classic choice," he said.

What was this guy, an arborist?

The terrain was more difficult off the path, so I held Gramps's hand while we navigated past roots and fallen branches until we were standing in front of the chosen tree.

"You remember what to look for when picking a good tree?" asked Gramps.

"Of course!" I lied, before making a show of walking around, inspecting it from every angle.

It was a couple of feet taller than I was. With branches. And pine needles. Or . . . fir needles?

Whatever. It was a tree. Bingo.

"It's perfect," I announced with a confident nod.

"What about this bare spot here?" said Gramps. I looked to where he was gesturing, and sure enough, I guess there was one side that didn't look quite as full as the others.

"We'll put that side to the back?" I said.

He pointed at the top. "The top is a little crooked. The star won't sit right on it."

Gee whiz. Everyone's a critic.

"That's how I like it," I said. "Gives character. No one is perfect, so why should we expect our trees to be, too?"

"Just like all characters in a book have flaws to make them interesting. You've been listening, my Holly Tree." His eyes twinkled at me. "All right, then. This is the one. You chop it down, and I'll hail someone to come help us get it on the car."

I slid on my gloves and crouched down next to the tree. Needles brushed against my arms and neck as I reached underneath and took hold of the trunk. I bet there were spiders crawling all over this thing! I pictured my mom, who would probably have a heart attack if she saw me, sure that I was about to saw off my own hand.

Once I started, I discovered it was even harder than it had looked, too. At first, I couldn't get the saw into the wood. The teeth finally sank in. Push. Pull. Back and forth and back again. I was sweating in Holly's flannel shirt by the time the saw broke through to the other side. The tree fell with a dramatic *kerflumpf* into the snow.

Breathing hard, I stood up and surveyed my work. A hand

landed on my shoulder, and I glanced up to see Gramps smiling proudly. "Nicely done."

I beamed. I might be covered in tree sap and spiderwebs (*but please, please not any spiders!*), but so far, I was totally nailing this Christmas thing.

CHAPTER 22

Holly

HEBREW. I'D NEVER EVEN HEARD HEBREW SPOKEN, SO there was no faking it. But I had to do *something*. Aviva's family was staring at me expectantly.

My heart raced as I tried to figure out my next step, standing there in their front picture window.

I was moments away from confessing everything when I realized what I needed to do.

I turned toward Bubbe. "I've been thinking, and I thought that you could do it for tonight. You're the guest of honor, so . . ." I made a show of stepping back from the menorah and sweeping my arm toward it.

"But you've been practicing!" Bubbe helpfully reminded everyone.

I shook my head. "I'll do it tomorrow. Please, I think you should do it today. Show us how it's *really* supposed to be done." Then I gave her a wink. I'd never winked at anyone before in my entire life, but it felt like such an Avivacious thing to do.

"Well," Bubbe said, her shoulders straightening as she took the spot I'd been in a second before. "If you insist."

Oh, I do, Bubbe, I thought. *I absolutely* do *insist.*

She picked up the pack of matches and struck one, using it to light the candle set in the middle. Then she waved out the match, put it on the tray, and picked up the lit candle.

She began to sing what had to be the blessing in Hebrew.

It was short, maybe twenty words. She took a breath and sang another that started the same but had a different ending.

Then, while I was thinking about how lovely it sounded, she reached forward and used the candle in her hand to light the other two. First the one on the left, closest to the center, and then the one on the end. Then she replaced the first candle in its holder.

"There," she said, turning back to us. "The whole neighborhood can see that we put light out into the world."

Everyone stood there for a minute, watching the flickering candles as they danced, their reflection in the window making it seem like there were six of them. It felt like an important moment. I didn't know why, but it felt good to be a part of it.

"All right, mishpocheh," Bubbe said. "Let's eat!"

Everyone laughed. But her wide smile, and the sheen of tears in her eyes, told me that letting her light the candles hadn't just been a way to save my butt, it had been exactly what she'd needed.

I'D HAD NO IDEA WHAT TO EXPECT FROM MY FIRST Hanukkah dinner, but the feast I got was like something out of a fantasy novel. If I'd been given a writing prompt to create a Hanukkah meal, I never would have been able to do it justice if I hadn't experienced it with my own two eyes. And my nose. And, thankfully, all my gloriously happy tastebuds.

Not knowing where I was supposed to sit at the dining room table, I excused myself to the bathroom (which I had to find on my own, as though I knew where it was!) while everyone got settled.

When I returned, Aviva's family was already seated, allowing me to confidently take my chair between Aviva's mom and Bubbe. I tucked myself into the table, which was covered in all those plates and platters I'd seen in the kitchen, now overflowing with food.

Yum, I thought, taking a big sniff, my mouth flooding with anticipation. But then I remembered I was supposed to be Aviva. She wouldn't just say yum to *herself*.

"Yum! This all looks and smells ah-may-zing!" I announced. "Can we dig in or what?"

I almost cringed at my boldness, but it must have hit the mark because Aviva's mom laughed. "Now that you're here, we can," she said as she picked up a platter off the table and held it in front of me. "I'll hold it for you while you serve yourself."

"Oh, uh, thanks!" I said brightly as I dished out what looked like a white hamburger, without the bun, but with a round slice of carrot on top, and put it on my appetizer plate. As the platter made its way around the table, I tried to discreetly figure out what the patty was. Fake meat of some type? How was I supposed to even eat it?

When they all had their portion—except for Benny, who made faces at it while the platter passed him by—as one, they reached for their small forks.

Okay, so buns weren't coming. Not a burger, then. I picked up my fork and watched out of the corner of my eye as Bubbe dug into her patty. I followed her example, with less enthusiasm. Sure, everything smelled good, but what *was* this? It had the texture of meat loaf but was the wrong color. Was it chicken? Or maybe pork? Wait, no, Jewish people didn't eat pork . . . did they? I felt like I'd heard that somewhere before. What was the word . . .

kosher? But I didn't really know what that meant, other than it had something to do with pork. Also, there were kosher pickles. And salt? Wait, did they eat pork, but just on special occasions and with special pickles and salt?

I wished Aviva was there so I could ask her before I said some clueless thing that would out us both.

"Ma, here's the chrain," Aviva's mom said as I was still trying to sort it out. She put a dollop of some beet-red-colored stuff on her whatever-it-was and then passed the little pot of it to me. "Here, Vivvy, pass this to your grandmother."

I was about to take some for my own whatever-it-was patty, but just a whiff made my nose burn and my eyes water. "Ugh!" I said before I even realized it.

Bubbe laughed. "I guess that answers my question about if it's hot."

I quickly passed her the stuff and watched her put a huge spoonful on her plate.

"You want to try it?" she asked.

I shook my head vehemently. "No, thanks. It's so strong!"

"Why bother with horseradish if it's not hot?" Aviva's dad said, grinning at me. "And when you get older, you'll learn to like it on your fish."

Fish?

Oh, fish! The patty was fish! That explained it. It still seemed kind of odd, but I liked fish. Sometimes, on Fridays, especially if Mom was working late, Gramps would take me for fish and chips.

I looked around the table but didn't see any tartar sauce. Aaron was eating his plain, so I lifted up my fork to dig in.

But then a thought occurred to me: Was Aviva right-handed or left-handed like me? Were identical twins the same? Or maybe we were mirrors of each other. There was no way to know. I couldn't exactly pull out my phone to ask her. Would anyone notice if I used the wrong hand?

"Vivvy?" Bubbe said. "Aren't you going to eat your gefilte fish?"

"Yes," I said. "I mean, yeah, of course!"

With my left hand, I used the side of my fork to slice off a bite of the patty. Then I moved the fork to my right hand to stab the food and raise it to my mouth. Because this was how I was going to have to eat now. At least until I could get a hold of Aviva to find out for sure which was her dominant hand.

Until then, I had this entirely new food in my mouth. It was delicious, but different than anything I'd ever had before. It was chilled, and the texture was like a hamburger but more delicate and with a bit of sweetness to it. I was going to ask for another piece, but if this was just the starter and it was this incredible, I wanted to save room for all of it.

BY THE TIME DINNER WAS OVER, I WAS SO FULL, I COULD barely breathe. Totally worth it. And I'd even managed to make it through without getting found out. Although I have to say, the right hand–left hand routine got old very quickly. But when Benny asked what I was doing and I'd explained that I was trying to learn to be ambidextrous, no one seemed to think it strange. Like maybe Aviva did stuff like that all the time.

Halfway through the meal, when I was starting to feel

comfortable and had begun to let my guard down, I realized the talking had stopped. The eating had stopped. *Everything* had stopped.

I looked up to see everyone staring at me in horror. I was in the process of squeezing ketchup on my latkes. I froze for a second, realizing my faux pas too late. Apparently, the proper toppings for latkes are either applesauce or sour cream (or, in the case of Aaron and Benny—both).

How was I supposed to know? Latkes are fried potatoes. French fries are fried potatoes, and you eat *those* with ketchup. *Why was ketchup even on the table?* I wondered, until I later saw Aaron squirt a giant blob of it onto his brisket.

But by then I had shrugged and owned it, saying I was just trying something. After a couple of eye rolls, everyone went back to talking and eating like nothing had happened.

No one seemed to think that Aviva acting odd was, well . . . odd. Which made me wonder if we really could pull this off.

"Time to play dreidel!" Aaron announced. He still had powdered sugar and jelly all over his face from the donuts. Plural. Where did such a small kid put all that food?

Everyone else moaned.

"Buddy, maybe we'll play tomorrow," his dad said, leaning back from the table and patting his belly.

"Aw, come on, guys!" Aaron whined as he looked at me. "You'll play with me, Vivvy, won't you?"

I felt bad. I could totally see how fun it would be to have Aaron as my little brother—something I'd always wished for.

Although, as Aviva's little brother, he was kind of, sort of mine, too, wasn't he?

But the truth was, in that moment, all I knew about "playing dreidel" was that you spun a clay top-like thing and that there was a song we'd learned in fourth-grade music class.

But Aaron made it sound like there was more to it than that. Like maybe there was a whole game involved? I loved games, but how would it look when I didn't know any of the rules? I was already exhausted from pretending to be Aviva all evening.

So while I didn't want to disappoint Aaron, until I could look up how to play, I took the easy way out. "I'm sorry," I said. "Too full. Tomorrow, okay?"

His shoulders slumped. "Promise?"

I hesitated. Would I even be here the next day? But as he looked at me with those hopeful, puppy-dog eyes, I said, "You'll get to play tomorrow, I promise."

And I meant it. Even if I couldn't play with him, I'd make sure Aviva did.

CHAPTER 23
Aviva

"WHY DON'T YOU TEXT YOUR MOM AND LET HER KNOW we're almost home?" said Gramps as we turned onto Westford Lane. "She can come down and help get the tree into the elevator."

"Oh, sure," I said, automatically reaching for my phone, which was tucked into Holly's backpack by my feet. But I had just opened the flap when I realized that Gramps didn't mean *my* mom, obviously. He meant Holly's mom! And I didn't have her phone number.

I considered texting Holly and having her send the message for me, but then I checked the clock on the dashboard. Holly was probably right in the middle of dinner now. Maybe even the traditional Hanukkah feast that had been promised. *If* my parents had managed to follow through this time ...

I hoped Holly was doing okay. I hoped she was enjoying Hanukkah. I felt a tiny stab of regret, wishing I could be there, too. With her, celebrating my holiday.

At the same time, I was also really looking forward to trimming my first tree.

"Oh, I just remembered that my battery is dead," I said.

"Here, you can use mine." Gramps handed me his phone.

I opened up the contacts and searched for *Mom* but nothing came up. Obviously, he wouldn't call his own daughter Mom! What was Holly's mom's name again?

Think, Aviva, think!

Growing nervous, I opened up the text messages. Right at the top was a message from someone named Charlie. Charlie! Right, that was it. And the most recent texts were talking about setting up the tree and stopping by the grocery store, so this had to be her.

I typed out a quick text letting her know we were almost home. She responded with a thumbs-up emoji seconds later.

Whew. Okay. I've got this.

The apartment building was four stories tall, one of those square classic red brick buildings. As Gramps pulled into a parking spot out front marked with a wheelchair sign, a woman came out of the building, zipping up a hoodie. The sun had set, and a chill was definitely coming on. The sky was clear, though, with a sliver of a crescent moon visible over the roof of the next building over, so I didn't think it would snow again. Not tonight, at least.

"How was the tree farm?" the woman who had to be Holly's mom asked, her words making clouds of steam in front of her face. "Wait a second. What did you do to your hair?"

I smiled brightly. "Just trying something new . . . for Christmas! What do you think? The bangs are cute, right?"

She frowned.

Uh-oh. "Anyway, the tree farm was great!" I chirped. "Best ever!"

She gave me another surprised look. "Well, I'm glad you had a good time. Dad, why don't you head on inside? Holly and I can handle this." She began undoing the straps that held the tree on top of the car's roof. I waited for instructions, hoping I wasn't expected to know how to do this already. Once the straps were off, Holly's mom hauled the tree from the roof and told me to grab it up at the top. It was heavy, but I could handle it as we carried it into the lobby where Gramps stood holding the elevator doors open.

I noticed we were leaving a trail of needles on the lobby's carpet, but no one seemed bothered by it as the elevator doors closed behind us. We went up to the second floor and carried the tree into an apartment. I helped Holly's mom wrangle it into a stand, then it was my job to screw four bolts into its trunk to keep it upright while Gramps barked orders at us, like "more to the left" and "back to the right again," and "that's too far!"

Finally we stood back to admire our work. The tree stood in front of a window in the living room, looking like . . . well, a tree in a living room. I'd never given it much thought before, but confronted with the reality of this tradition, I couldn't help feeling like it was pretty strange. Who wants a tree in their living room? I guessed it didn't really become magical until there were lights and decorations on it.

It did smell nice, though, like the air freshener in Dad's car times about a thousand.

I took the opportunity to check out the room, too. The furniture had a retro vibe, with a blue velvet sofa and a leather recliner facing a fireplace, the TV mounted on the wall above. There was a small dining table to one side, and a hallway stretching toward the back of the apartment. There were some Christmas decorations scattered about—three stockings on the fireplace mantel, along with framed photos of mini-Holly sitting on Santa's lap. Some porcelain angels stood on a side table, and a couple of wooden reindeer acted as a centerpiece on the table.

It was nice and all, but . . . where was the mistletoe? Where were the snow globes? I couldn't help feeling that it was a little lackluster when compared to the houses on the Hallmark Channel, where every single surface was covered in garlands and lights. I'd assumed that was how everyone decorated for Christmas.

"Why don't you go get your pajamas on?" said Holly's mom. "I've got some soup in the slow cooker. We'll eat, and then—we'll do the tree!"

"On it!" I bounced toward the hallway and started opening doors. First a bathroom. Then a room with a king-size bed draped in white chenille. *Hmm*, probably not Holly's?

I kept going.

On the third try, I knew I'd found my sister's bedroom. I grinned as I went in and shut the door behind me. So. Many. Books. A tall bookshelf next to her dresser was seriously overloaded. Like—if there was an earthquake right now, I would probably be buried beneath an avalanche of books. I was amazed the shelves hadn't collapsed! Had she read them all?

There were even more stacked up next to her bed and on another shorter shelf in the closet.

The bed was actually *made*. (I never made mine at home—why bother when you're just going to get back into it?) And the walls were decorated with some magazine pictures of horses, a poster of an anime that I didn't recognize, and drawings of dragons and fairies. Did Holly make these? She hadn't told me she liked to draw, too. I felt suddenly overcome with pride. My sister was so talented!

I pulled out my phone, dying to text Holly and ask how things were going and tell her that I was standing *in her bedroom*! But I hadn't heard from her yet and didn't want to interrupt dinner. Dad got very grumpy about phones at the table, and I didn't want to get her in trouble.

I dug through her drawers until I found a pair of pajamas. Not just any pajamas. Christmas pajamas! They were flannel (my sister sure loved her flannel), with a pattern of snowflakes and gingerbread men. I giggled to myself as I pulled them on. They were super cozy and smelled like laundry detergent.

As I finished pulling them on, I turned around and froze.

A gray tabby cat was on my bed. Er, Holly's bed. This must be Sherlock, the friendly cat from the picture on Holly's phone, except . . . he was staring at me in ferocious judgment, eyeing me like the impostor I was.

I didn't know a lot about cats, since Mom was allergic to, like, everything, but at friends' houses they usually snuggled right up to me.

Not this one. His back was arched, hair standing on end. His slitted green eyes burned with distrust as he started to hiss.

In short, this creature was *terrifying*. I gulped, backing away.

"It's okay, kitty," I said, my voice pitched high. My hand fumbled for the doorknob. "I'm a friend of Holly's. Don't be scared."

It was a ridiculous thing to say. *I* was the terrified one!

Sherlock hissed again, and I found the doorknob. Yanking open the door, I slipped back out into the hallway, heart racing even as I rushed back to the relative safety of the living room. I just hoped that angry furball wouldn't attack me in my sleep.

THE SMELL OF THE FIR TREE HAD SPREAD THROUGHOUT the whole apartment by the time we sat down at the small dining table. A bowl of steaming leek and potato soup sat before me, with a platter of garlic bread, and . . . cookies! A whole plate of sugar cookies sat on the table, decorated with white icing and red and green sprinkles.

"Yum!" I said, grabbing a cookie from the plate and taking a huge bite. I moaned in delight as the buttery cookie crumbled in my mouth and the icing melted against my tongue and the sprinkles crunched between my teeth. "So good!"

"Holly!" Charlie said sharply, pulling the plate of cookies away. "What are you doing? Those are for dessert!"

I stared at her, the half-eaten cookie inches from my mouth.

Uh-oh. I was very much raised in an eat-dessert-first type of family. Or, at least, my parents didn't mind if my brothers and I sampled the sweets before eating our meal.

Clearly, it was not the same here.

I swallowed and set the cookie down on the table. "Sorry," I said. "They looked really, really good."

Charlie gave me another warning glance, then took her seat and passed napkins around to me and Gramps. Still feeling scolded, I tried the soup. It was deliciously creamy and warmed me from the inside out. I wondered if I could somehow get the recipe for my dad.

My knees bounced under the table as Gramps and Charlie talked about their days. Charlie asked about the pageant rehearsal, and I did my best to talk about sets and props and lighting when what I really wanted was to figure out how to get Holly to perform in the pageant with me. There had to be a way! But blowing my cover with her mom and grandpa wasn't it.

Finally, dinner was over and the dishes were cleared and it was time to trim the tree. After pulling up a Christmas music playlist on her phone, Charlie brought out two huge plastic totes, one marked TREE LIGHTS, and the other ORNAMENTS. We opened the box of lights first, and . . . holy moly. They were a mess! Imagine a ball of yarn after it had been mauled by an enthusiastic cheetah.

We got to work, trying to untangle them all. Whenever we found a string's plug-in end, Gramps would put it into the electrical outlet on the wall, and half the time, the lights didn't even work. Or half the lights were burned-out, or they would blink randomly on and off. We ended up with two strands that worked, which seemed like plenty to me, but then Charlie produced two more unopened boxes of lights from the hardware store.

"Seriously?" I said. "You had those the whole time? Why did I spend twenty minutes trying to untangle all of these?"

Charlie's eyebrows went up for a second, making me think Holly never would have said something like that. I froze until Charlie laughed and shrugged. "We had to figure out which ones were still working somehow, didn't we?"

I wrinkled my nose, not sure that I agreed.

A growl drew my attention down to the lights I was working on. The cat had reappeared. He was tucked under the tree, his eyes laser-focused on me, body puffed up.

I tensed.

"Sherlock, what's gotten into you?" said Charlie. "Don't you like the tree?"

I laughed nervously. Sherlock was a fitting name. He surely suspected me, after all!

"Maybe he wants to play with the lights?" I said, wondering if *he* was the enthusiastic cheetah. Taking one of the burned-out strands, I dangled it playfully in front of the cat.

He hissed and backed farther beneath the tree.

"Or not . . ."

"That old crabby cat," said Gramps. He was sitting on the recliner with the box of ornaments at his feet, gently pulling them out one by one and removing their protective tissue paper. "He doesn't like change, just like me." He stared at Charlie when he said that last part.

"Oh, don't start," she said. "Even you have to admit that Rowena Village was nice. And you liked the food!"

Gramps harrumphed. "I said it was *edible*. That's hardly a glowing review."

With a roll of her eyes, Charlie picked up a box of lights and started tearing it open. "I wish you'd stop making me out to be the bad guy, here. I'm concerned, Dad. Your balance has gotten so bad lately. If you had a fall, and Holly and I weren't here to help you—"

"Charlene, this is my decision to make," Gramps barked. "And I've already told you, I'm not ready to move into a home. Besides, it was just a small fall. I'm fine. Barely even bruised." He turned toward me. "And Holly wants me around. Don't you, Holly Tree?"

I stood, frozen, not sure how to respond to what felt like a really important question. I darted my eyes between Gramps and Charlie, my insides squirming from the sudden tension in the room.

What would Holly say?

"Of course, Gramps!" I said, hoping I'd gotten it right. "I love having you here with us!"

Gramps swiveled his head to give Charlie a smug look.

Charlie sighed and said, "All right, no need to gang up on me. *Again.* Let's get those lights up."

"Yes!" I'd been waiting for this all night. I took the strand I was holding and threw it into the tree branches.

Charlie laughed. "What are you doing?"

I paused. "Um. Putting the lights on the tree?"

"Ha ha. Very funny. Start at the bottom, like usual, twining the lights in and out so the whole tree is covered. You know I like *lots* of sparkle!"

Sparkle! Charlie was a woman after my own heart!

I started over, at the bottom this time, wrapping the lights around the prickly branches. Back and forth, back and forth. At first I was sure we had way more lights now than we needed, but Charlie wasn't kidding. She truly did like lots of lights. I kept getting tangled up in them as I worked, and more than once had to backtrack as the strands twisted around my arms and legs. Soon my hands were sticky with gunky tree sap stuff and there were pine needles in my hair, but I was loving every second.

Charlie brought out a step stool so I could get the lights on the highest branches. Once I was done, she plugged in the strands, and *boom.* The tree lit up in colorful twinkles—red, orange, blue, green, and pink. It was stunning!

"Now for the fun part," said Gramps.

"Don't forget," said Charlie. "Sherlock loves to play with the low-hanging ornaments. Remember to hang the special ones up high so he can't reach them."

"Right!" I said, looking at the growing pile of ornaments at Gramps's feet. Everything from fragile glass balls to felted snowmen to crafty reindeer made out of wine corks and pipe cleaners. How would I know which ones were special?

Gramps put little wire hooks on each ornament and handed them to me and Charlie to hang up. We sang along to "Jingle Bells" and "Deck the Halls" while we worked, and every time Charlie held up an ornament and proclaimed, "Oh, do you remember this one?" I would squeal, "Yes! I love this one!" even though I was seeing it for the first time.

"The macaroni snowflake you made in second grade!" Charlie said.

Gramps pulled a ballerina from the box and declared, with tears in his eyes, "I gave this one to your grandmother on our last Christmas together." I offered him a hug after that—he looked like he needed one.

Charlie had said to keep the special ornaments out of reach of the cat, but it felt like they were all special. I marveled at each one, wishing Holly was there to tell me her own memories about them. I wanted to know which ones were special to *her*.

There was one glittery ceramic ornament with the comedy and tragedy masks I knew so well from the theater, and I knew immediately that this one was my favorite. And right after that, Gramps handed me a small glass typewriter, and I wondered if Holly liked this one the most. No, of course she did. My twin brain told me this one was definitely her favorite.

I hung our two favorites together.

CHAPTER 24

Holly

EVERYONE PITCHED IN TO HELP CLEAN AFTER THE FEAST. Aviva's parents wrapped up all the leftovers, including making up a "care package" that would go home with Bubbe, and then arranged all the containers like a Tetris game of deliciousness in the already-full fridge.

My job, as I learned from Benny when he barked at me to get out of his way, was to collect all the dishes and glasses from the table to hand to Aaron, who then scraped off all the food into the compost bin and placed them in a neat pile by the sink. Benny then took the dishes and stacked them in the dishwasher and washed the big platters that wouldn't fit.

After I finished clearing the table, it was up to me to dry the clean platters. Once I figured all that out, I became part of the incredibly efficient Davis cleanup crew.

Bubbe sat on a stool at the island, but as I dried the last of the platters, I could see that she was sagging a little. "You okay, Bubbe?" I asked, sliding the platter on the counter, hoping someone else would put it away because I had zero clue where it should go.

Her eyes widened. "Oh, yes, Vivvy, of course. Just a little tired after that big meal."

"Why don't I drive you home, Ma," Aviva's mom said, coming around the island to stand in front of Bubbe.

Bubbe glanced up at the clock on the microwave. "But it's still early. And it's Hanukkah!"

"We're doing it again tomorrow," Aviva's dad said. "Vivvy wanted a Hanukkah extravaganza, and she's getting it. Just wait until you see what's on for tomorrow."

Well, *that* was intriguing. I swiveled to look at him. "Really? What?"

He aimed a sly grin at me. "All in good time, daughter. But don't you worry, it will be—"

"EPIC!" I blurted out Avivaciously, doing a fist pump in the air.

Everyone laughed. I was starting to get why Aviva loved being on the stage. She wanted to entertain people. She wanted to make people happy with her performance. It made sense. And somehow, it was easier for me to be the center of attention when I was pretending to be Aviva. Was it possible there had been a bit of an actress inside me this whole time?

Bubbe slid off her stool with a grunt. "Maybe I should go. These old bones could use a hot bath."

Aviva's mom grabbed her keys and purse and took Bubbe's arm. Over her shoulder, she said to me, "Vivvy, can you grab your grandmother's leftovers and help us out?"

After Bubbe gave everyone—including me—a hug and a big kiss goodbye, I followed them out with the shopping bag that contained three patties of gefilte fish, brisket, and a few latkes smothered in sour cream. Once Bubbe was buckled in the passenger seat, I placed the bag in her lap and, before I even realized it, leaned over and gave her another kiss on the cheek. It was an

Aviva thing to do, but, at least in this instance, it was a Holly thing to do, too.

I waved as they pulled out of the driveway. When I turned back toward the house, the lit menorah in the window caught my eye, the three flames flickering cheerily. I had a sudden pang of homesickness as I thought about how Aviva was trimming *my* tree, but at the same time, I felt bad that she wasn't here with me, seeing *her* menorah lit in *her* window. I pulled my phone out of my pocket and took a photo to send her so she wouldn't feel like she was completely missing her holiday.

I wasn't exactly missing mine, since Christmas was still a few days away, but one thing I was missing in that moment was my sister.

ONCE BUBBE HAD LEFT, IT WAS LIKE THE HOLIDAY SWITCH had been turned off. The candles on the menorah burned down, and life was back to what seemed to be normal for Aviva's family.

Everyone had basically scattered: Her dad pulled out folders of paperwork and sat down at the kitchen island with a pen and a calculator, while Benny escaped downstairs and Aaron plopped himself in the living room to watch TV.

No one seemed interested in what I was doing, so it felt like a good time to investigate Aviva's room. I headed down the hall and was easily able to identify it by the collage of Broadway posters on her door: *The Lion King*, *Hamilton*, *Fiddler on the Roof*, and of course, *Cats*. I went inside, only to find that the door had just been the beginning. The entire room was papered with posters, photos, and even colorful word cutouts that said things like SUPERSTAR! and BELIEVE! and, over the bed, LIVE YOUR DREAM!

"Whoa," I said out loud. "This is definitely your room, Aviva."

I loved it. Even down to her messy, unmade bed, which was totally on-brand.

On her desk was a cardboard box that caught my attention. She'd never said I couldn't look at anything, so despite its slightly musty smell, I dug in and found some pink satin bags closed with drawstrings. I opened one up and almost screamed when I thought there was a rat in there! But no, it was . . . a wig?

I carefully pulled it out. Long blond hair. I studied it a moment before hesitantly trying it on. I peered at myself in the mirror. Between the Sharpie freckle and this long, luxurious hair, I looked totally unlike me. Which, I guess, was the point.

Returning to the bags, I pulled out a bunch of costumes that must have been from a theater, or that maybe she'd borrowed from the senior center. At the bottom, I found another wig. This one was ice blue at the roots and phased into dark blue at the ends. I put it on and took a selfie and sent it to Aviva. **Your costume for the pageant? What do you think?**

When she didn't respond, I put the phone down on her desk and sat on the bed, overcome by a big yawn. What a day it had been! I glanced at her bedside clock. It was almost eight thirty, about the time I'd be sitting with Gramps, both of us reading side by side, or me working on my newest story.

Wait. My stories! My notebook, with all my stories in it, was in my backpack. Which was with Aviva.

My phone buzzed.

There was a line of hearts and heart-eye emojis and then, **I had the same thought! Totally for PAGEANT!**

I grinned. I'd been joking, but something told me she wasn't.

> **How's it going there?**

> **Great, sis! Xmas rocks!**

> **You have my backpack and notebook, right?**

> **Y!**

So that was a relief.

"How was tonight?"

I looked up to see Aviva's mom standing in the doorway. "Oh, hi. Pardon?"

"Did our do-over of night one meet your expectations?"

Oh, right!

"It exceeded them," I said truthfully.

She smiled and came into the room, sitting on the bed beside me. I swallowed, instantly nervous. It had started to feel easy pretending to be Aviva when I was surrounded by the whole family. I could blend in and just go with the flow. But being one-on-one with her mom felt . . . dangerous. Like any second she could realize that I was a fraud.

"Good," she said with a smile. "Bubbe had a good time, too. You two are alike in so many ways. Sometimes I think you really must have her DNA in you." She paused before adding, "She loves that you're in the pageant, by the way."

"Me too," I said, channeling Aviva.

"You can stay up late tonight since you're on holidays this week, but don't forget to brush and floss."

She kissed me on the forehead, just like my mom often did. It felt nice. Like maybe in a weird way, I really did belong there. "Anyway," she said, getting up from the bed, "I'm off to go escape into my reading cave."

"What are you reading?" I asked with genuine interest.

Her eyes lit up. "Oh, this fun mystery that my book club started reading last month, but I'm only getting to now. What's it called . . . ?" She looked up at the ceiling, trying to remember. "Oh, right! *Checkmate*. By Ed Martin. Apparently, he's local."

My jaw dropped. Yes, he was local. Like, he's-my-grandpa local! I snapped my mouth shut and bit my lip to keep from blurting out that she was reading a book written by my own grandpa, because, well I couldn't tell her that. But I really, really wanted to.

Aviva was going to faint when she heard this coincidence.

I knew Gramps wrote great books, even though I wasn't allowed to read them yet. He said there was too much PG-13 content in them. But the second he and Mom would let me, I was going to devour every single one.

"Cool," I said, suddenly struggling to think of how Aviva might respond. "I'm glad you're enjoying it."

"I am. I might grab a few more of his titles at the library to get me through the holidays. Feel like going with me?"

"To the library?" I perked up. "Yes! You don't have to ask me twice!"

She tilted her head, frowning. "Really? You never want to go to the library."

I stilled. "Oh. Right. But, I mean, it's something to do over the holidays, I guess?"

She started toward the door. "Oh, Aviva, daughter mine, you never cease to surprise and delight me. I'll check on the office schedule and will let you know when we can go. Anyway, don't forget your teeth."

After she left, I glanced at my phone, and when I saw that Aviva still hadn't texted me back, I figured it was as good a time as any to get ready for bed. After putting all the wigs and costumes carefully back into the box, I turned to Aviva's dresser, looking for pajamas. It only took two drawers to find what I was looking for, and when faced with the choice of Hello Kitty or tie-dye, I went full-on Avivacious: tie-dye bottoms and Hello Kitty top.

I padded down the hall to the bathroom. The door was open, but the room wasn't empty. Aaron was in there, brushing his teeth with an electric toothbrush, looking like a rabid dog with the foam that was dripping out of his mouth into the sink. He must have used half a tube of toothpaste.

I hesitated. "Sorry, I'll give you a minute to finish up."

That was clearly the wrong thing to say. He made a face and said, "What for?" He spat some of that froth onto the counter. "I already peed."

Okay, then. Apparently, Aviva shared the bathroom with her brothers. He slid a package of flossers toward me. They were in the shape of giraffes. How cute. We only got the boring string kind at home.

I took one of the picks and started flossing, sneaking glances at Aaron in the mirror as he finished up and spit all that foam into the sink. He was so adorably slobby.

"What's the deal with you today?" he asked suddenly.

I stilled, blinking at him in the mirror. "What do you mean?"

He didn't respond, just stared at me, suspicious. Very suspicious.

I swallowed, trying to figure out what to say while not looking guilty. "I'm not being weird. You're being weird. I'm just excited about Hanukkah and the pageant and everything."

He stared at me for a long time, but I forced myself not to look away.

Finally he shrugged and walked around me toward the door. He didn't seem fully convinced, though, even as he muttered, "You're always weird, Aviva."

I exhaled in relief. Somehow, I felt like my sister would have taken that as a compliment.

CHAPTER 25

Aviva

I WAS EXHAUSTED BY THE TIME I FINALLY GOT TO TOP THE tree with a shiny tin star. Gramps was right: The crooked branch on top did make the star tilt at a precarious angle, but as I stood back and took it all in, I was in love with this Christmas tree. It was probably the best ever! At least, the best ever first time decoration attempt by a Jewish girl who had literally no idea what she was doing.

Charlie put her arm around me, surprising me at first. But it felt good and like what my own mom would do, so I leaned into it. I am a natural hugger, after all.

"I'd say it's the best tree we've ever had," said Gramps.

See?

"I can't disagree," said Charlie. "But now it's time for bed." She kissed the top of my head, and I squirmed happily. My mom always did that, too. "Go brush your teeth, and I'll come tuck you in."

"Yes, ma'am!" I said, saluting her.

Charlie chuckled. "You're in a funny mood today, Holly."

"She's been like that since we left the center," said Gramps. "Must be the influence of all those pageant kids bringing you out of your shell."

"Maybe!" I said, but this felt like dangerous territory, so I turned away from them both.

But as soon as I set foot into the hallway, I hesitated. I rushed back to Holly's grandpa and threw my arms around him. "G'night, Gramps!" I said, kissing him on the cheek.

Then I hightailed it off to the bathroom before I could find out if that was un-Holly or not.

It took me a while to do things that are normally second nature, like brushing my teeth and flossing and washing my face, because nothing was where it was supposed to be. The washcloths were in a drawer, not under the sink. The toothbrush was in a medicine cabinet, not a cup on the counter. And where were the fun giraffe-shaped flossers that I used at home? (Nowhere. Holly just used regular string floss. Boring.)

Finally I finished up and made my way to Holly's bedroom. I pulled back the covers and slipped in between the sheets, and . . . Were these flannel, *too*? I laughed out loud at my warmth-obsessed sister but snuggled in deeper. The bed was extra cozy, like it was giving me a hug. Which was welcome after the mind-warp of a day I'd had.

Holly's mom came in a second later to say good night. She tucked the covers around me and gave me another kiss on my forehead. I wiggled my toes happily under the blankets. "Get a good night's rest," she said, as she flipped off the light. "We're going to have a fun day tomorrow."

"Okay. Good night," I said.

Only after she'd closed the door did I wonder, *Wait. What's happening tomorrow?* Holly had mentioned getting the tree today, but nothing about tomorrow. Didn't her mom have to work?

Whatever. Time would tell soon enough.

I sighed contentedly and nestled into the blankets. I'd hardly had time to think about everything that had happened, but here I was, sleeping in a strange apartment, in a strange bed. Pretending to be my sister, who I'd just learned about and who was, in some ways, a complete stranger. Her mom and Gramps were definitely strangers.

And I was playing the part of someone who celebrated Christmas. As an actress, I felt comfortable playing that role, but did it feel like me?

Not really.

I was starting to drift off when . . .

Meeeeeooooooowwwww . . .

I bolted upright, my heart jumping.

There, on the dresser.

Two eyes glowed in the moonlight. An angry tail swished back and forth.

Sherlock. Watching me.

And waiting.

Aviva! Are you there?

911!

!!! U ok? Fam ok?

Fine! Need intel. Wait: are YOU okay? Gramps okay?

All ok. Tree is *chefs kiss* U will 🖤.

Can't wait to see it!

how was hanukkah?

Delicious! Fun. A little overwhelming.

Q: Are you left or right-handed?

Left-U?

Same! Okay good, I was worried I'd have to become a righty. Also is your family kosher?

Nope. Yours? HA JK!

Oh okay. And why didn't you tell me I was supposed to give the blessing? IN HEBREW

Oops? Sorry? I forgot!

But U didn't tell me bout yr killer 🐆!

Sherlock? He's an old sweetie!

Pls! Wants to murder me in my sleep.

151

If u dont hear from me in a.m. send help!

HA!

Oh here is a pic of your notebook with the song Download .png file

Thank you! Want to FaceTime?

2 Tired ,z^z

Good night, sister. 🌙

Gnight, sis.Luv U.xoxo

Love you, too.

CHAPTER 26
Holly

"VIVVY? YOU OKAY?"

The voice seemed to come from far away. I was standing alone on the stage at Rowena Village, a huge audience in front of me, getting ready to sing the blessings over lighting the menorah. In Hebrew. All those eyes on me, I was terrified I was going to mess everything up. The voice had come from the wings. I looked over and saw Gramps and was about to tell him that I wasn't Aviva but his granddaughter, Holly. No words came out of my mouth, though. But then I remembered I wasn't even supposed to be doing the pageant. So why was I standing on this stage, completely and utterly unprepared? Everyone was going to laugh at me! I was going to—

"Vivvy?"

A giant lump of kid landed on top of me, yanking me from the nightmare.

"Ughhhhh! Aaron!"

"Mom sent me to wake you up."

"By jumping on me? Please get off me!" I rolled to the side to dislodge him. I was so not a morning person, and even if I had been, well, I couldn't think of a worse way to be woken up.

He didn't go very far. "Aw, Vivvy, don't be mad," Aaron said, looking at me with a ridiculously sweet grin on his face—a couple of teeth missing. "Mom wanted me to make sure you were okay. You never sleep this late."

"So you thought jumping on me while I was sleeping was a good way to find out if I was okay?"

He shrugged but looked gleefully guilty.

Well, that simply would not do.

So I tickled him. I tickled him until he begged me through his giggles to stop. Although he wasn't exactly trying to get away from me. I tickled him some more until he threatened he would pee.

That did it.

"What's going on in here?" Aviva's mom stood in the doorway, arms crossed, but with a smile on her face.

"Aviva was tickling me, trying to make me pee!" Aaron blurted.

His mom and I exchanged amused glances. His false accusation was deeply flawed. "Right," I said. "Because I *want* your pee in my bed." I gently shoved him with my foot as I sat up.

"I was just trying to make sure you weren't dead!" Aaron announced.

I laughed. Although I could have used more sleep. I'd stayed up late, working on Aviva's pageant song until I'd realized, rather suddenly, that if this ruse lasted for another full day, I really was going to have to give the blessings over the menorah. So then I'd switched to trying to learn them. Thank goodness for YouTube! I'd watched the videos, following along with the phonetic subtitles, and practiced over and over until I couldn't keep my eyes open.

"So," Aviva's mom said. "Still want to go to the library? Appointments are finally starting to taper off as we're getting into the holidays, so I thought I'd take the morning off."

I did very much want to go to the library, but my enthusiasm the night before had obviously been un-Aviva-like, so I made a face and shrugged. "I guess so."

"Or you could stay home with me and Benny and play video games?" Aaron said, a hopeful look on his face.

For half a second, I was torn. Not because of the video games but because, earlier pounce aside, I was really starting to warm up to that little brother thing.

"We can hang out later," I promised.

"All right," Aviva's mom said. "Wash up and get some breakfast. We'll leave in an hour."

CHAPTER 27

Aviva

MY SHOULDER WAS THROBBING PAINFULLY WHEN I WOKE up the next morning, my palms felt like they'd been rubbed raw, and there was a weight on my legs, like I had a heavy blanket at the foot of my bed. Sunlight was streaming in through my curtains, making me squint as I opened my eyes.

Hold on. Why was the window on my left? Was I sleeping with my head on the wrong end of the bed? I groaned and rolled onto my side, kicking away the blanket.

The blanket that hissed and dug sharp claws into my ankles.

I yelped and bolted upright.

Not a blanket at all—it was the Demon Cat of Fleet Street!

I instinctively kicked again and Sherlock launched to the floor. He turned and glared at me.

"Sorry not sorry," I muttered, rubbing my ankle, surprised he hadn't drawn blood.

I looked down at my raw and aching hands. They were a wreck. There were red scratches from carrying the tree and even a blister where I'd gripped the saw handle. All that work explained my sore shoulder, too.

They never showed *that* on the Hallmark Channel.

The cat started to growl, likely still annoyed that I'd kicked him.

"What?" I said. "You were the one sleeping on me!"

That thought made me pause. Sherlock had been sleeping on

me. Like . . . practically cuddling. Did that mean he liked me? Was he my feline buddy now? You didn't just snuggle with your mortal enemy all night, did you?

I looked hopefully back over at the cat, who had skulked over to the bedroom door and sat down on his haunches, evidently waiting to be let out of the room. The look he was giving me was . . . let's just say, *not* of the "besties" variety. Pretty sure he was plotting my doom.

That was okay. I could make anyone like me, even Holly's vicious cat. And I was going to prove it!

"Here, kitty, kitty," I sang, patting the blankets in hopes that he might come back and curl up next to me again.

Sherlock bared his fangs and hissed—louder than the last time.

I shuddered. Okay, I would prove it *after* breakfast.

Climbing out of bed, I opened the door and Sherlock disappeared down the hallway.

I headed in the opposite direction. There were some noises coming from the kitchen, and as I turned the corner, I saw Charlie, pouring herself a cup of coffee.

She glanced up and startled, her eyes going wide.

Oh no! Did I forget to put on my disguise?

Wait . . . no. I *am* the disguise!

"Morning!" I chirped.

But her expression just became more bewildered as she looked at the clock on the microwave.

"Morning . . ." she said uncertainly, turning back to me. "What are you doing up so early?"

I blinked. It was almost eight. I'd actually slept in!

Oh, right. My sister was not a morning person.

I shrugged and sat down at the table. "You know how excited I get for all the fun Christmasy stuff this time of year. I couldn't stay in bed a second longer! Yay, Christmas!"

"Okay," Charlie said suspiciously as she added a splash of something thick and yellow-tinged to her coffee. At first I thought it was coffee creamer—my parents liked French vanilla—but then I saw the carton.

Eggnog!

I nearly gasped. Of course I'd heard of eggnog, but I'd never tried it. The name sounded kind of gross, but . . . "Can I have some?"

Charlie lifted an eyebrow at me. "I thought you didn't like eggnog," she said, even as she reached for a glass in the cupboard.

"Really?" I said. "I mean . . . I didn't used to. But it never hurts to try again."

"All right," Charlie singsonged suspiciously. She poured a small amount before handing me the glass.

Eggnog had always sounded like some mythical beverage that was only allowed to be enjoyed during the holidays. All the stores would boast *eggnog latte* this and *eggnog cookies* that, but I'd never had the real stuff.

I giddily lifted the glass to my lips and took a sip.

Then another.

It was . . . thick. And sweet. And creamy. And not really *eggy* so much as . . . cinnamony?

And I *loved* it. I drank the rest in three big gulps. "O-M-G! That is so good!" How could Holly not like this stuff?

Charlie laughed. "I guess tastes do change. Want some more?"

I shook my head, because even though it was delicious, it was also extremely rich, and I didn't want to get a stomachache before breakfast.

"So?" asked Charlie, sitting down across from me. "Aren't you going to ask why I haven't left for work yet?"

Oh! "Why haven't you left for work yet?"

She beamed and leaned forward, her eyes glinting with mischief. "I decided to play hooky today."

"What?" I squeaked. Then tried a smile. "I mean, you're taking the day off?"

She nodded. "I know how much you love this time of year, and I feel bad that I haven't been around more, and what time we have had together has been focused on Gramps and this whole assisted living thing. And I thought—well, I have a couple vacation days saved up, so why not take some time off?"

"Oh great!" I said, trying to sound convincing. "How much time?"

"Today and tomorrow," she said. "I'll have to go in on Thursday and Friday, but then I'm off for the weekend and Christmas . . . and to see your pageant! I know you're not going to be onstage, but I still want to go and support your . . . well, your contribution. Plus, maybe your grandfather will warm up to the place."

My mind whirred. Holly's mom was taking *two* days off. That hadn't been a part of the plan! I'd figured I could fool Gramps pretty well—I'd knocked it out of the park during our tree hunting mission yesterday. But to have to fool both of them?

Although that was what Holly was doing at my house. Fooling both my parents *and* my brothers. And I was supposed to be the actress, wasn't I?

Of course I was. I could do this. I could be Holly! I would just have to up my game a little . . . get into character and *be* Holly.

"Holly, what's wrong?" said Charlie, reaching across the table and putting a hand over mine. "I thought you'd be happy about this!"

"I am!" I said. "I definitely am. I . . . um . . ." I swallowed, thinking hard. Then—*aha!* "I just know that Gramps really doesn't want to move. Even though it's nice. But if he did move, I'd miss having him around."

Charlie's expression softened. "Me too, sweetheart. And I wouldn't even be considering it if I didn't honestly think it would be the best thing for him. More people to care for him, facilities that were designed with his needs in mind, and . . . I think the biggest thing of all is the social aspect. I would really love to see him make some friends. You know, besides you and me."

"Yeah, me too," I said, thinking again of the way he'd looked at my bubbe. Had that really only been yesterday? It felt like a week since I'd swapped clothes with Holly, trimmed her bangs, and left her in the bathroom with my grandmother. "I think he will make friends," I said. "You know that Sylvia lady? I'm pretty sure I saw him flirting with her."

Charlie's eyes widened. "Do tell!"

"Holly Jo Martin," boomed a stern voice. I shrank into my chair as Gramps—nope, nope, this was definitely *Grumps!*—walked into the kitchen, his cane thumping on the linoleum. "I've never known my granddaughter to be a gossip."

He gave me a disapproving look that made me squirm, but Charlie rolled her eyes. "Oh, come on, Dad. You can't blame us for being curious. Maybe *you* can tell us more about Sylvia."

"There is nothing to tell," he said, huffing. "And for the last time, I'm not moving into some old folks' penitentiary!"

Charlie held up her hands in surrender. "Message received. I didn't bring it up. Can we please have a nice holiday without any drama?"

Gramps muttered something I couldn't hear as Charlie got up to pour him a cup of coffee. "Now that you're here," she said, "I actually had something I wanted to talk to you both about."

"Wonderful," said Gramps, shooting me a wry look. "Last time we had a family heart-to-heart, she tried to ship me off to Rowena Village. Do you think this time it'll be the North Pole?"

I stifled a laugh. It was becoming clear to me that his grumbling was an act, at least a little bit.

"I would ship you off to the North Pole," said Charlie, setting the coffee down on the table, "if I didn't think Santa would send you right back! But no. I've been thinking, and you know what I want us all to do this morning?" She looked from me to Gramps, grinning ear to ear. "We're going to take a Martin family portrait for this year's Christmas cards!"

My eyebrows shot up. Christmas cards? A family portrait?

Great. I guess I was about to take this twin impostor thing to a whole new level. Complete with photographic evidence.

CHAPTER 28
Holly

AH, THE LIBRARY. MY SANCTUARY. MY HAPPY PLACE.

It wasn't until we were inside that I realized my tactical error. I glanced over at the checkout desk, like always, ready to say hi to whoever was working.

Because I knew every single staff member. And every single one of them knew *me*. Holly Martin, granddaughter of Ed Martin, famous local author who sometimes gave seminars about writing in this very building.

For a minute, I wished I'd worn one of Aviva's disguises—the blond wig or even the pink one. Her family wouldn't have blinked an eye, but it would have kept me from being recognized.

At least I was wearing clothes that were totally Avivacious: a baggy pair of army-green cargo pants with loads of zippered pockets, a pink-and-green camo top that had a glittery GIRL POWER decal, her purple puffy winter coat, and her beige UGG boots. It was an outfit that I never would have chosen for myself in a thousand years (Aviva didn't own even one flannel shirt—I had searched her entire closet!), but now that I was wearing it, I kind of loved it. The pants held all my stuff in the pockets, the shirt was colorful and cute, and the UGGs were really comfy. My sister had style.

"I'm going to ask about those mystery books," Aviva's mom said, pointing to where Ms. Clark, the librarian, stood, checking in books with her barcode scanner. Thankfully, she hadn't looked our way.

"Oh, um, I'm going . . . to go look up books about . . ." I shuffled through topics in my mind, trying to guess what would interest Aviva. Broadway? Fashion? Celebrity twins throughout history? "Uh . . . Hello Kitty." I finally blurted out, then cringed. Seriously, brain? I might be wearing Aviva's clothes, but I was still awkward Holly on the inside.

"Okay, well, I'm not sure how much one needs to know about Hello Kitty, but you do you."

She turned toward the front desk, which was my cue to escape before Ms. Clark saw me.

While I was itching to check out the new arrivals section to see what fantasy books had hit the shelves, I decided it was a good idea to find books on Hanukkah instead. While I'd learned the blessings, I still didn't feel like I knew enough about the holiday to finish the song.

After a trip to the self-serve computer to find out where the books would be shelved, I found several on the subject and took them to my favorite reading nook, dropping contentedly into the beanbag chair.

But as I opened the cover of the first book, I thought about the last time I'd been in that very spot and how I'd been working on my Christmas story for Gramps. I hadn't touched it in days, and now I wasn't sure I'd finish it in time for Christmas, especially since I didn't even have my notebook. Maybe when I got back to Aviva's house I could track down another notebook, and work on it when I had time.

"That doesn't look like Hello Kitty."

I looked up to see Aviva's mom standing over me. "Oh, no, I guess you were right. What more do I need to know about Hello

Kitty?" But then I worried that looking up Hanukkah was making Aviva look bad. Although it was too late to try to hide the books.

"You about ready to go?"

I nodded and hauled myself out of the chair.

"Do you want to check those books out?" she asked.

"Oh, uh, I mean . . ."

Aviva's mom smiled. "Don't be embarrassed. I'm glad you're interested in learning more about the holiday." She put her arm around my shoulders. "We've been pretty terrible at teaching you about your culture, and obviously you want to know. You deserve to know. Get the books. We could all use a refresher."

"Thanks," I said.

She gave me a squeeze before letting go.

"Didn't you find anything?" I asked.

She smiled. "Oh, my books are at the desk waiting for me. I thought I'd see what you might want before checking out."

Checking out. At the desk. Where Ms. Clark was there with her trusty scanner. "Oh," I said. "I have to use the bathroom. I'll meet you by the door."

Whew. Close one! I turned away, heading toward the bathroom . . . only to run into Mr. Merino, the youth librarian.

"Hey, Holly!" he said, so loud I actually jumped. "Here for the new Dragon Lore Chronicle? I can grab it off the new releases shelf if you want to take it with you today."

Usually I liked running into Mr. Merino. He was so friendly and nice, always finding the perfect books for me. (How badly did I want to take home that new Dragon Lore book? *So badly!*) But not today. Today, Mr. Merino was a complication.

I glanced over at the front desk. Aviva's mom was slipping her library card back into her wallet.

"Oh, uh, no thanks! I'm good for now."

He paused, giving me a funny look.

Which . . . fair. I'd probably never said no to being handed a book before.

I smiled sheepishly. "I've just got so much on my TBR pile already. Trying to make a dent in it before adding more, you know? And I'll probably get some books for Christmas, too."

Understanding dawned on his face. If there was anything bookish people could bond over, it was the never-ending to-be-read pile.

"It'll be here for you when you're ready for it," he said, before looking around. "You here with your grandpa?"

Another quick glance told me Aviva's mom was sliding the stack of books into her arms.

"Nope," I said. "He's not here. But, uh, I should—"

"Your grandpa's such a great writer," Mr. Merino said. "His books are some of our most checked out. Maybe he'd like to do a reading after the holidays?"

Aviva's mom was now on her way toward me.

"Yeah, maybe," I said. "I'll mention it to him. Anyway, I have to run now. Bye!"

"Merry Christmas!" Mr. Merino called out.

Just in time for Aviva's mom to hear it.

"Oh, uh, happy holidays!" I said back as I hurried toward the door so he wouldn't try to introduce himself to Aviva's mom. I'd be found out for sure if that happened.

"Who was that?" she asked.

"Uh, I think he's the youth librarian? He was recommending some new fantasy book, something about dragons. I don't know. Not really my thing, right?"

Aviva's mom lifted an eyebrow. "The graphic novels you normally read are great, but you know, it can be good to try new things once in a while."

I nearly choked on my saliva.

If only she knew.

CHAPTER 29
Aviva

I'D WATCHED LOTS OF INTERVIEWS WITH THE BROADWAY and Hollywood performers that I idolized, the ones I totally wanted to be when I grew up, so I'd heard a thing or two about "impostor syndrome," where legit celebrities felt like they didn't deserve their fame.

But let's face it. Today, I was taking impostor syndrome to new heights. As in, I totally *was* an impostor.

I stood in front of Holly's mirror, frantic. A family portrait, her mom had said. A *Martin* family portrait! They had no idea they were missing one very important Martin!

Maybe I should have said something. Was it wrong to pretend to be Holly for this piece of family history?

But I wasn't ready to be done with our act. Especially when I hadn't yet had a chance to find the letter from our birth mom that I was sure was tucked away somewhere. I hadn't figured out whether to search for the letter myself or broach the subject with Charlie.

Now this picture thing was completely stressing me out.

I mean, don't get me wrong, I was *very* photogenic and normally had no problem cheesing for the camera. I'd spent a lot of time practicing my best poses and award-acceptance faces. But I wasn't me, Aviva Davis, future superstar, right now. I was Holly, smart and bookish member of the Martin family.

And Holly . . . Well. Holly had nothing to wear for the family portrait!

I spun around, looking at the absolute mess I'd made of her room over the past hour. Clothes and jewelry were scattered across every surface. I'd dug everything out of her closet and every drawer of her dresser, searching for . . . I don't know. Sequins? Glitter? I would have even settled for one of those trendy ugly Christmas sweaters, but nope! Holly had one tasteful (boring) black dress that looked like it was years old and barely fit anymore, and . . . flannel. And plaid. A *lot* of plaid.

I had to face the truth: My identical twin sister did not share my fashionista genes. And as I thought about how cute and bookish she looked, I realized that was okay, but I wanted "her" to look good in the photo—her very best self. Pictures are forever!

I'd finally settled on a denim skirt with a red sweater, both of which I'd found buried in the back of the closet, so something told me it had been a while since Holly had seen them. They were cute enough, even if they were a smidge on the small side. But that only led to my next problem.

Where did she keep her makeup? Did she even have any?

I scoured her bedroom. I searched every nook and cranny of the bathroom. All I found was one tinted ChapStick and a bottle of crusty mascara that I tossed in the garbage.

Luckily, her mom's makeup bag, which I found under the bathroom sink, was much better stocked. I tried not to go overboard. A swipe of eyeliner, and a dab of blush . . .

"Holly, what are you doing back there?" called Charlie from the living room. "Primping for the Oscars?"

"That would be less stressful," I muttered to myself. Charlie had explained that she was going to use this photo for their "digital Christmas cards" this year, since she didn't have time to get real cards printed and mailed out. Which meant that this portrait was sort of a big deal—it could even go viral!

I sighed heavily, looking at myself in the mirror. I'd opted to wear my hair down, like Holly had worn it at the pageant rehearsals, but I'd added a braid crown for a little extra jazz, plus I'd clipped on a pair of pearl drop earrings I'd found at the bottom of a jewelry box in her room. A jewelry box that had been filled mostly with *colored pencils*, not jewelry.

"Okay," I said, letting out a slow exhale. I'd done the best I could. Time to shine!

I was about to head out the door when I paused to look around. Yikes—I had really made a disaster of Holly's bedroom, which had been perfect and neat yesterday. Something told me that Holly never let her things get this messy.

Maybe I'd do some tidying up after we took the photos?

Or . . . maybe I could just keep the door closed so her mom wouldn't notice.

I slipped into the hallway and shut the door quietly behind me. Voilà—problem solved and already forgotten by the time I made my grand entrance into the living room and declared, "I'm ready!"

Charlie and Gramps looked at me, and their eyes widened.

"Wow," Charlie said, after a beat of silence. "You look nice, honey."

"Thanks!"

She tilted her head to the side. "Is that the sweater your great aunt Linda gave you for your birthday a couple years ago? I thought we got rid of that. Amazing it still fits you."

I tugged at the fabric. Truth be told, it was pretty itchy, so I was beginning to see why it had been banished to the back of the closet.

Charlie had placed a camera on a small tripod on the coffee table, aimed at the Christmas tree, with all its twinkling lights. "I'll set it on a timer, and we'll take a few and then pick our favorite."

Gramps went to stand in front of the tree. He had gussied himself up, too, in a jacket and a tie with classy little blue snowflakes all over it. His hair was neat, and he'd even shaved.

I went to stand next to him, but Charlie stopped me, looking at my face and frowning.

I smiled at her, knowing she wasn't used to seeing Holly so dolled up. "I look pretty good, right?"

Without a word, Charlie licked her thumb and rubbed it against the side of my nose.

I recoiled. *Ew!* It was bad enough when my own mom did that!

"You have something on your face," Charlie said. "Is that what was taking so long back there? You had to jot down some brilliant story idea and ended up getting pen ink on your face?"

My heart jolted, and I reached my hand up to cover my freckle. *Gah*, I'd forgotten that Holly didn't have one! Of course the makeup I put on yesterday had worn off by now, and looking at myself in the mirror, well, it was always there, so I'd forgotten to cover it up.

"Uh . . . I'll go wash it off," I said. "Be right back!"

I turned and dashed back to the bathroom. I dug through Charlie's makeup bag again until I found the concealer and foundation. I was extra grateful for all those makeup lessons I'd gotten from the stage crew during drama classes over the years. It only took a minute to disguise the freckle again.

I put away the makeup and double-checked my reflection before heading back out. "Now I'm ready."

Charlie posed us in front of the tree with me in the middle. The camera made little beeps as the timer counted down, letting us know when it was about to snap the photos.

"Everyone say *jolly*!" I cheered, just as the tree began to make a weird rustling noise.

"Sherlock!" Charlie yelled as she swiveled toward the tree. "Get out of there!"

Click. The camera flashed.

The tree tilted.

Click.

Gramps grabbed the tree before it went over.

Click.

"MRREEOOOWWW!"

Click.

Once we shooed the cat away, righted the tree, and stopped laughing, we finally managed to get the perfect shot.

CHAPTER 30
Holly

THANKS TO ALL MY SLEUTHING, WHEN IT CAME TIME TO light the menorah and say those blessings, I was ready. Well, as ready as a person with excruciating stage fright could be.

I was now basically a Hanukkah expert. Besides the blessings that I could recite by heart *in Hebrew*, I now knew that the holiday was about how Judah and his army, called the Maccabees, defeated a much bigger army that was trying to make them denounce their Jewish religion and beliefs. Despite their victory, Judah and his people returned to their temple . . . only to find it destroyed. They discovered one tiny pot of olive oil—the fuel they used to light their menorah. While it should have lasted for only one night, it lasted a miraculous *eight* nights. Hence, the eight nights of Hanukkah— also called the Festival of Lights.

I learned about how some people still used menorahs that burned olive oil, like the one in the story, but in modern times it was also common to use wax candles, or even electric ones. Aviva had been right about eating fried food because of the oil miracle.

But the holiday was about more than food and lighting candles. The more I thought about Judah and his people, the more I felt proud of them for fighting for their rights to be who they were and not bow to what someone else thought they should be. I was also proud of Aviva. She wanted to participate in the pageant, celebrating her own Jewish culture, even though the other kids were doing Christmas skits. Her confidence and bravery to be who she was, was one of the many things I already loved about her. This made me love her even more.

As I'd read the books, I texted her the important points so she wouldn't feel guilty about not knowing everything about her own holiday anymore. Plus, I promised to leave the books in her bedroom so she would be able to read them before they were due back at the library.

Not only had I watched YouTube videos and read books, but I'd helped Aviva's mom make a whole new batch of latkes for the evening meal. They weren't difficult to make, especially since we got to use a food processor to shred the potatoes and onions, but they took a lot of work to fry in small batches in the big cast iron pan. Totally worth it, though. Even without ketchup, I couldn't wait to devour them at tonight's meal.

All that research came to this moment when I stood in the living room, facing the menorah that was set with three regular candles and the shamash—the helper candle—that I was going to light.

I was surrounded by Aviva's family, including Bubbe, who had Ubered over from Rowena Village. I was still nervous, but not because I didn't know what I was doing. This was the same old familiar performance anxiety I'd had my whole life.

I reached for the box of matches, realizing that while I knew the blessings, I didn't have to recite them alone. "I'll light," I said, "but maybe we can all do the blessings together?"

"That's a great idea," Bubbe said, giving my shoulder a squeeze. "As a family."

I struck a match and lit the shamash. Then, as I carefully took it from the holder, we all began to sing. "Baruch atah Adonai . . ."

I'm not going to lie—it was pretty beautiful.

❄ ❄ ❄

DESPITE ALL THE DELICIOUS FOOD—LEFTOVER BRISKET, chicken soup, some kind of carrot side dish that I couldn't pronounce, and, of course, latkes with sour cream and applesauce (applesauce was my favorite legit topping), and more jelly donuts—I managed to not eat so much that I was on the verge of exploding. Bubbe had said that Hanukkah, being eight nights, was a marathon and not a sprint, and I was starting to understand what she meant.

After we were done cleaning up and the dishwasher was humming along in the background, Aviva's dad went into the pantry and took down a bag that had been hiding on the top shelf behind cereal boxes.

"Ah!" Benny blurted out. "That's where they were!"

Aviva's dad lifted an eyebrow. "You think this is my first day here?"

Benny screwed up his face as we all laughed.

The bag contained about a dozen wooden dreidels and mesh bags of gold- and silver-foil-wrapped chocolate coins. They were similar to the bags of chocolate coins I usually got in my stocking on Christmas morning, except instead of George Washington's head on them, these ones had a menorah. From my research, I knew that the coins—called gelt—were used in the game to make bets, and at the end you got to keep whatever you won.

The boys each picked up a dreidel and started spinning it on the table, grabbing another once they got one started. Benny even got a couple spinning upside down, on their handles, until there were several spinning away.

"Show-off!" Aaron yelled when he tried it the upside-down way and couldn't manage it.

I grabbed one and gave it a try, holding the little handle and quickly spinning it as I let it go, watching it take off across the table as it spun and spun, on and on before finally losing speed, wobbling for a few turns, and then falling on its side with a soft clatter.

"Come on!" Aaron said after a few more practice spins. "Let's play the real game."

I watched as they divvied up the coins, and told everyone that I would go last—which, judging from the surprised looks I got, maybe wasn't very Aviva-ish? But it gave me a chance to see them play and get comfortable with the rules, because watching a game played on YouTube wasn't exactly the same thing as playing it yourself.

We went around the table, putting our coin ante into the middle and taking turns spinning our tops. Each side of the top had a Hebrew letter, which corresponded with an action: do nothing, take the whole pot, take half the pot, or add a coin to the pot.

It was totally a game of chance, but it was fun, and I got caught up in it, enjoying myself as much as everyone else. Or maybe it was the family that made it fun. Or that, in the end, I was the big winner. Beginner's luck, I guess?

My winning prompted a noisy huff from Aaron who was left with zero chocolate coins (although the smudge of chocolate by his mouth was a sure sign that he hadn't suffered through the game without sneaking at least one).

"Here," I said, pushing a couple of coins toward him and then divvying up the rest around the table.

"What's this?" Benny said, looking down.

I shrugged. "I'm sharing."

Benny and Aaron exchanged a glance.

I looked around the table. "What?"

Everyone stared at me.

Benny was the one to break the silence. "You always want to go first when we play games," he said, "and you never share your candy."

"Like, *never*," Aaron agreed, then gave me a sideways glare. "Did you poison it or something?"

Bubbe unwrapped one and took a nibble. "Tastes fine to me."

"Boys," Aviva's mom warned. "Your sister is being generous. Maybe she's done with her candy hoarding days."

I started to panic. How was I supposed to know my sister was a candy hoarder?

Aaron's eyes narrowed. "It's like you're not even you."

"Fine, then," I said. "I'll take it all back!"

Never have I ever seen anyone move so fast as Aaron did then, sweeping his arm out to block me as he grabbed the coins with his other hand.

"Nope! Mine now!" he yelled, and then ran away, still hollering as he thumped away down the hall. "Sorry not sorry!"

The rest of us laughed.

Although, even as I chuckled along, alarm bells were going off in the back of my head. Aaron's words kept echoing in my thoughts.

It's like you're not even you.

CHAPTER 31
Aviva

IT TOOK AWHILE TO GET THE DIGITAL CHRISTMAS CARDS just right, with plenty of stickers and emojis and a thoughtful message composed by Gramps—even though they'd tried to get me/Holly, the family's *other* writer, to do it. Once we were finally finished, Charlie asked me what I wanted to do next.

And I knew exactly what I wanted to do. The most awesome Christmas tradition of all. "Let's go caroling!"

"Caroling?" said Charlie, trading a confused look with her dad. Then she chuckled. "Good one. How about we watch *Elf*?"

I wasn't sure what she meant by "good one," but when I glanced out the window, I saw that it had started snowing. I guessed that would make it hard for Gramps if the sidewalk got slippery, so maybe Charlie was right. We could always go caroling another night . . . if I was still here, that is.

"Okay, *Elf* sounds great."

We all got out of our camera-ready outfits and into our "cozy clothes," as Charlie called them. She and Holly were clearly cut from the same (flannel) cloth.

Sherlock joined us as the movie was starting, but instead of watching the TV, he sat on Charlie's lap and glared at me with fierce, judgment-filled eyes. *The entire time.*

As the movie played, I was itching to grab my phone and text Holly about all my favorite parts to see if they were her favorite parts too. The story was about a human who had been adopted (!)

by an elf in the North Pole, but then decided to go to New York City to find his biological father, who turned out to be a total Grinch. It was hilarious, and while I hadn't gotten to go caroling, there was some singing in the movie, and I got to sing along, so that was cool, too.

Gramps had fallen asleep toward the end, so once it was over, Charlie and I moved into the kitchen where I helped her put together a casserole for dinner. After it went into the oven, Charlie looked at me, beaming. "I have an idea for what we can do next," she said, disappearing down the hallway.

She came back a few minutes later carrying a couple of plastic totes. She set them on top of the table, and when she pulled off the lids—I couldn't help it. I gasped in absolute glee.

So! Much! Glitter!

The bins were full of crafting supplies. Turned out, Holly's mom was a major crafter. She had it all—glue guns, stickers, fun papers, beads, sequins . . . the absolute works! Why couldn't *my* mom be a crafter? All she ever wanted to do in her spare time was read novels, and not even graphic novels!

Charlie suggested we make some new decorations for the apartment. Maybe crafting new decorations was a Christmas tradition? Either way, I was in.

She pulled up some ideas for us on Pinterest, and over the next hour I made glittery snowflakes, a squishy snowman with a glittery multicolored coat, and a miniature Christmas tree out of beads and wire and . . . you guessed it. *Glitter*.

I was having a great time, and the casserole in the oven was beginning to smell incredible, but as we worked, my mind started to wander. I thought about the dinner Holly was enjoying on the other side of town. My mouth watered, just thinking about the latkes, carrot tzimmes, the *donuts* (donuts plural because I would totally steal one before dinner and then have one after). My heart ached a little when I thought about what I was missing.

Not that I wasn't having fun. I was. But I felt a little sad to be missing out on Hanukkah when my family was finally honoring all the traditions.

And I missed my family. Benny being a dork and talking about hockey nonstop and chewing with his mouth full. Aaron and his earnest curiosity about everything. Mom and Dad and how they joked with each other, and with us.

I liked Holly's mom and grandfather, but they were so quiet. Dinner at the Davis house was never quiet!

And also, if I was being honest, a part of me felt sad to think that Holly was there in my place . . . and somehow, no one had noticed. I mean, that was the whole point. I got that. And I was proud of Holly for pulling this off so far.

But was I really that . . . I don't know. Replaceable? Or was she a better version of me? Aviva 2.0?

"I think I hear your grandpa stirring in there," said Charlie, craning her head to peer toward the living room. "I'm going to start some green beans, okay? We should probably think about clearing the table so we have a place to eat."

"Okay," I said. "I'll take care of that."

As Charlie got up and started bustling about the kitchen, I began packing up the craft supplies, still distracted by thoughts of my family back at home, and the traditions Holly was getting to experience. I was struck with a serious case of FOMO. I was happy for my sister, who I hoped was having the time of her life, immersed in Hanukkah. But it also hit me all at once that it was a little unfair. She was getting to enjoy the holiday that I had asked for, the one that was supposed to help me feel more Jewish.

And here I was, watching Christmas movies and making Christmas crafts. Sure, the swap had been my idea, but now I was wondering if it had been a mistake.

I returned a pile of Popsicle sticks to their box and was gathering up all the scattered puff balls when suddenly, sharp pain lanced up my leg.

"Ow!" I cried, instinctively kicking out my foot. It hit a soft lump beneath the table, and I heard the telltale yowl of an angry cat.

I looked down to see Sherlock, his fur standing on end as he growled at me.

"What?" I said, tempted to growl back. "*You* scratched *me*!"

"What is going on over there?" said Charlie.

"Nothing," I said with a huff. "Just the cat being . . . feisty."

The cat growled at me one more time before darting away.

So there was definitely one member of this household who was missing the real Holly.

It made me sad all over again to think that no one back home was missing me.

Aviva! How did you not tell me how amazing Hanukkah food is?!

I did! It's the best. Whats ur fav?

All of it! Maybe the carrot stuff?

Tzimmes? SO GOOD.

Right? Latkes too!

SO JELLY, SIS!

OH! And the jelly donuts!

How's it going there?

GR8! Except. Sherlock tried to kill the tree.

Oh no!

We saved it.

And dont worry. I hv a plan to win him ovr!

I'm sure you will!

BTW, I won at dreidel!

👏 did Aaron whine?

Ha! Yes. He's so cute, though.

🥹 I miss him a little, TBH. GTG! TTYL

Bye!

CHAPTER 32
Holly

SOMETHING WOKE ME UP. I BLINKED MY TIRED EYES OPEN.
The glow of the streetlight outside coming in on the wrong side
of the room reminded me I was in Aviva's bed. A quick glance at
the clock told me it was the middle of the night: 3:21 A.M.

"Are you an alien?" whispered a small voice.

Somehow, I managed not to scream.

"Aaron!"

"Are you?"

Am I what? I rubbed a palm into my sleepy eyes. "Am I what?
An alien? What are you talking about?"

"I had a bad dream that you were an alien and you landed
here in an invisible spaceship and took over the family, starting
with Aviva. Then when I woke up, I thought about everything
that's happened since Hanukkah, and I know that it's true." He
paused to take a breath that hitched. "You're not my sister. I just
know it."

Oh no. This is bad.

Then he began to cry.

Oh no. This is really bad.

"Aaron," I said softly. "Come here."

He didn't move.

"Please. Come on, I'm not going to hurt you. I'm not an alien.
It was just a dream."

He padded suspiciously into the room. I scooched over and

smoothed the blankets out beside me. He sat down, keeping some distance between us.

"Do you really think I'm an alien?" I asked. It seemed Aaron and I both had overactive imaginations.

He drew his knees up to his chest. "You're not her, and I miss her and want to know what you did with her, and is she dead?"

And okay, it just got worse. But at least I could answer that last question honestly.

"Aviva is not dead, I promise you."

He sniffled and wiped at his tears. "So I'm right! You're not her. Where is she? Is she ever coming back?"

I passed him a tissue from the box on the nightstand as I thought about what I was supposed to say. I didn't want to lie to him, especially since he was looking at me with such anguish, his eyes glassy in the dimness.

I sighed. "Your sister is fine. You're right that I'm not her. But I am her identical twin sister. Twins, not aliens."

Those glassy eyes narrowed in suspicion. Was *twins* less plausible than *aliens*?

"Really?" he asked.

I nodded. "Really. I was adopted, too, and we think we must have gotten separated as babies. We met for the first time at the senior center during pageant sign-ups."

Aaron considered this for a long moment, his gaze searching my face.

"That's . . . that's kind of cool," he said, his anguish starting to fade. "But where is she?"

"At my house. Hopefully sleeping, considering it's the middle of the night."

"So, you live here now?" he asked. Then half a second later, his face crumpled, his sadness returning. "Does she not love us anymore? Did I do something wrong? Is that why she left?"

"Oh! That's not it at all," I assured him, reaching out to rub his back. "You didn't do anything wrong! She loves you and even said she misses you!"

When he gave me a skeptical look, I grabbed my phone and showed him the text thread where she'd admitted as much.

"We just thought it would be fun to swap lives for a while. We're going to swap back."

"Okay," he said, still sounding a little uncertain about everything. I guessed I would have, too, if I'd just found out my sibling really had been replaced with an impostor. But I swear I was a nice impostor! "So . . . is your name Aviva, too?"

"No." I laughed. "I'm Holly."

That must have made it feel real, because he was silent for a long time after that, processing it all. Finally he nodded, like it was all starting to make sense. "Who else knows?"

"No one," I said. "And you have to keep it a secret."

"Okay," he agreed without hesitation. But then he frowned. "But . . . does that mean . . . Are you my sister, too?"

"Sort of?" I said, because I wasn't really sure what it made us. "I mean, I think so. I want to be. Does that count?"

He grinned, showing off his missing front tooth. "Yes."

"Well, it may not be official, but I now declare us siblings."

He nodded and put up his pinky, which I looped with mine.

"All right," I said over a yawn, "now go back to bed."

He didn't move.

I lifted my eyebrows.

"Sometimes when I have bad dreams, Aviva lets me stay with her."

When I was his age, I would sneak into bed with Mom whenever I had a nightmare. If I'd had an older sibling, maybe I would have crawled into bed with them, too.

"All right," I said, moving over so he could get under the blankets.

"She sings to me," Aaron said hopefully.

"Yes, well, that's Aviva, and I'm Holly."

"If I'm supposed to pretend you're Aviva, you should sing to me so I can fall asleep," he reasoned.

I had to respect his canniness.

"Yes, well, I'm more of a storyteller person than a performer person," I said.

"Then you'd better tell me a story," he said as he snuggled in and closed his eyes.

"Fine," I said with fake irritation. I wasn't going to mind going home at the end of this adventure, but I sure would miss this kid.

Normally I read my stories to Gramps, but without my notebook or the willingness to get out of bed to find a book, I was going to have to come up with something on the fly.

"Once upon a time, there were two sisters," I started, "and one of them badly wanted . . . a pet dragon . . ."

CHAPTER 33

Aviva

I WOKE UP EARLY, LIKE USUAL, AND WHEN I LEFT HOLLY'S room, the apartment was quiet.

Perfect—this was my chance to go search out the letter. I was about to text Holly to see if she had any tips on where I might find it, but (A) I was sure she wouldn't be up yet, and (B) she hadn't been willing to go search for the letter herself and I didn't want her telling me not to, so . . .

I snuck down the hall to the living room where I'd seen the filing cabinet. I hadn't done a lot of snooping in the apartment, but I had to assume if the letter was tucked away with Holly's adoption papers, everything would be in there. It was a starting point, anyway.

"Please don't be locked, please don't be locked," I chanted softly as I tried the handle on the top drawer.

Success! The drawer opened, although not without a loud squeak.

I froze, listening for anyone coming down the hall.

Still nothing. Except . . .

"Mreow?"

I looked down at Sherlock, the detective cat, who was looking up at me quizzically. Or accusingly. It was hard to tell—I mean, he was a cat.

"Mind your own business," I hissed at him.

He hissed back but didn't make a move.

Daring to turn my back on Sherlock, I returned to the files

and began thumbing through folders. Each one had a perfectly printed label on the tabs.

"Thanks for being so organized, Charlie." She seemed to file everything: bills, report cards (of course Holly was a straight A student—my twin is an Einstein!), insurance papers, her apartment lease, taxes . . . wait! There! On a blue folder near the back:

HOLLY JO—ADOPTION

My heart started to race. This was it. This was where I was going to find out if we were twins. I mean, I knew we were, but this would be proof. Legal, biological proof. And there had to be a letter in there from our birth mom. There had to be!

I opened the folder, and there were a bunch of legal-looking papers with tiny print and lots of signatures. I pulled the stapled stack out and scanned quickly, but it was all legal gibberish and I didn't see any mention of a sister, or a twin, or any sibling at all. I was turning to the second page when something fell on the floor.

I looked down. My heart, which had already been racing, started to beat double time. Because what had fallen on the floor was a yellowed old envelope. I stuffed the legal papers back into the folder and gently closed the filing cabinet before I kneeled down on the carpet.

As I reached for the envelope, Sherlock stuck out a paw at the same time, but I pulled it away before he could sink his claws into it. "No, kitty! Mine." Well, Holly's, but we had the same DNA, so it might as well have been mine.

On the front of the envelope, in beautiful printing, it said,

To my daughter,
To be opened on her 13th birthday.

Thirteen, just like my parents had said. But that was almost a whole year away. I wasn't even going to wait one more second! I stuck my finger in the little gap in the corner and was about to rip it open when—

"Holly?"

Urk! I looked over my shoulder, and there was Charlie standing behind me. Staring at me. Her eyebrows up high on her head.

"Good morning!" I singsonged, giving her my biggest smile while I inconspicuously slid the envelope under the cabinet, hoping she didn't see.

"What are you doing?"

Not snooping in your files, that's for sure, I was tempted to say. I glanced over at Sherlock, who was still sitting there, a smug expression on his face, as though he was saying, *Yes, impostor, what are* you *doing?*

"Nothing," I said with a shrug, reaching out to give Sherlock a scratch behind the ear. "Playing with Sherlock."

Of course, the feisty cat took a swipe at me, and I only barely pulled my hand back in time to keep it from getting shredded. Honestly, Sherlock! Work with me here!

"All right," Charlie said, and then did a little head shake before adding, "Anyway, since I've got today off from work, too, what would you say about . . ." She paused for dramatic effect, her eyes twinkling at me. "Going *ice-skating*?"

"Oh. Um . . ." The way she was looking at me, I could tell she expected me to be into it. "I would say . . . yay?"

It was the right answer.

"I thought you'd like that," she said. "We haven't gone yet this winter, and I know how much you love it. I thought it would be a great way to spend some time together since I've been working so much lately."

Only one problem: I was terrible at ice-skating! I'd tried a couple of times when I was little and had spent more time on my butt than standing upright. My brothers loved it—mostly because they played hockey—but after I'd twisted my ankle on the fourth or fifth time I went with them, I'd had enough. Besides, why would I want to be out in the freezing cold, falling repeatedly on the hard ice, when I could be on a stage in a nice, warm theater?

But judging from Charlie's expectant face, I couldn't say any of that.

"That sounds so fun!" I lied.

"Great. Come on, I'll make you breakfast."

"Oh, uh . . ." *What about the letter?* I could sense it under the filing cabinet, waiting for me. "I have to finish scratching Sherlock. We're having a moment."

On cue, Sherlock hissed and batted at my hand again before tearing off down the hall.

"What has gotten into that cat?" Charlie asked. "Anyway, how do pancakes sound?"

I glanced down and could see the corner of the envelope peeking out from under the cabinet. With Charlie staring at me, I couldn't grab it, but at least now I knew it existed. I'd have to figure out a time to come back and get it.

Until then, I had ice-skating to look forward to. (Not!)

CHAPTER 34

Holly

I DID NOT WANT TO GET OUT OF BED. BUT WHEN AARON woke up and muttered that he had to pee and scurried out of my room, I figured I may as well get up, too. Aviva was an early riser, after all. Maybe there was something to that.

Nope. Even after I showered and dressed, I still wanted to crawl back beneath the blankets, but I heard the family in the kitchen so I headed that way.

"There she is," Aviva's dad sang. "Just in time for Dad's famous omelet bar. The regular, madam?"

I couldn't help but smile. I liked Aviva's dad so much. In fact, I liked Aviva's whole family. Not that I didn't love my own, but if I could pick a surrogate family, this would be it. Brothers, parents, a fun grandma? They were the whole package.

"That would be great, thanks," I said as I sat down at the table. I had no idea what "the regular" was, but I had a feeling I'd like it. Benny was already stuffing his face with what looked like a cheese omelet, and Aaron had toast and scrambled eggs in front of him.

I gave him a pointed look that hopefully said, *Remember our secret!*

He grinned back at me. I took that to mean, *Message received.*

I reached for the big jug of orange juice to pour myself a glass.

"Hey, did you guys know that Hol . . . I mean, *Aviva* writes stories?" Aaron announced.

And cue the orange juice spilling all over the table.

I jumped up and grabbed a towel off the counter to soak up the puddle before it ran over onto the floor. Once the mess was cleaned, I sat back down and glared at Aaron. "I do not *write* stories," I said in my most Avivacious voice, kicking him under the table. "I perform them! Everyone knows that."

I hoped he would take the hint and change the subject, but that kid would not be deterred.

"Yeah, yeah," he said, waving his fork at me. "But last night, when I couldn't sleep, she told me this really cool story about dragons. Like, it could be a book, or maybe even a movie! It was that good!"

I had a thought of how maybe I should have poured the rest of the juice over his head, but then, as I watched in helpless horror while Aaron told the whole family what a great storyteller I was, it was clear that he meant every word. I mean, it was nice to hear that he'd liked my story, but seriously? He was going to get me caught!

I swallowed the first mouthful of my omelet ("the regular" turned out to be mushroom, goat cheese, and chives—yum!). "Ha ha," I said. "I was just making stuff up to get you to go to sleep. Random things. This omelet is delicious, by the way. Thanks, Dad," I added, hoping to change the subject and also not get sidetracked by how strange it was to call someone Dad.

Aviva's mom sipped her coffee and asked, "So, what are you kids doing today?"

I shrugged, since I hadn't given it much thought. If I had the day to myself, maybe I'd work on my story for Gramps. I really should work on Aviva's song, too, since the pageant was only a few days away. Now that I was a Hanukkah expert, I felt confident that I could finish it and make it Aviva-worthy!

Benny said, "Meeting my friends at the rink."

"Oh!" Aaron said, his eyes wide. "Can I come?"

Benny made a face like the last thing he wanted was his little brother hanging around.

"Wait, the rink?" I asked. "Like, the ice-skating rink?" I sat up straighter. I loved ice-skating. Finally, something that my sister and I had in common! "Can I come, too?"

Benny turned to me, stunned. "Seriously? *You?*"

I deflated, feeling a little hurt by his reaction. I guess he didn't particularly want a little sister hanging around, either.

"That's a great idea," Aviva's mom said. "Why don't you take your brother and sister with you, Benny. It would be good for all of you to get some fresh air."

"Yes!" Aaron said with a fist pump.

Benny whined, "Seriously? I'm going to meet my friends."

"Yes, seriously," his dad responded with a stern look. "Unless you'd rather not get your allowance this week."

"Fine." Resigned, Benny nodded before turning to me and Aaron. "We'll go after lunch."

AFTER BREAKFAST, AVIVA'S PARENTS LEFT FOR WORK, Benny retreated to his dungeon in the basement (that did not have any medieval torture equipment or shackles—I'd checked), and Aaron went off to build with Legos for a while. I returned to Aviva's room, resisting the urge to make her bed. Nothing would get me found out quicker than cleaning up her mess, even though I really, *really* wanted to.

I sat on the bed and pulled out my phone. I was going to see if Aviva wanted to FaceTime and work on the song when I saw that she'd texted me a bunch of times. But before I opened the thread, I saw in my notifications that my mom had uploaded a bunch of photos to our shared family album.

I opened the folder—only to burst out laughing. Oh, my cat! Sherlock had climbed the Christmas tree, just in time to be captured in a series of hilarious snaps of Mom, Gramps, and Aviva trying to take a sweet family photo. That mischievous cat had photobombed them! Each photo was funnier than the last, and I could only imagine Gramps yelling and Mom shrieking and Sherlock freaking out.

Aviva? She was laughing so hard she was actually doubled over in some shots, wiping tears from her eyes in others.

I was laughing, too, until I came to the very last photo. They had recovered from Sherlock's hijinks and managed to get a portrait with Mom, Gramps, and Aviva all looking like a normal, happy family, with the lights from the tree shimmering in the background. Aviva was wearing a sweater that I barely remembered owning. She'd done her hair in a pretty style, and her smile lit up her face, her cheeks still flushed from all the commotion.

The picture also had some digital stickers on it—Christmas trees and Santa emojis—that had to be Aviva's handiwork. It was cute and funny, and she'd done a great job fitting into my family's Christmas card photo.

A pang of regret hit me then, so sharp that I actually gasped from the sudden sting of it. I was staring at my family's Christmas card photo . . . and I wasn't there. I wasn't in it, and absolutely nobody even noticed.

It hurt to know that my own mom and grandpa hadn't figured out that it wasn't me standing there, laughing and smiling for the camera. Sure, it meant Aviva was a great actress, but still, was I really so replaceable?

I set the phone down in my lap, feeling truly homesick for the first time since Aviva and I had decided to switch places. When tears pricked my eyes, I sniffled quietly to myself and reached for a tissue from the box on the nightstand.

But after a few minutes, the feelings started to pass. I wiped my eyes, drew in a long, shaky breath, and forced myself to think of why I was here in the first place. Yes, Aviva might be having fun without me, but I was having a pretty good time with her family, too. A great time, actually. If we hadn't switched, I wouldn't have learned how to give the blessing in Hebrew, or played dreidel with Aaron and Benny, or tried so many delicious new foods. Not to mention that I was writing a song about Hanukkah. I only had one more day with the Davis family, and I was going to make the absolute most of it.

Besides, this whole experience was giving me so much fodder for my writing assignment. I was facing my fears—strangers, new situations, even speaking in a whole different language—like a boss.

My phone buzzed, and before I even picked it up, I knew it was Aviva.

I smiled as I opened up the text thread. Until I saw what she'd written:

I FOUND THE LETTER FROM OUR BIRTH MOM!!!!

CHAPTER 35
Aviva

ARRIVING AT THE RINK WITH CHARLIE AND GRAMPS MADE me almost giddy. Festive lights had been strung in every direction, creating a colorful canopy over the ice. It was crowded for a Wednesday afternoon, with people of every age in scarves and hats and puffy coats zipping around, holding hands and enjoying themselves. Big speakers were playing Christmas songs, and the air was crisp and delicious, thanks to the aromas of kettle corn and hot chocolate wafting toward me. I was starting to get why people liked ice-skating! All it needed was a Hanukkah song and some jelly donuts, and it would be perfect.

There was a skate rental stand, but amazingly, Holly actually owned her own ice skates. They fit me perfectly, of course. Charlie, Gramps, and I sat down on a bench off to the side of the ice, and I traded out my shoes for the skates, cinching up the laces. When I was done, I tucked my shoes into Holly's backpack.

"I'll be on shoe and bag guard duty," said Gramps. "You ladies have fun out there. Let me know when you want me to grab us all some hot cocoas."

"Can we have some now?" I asked eagerly—because there was never a bad time for hot cocoa.

Charlie gave me a look. "You sure have had a sweet tooth lately," she said. "Come on, let's do a few turns around the rink first."

Charlie took my mittened hand in hers, and we stood up. My feet were wobbly, my ankles feeling weak in the skates as I stomped my way toward the rink. I held on to the wall as the blades hit the ice. Charlie was already pushing off, heading toward the faster skaters in the center of the rink. She tugged me along, and one of my skates slipped out beneath me.

"Whoa!" I stumbled and dropped her hand, spinning back to grab on to the wall.

Charlie turned so she was skating backward, then came to a slow stop, frowning at me.

"Holly? What's going on?"

"Nothing! I'm fine! Just getting my bearings. It's been a while, remember?"

I straightened myself up, sent her what I hoped was a confident smile, and pushed away from the wall.

Left foot forward, right foot forward, left foot, right foot, left—

Whoops!

My arms pinwheeled as I nearly lost my balance, but I caught myself before going down. "Ha ha!" I bellowed triumphantly, righting myself again. I beamed at Charlie, but she seemed unimpressed.

Actually . . . she seemed concerned.

She skated effortlessly over to join me, taking my arm. "What's the matter?" she said, as we skated slowly side by side. "What are you doing?"

"Um . . . ice-skating?"

"Why are you so . . ."—she hesitated on the word—"clumsy . . . today? It's like you've forgotten how to skate."

Clumsy? I felt like I was doing really well, all things considered!

Wait a second . . . her own skates, her mom knowing she'd be excited . . . Was it possible that Holly, my bookish, quiet, introverted sister, was . . . *an ice-skating queen*? Was she really good?

Like, championship good? Like, triple-axel-ice-dancer-going-to-the-Olympics-someday good? I hoped so! How cool would that be?

Except . . . "I'm just getting warmed up," I said.

Charlie shrugged. "All right. Well, I'm going to do a few laps. Once you're *warmed up*, I'd love to see those moves you told me you wanted to try."

Moves? What moves?

Holly Martin, you have been holding out on me! I couldn't wait to get back to my phone so I could text her and get all the deets on her secret figure-skating-superhero identity!

But in the meantime . . . how was I going to fake my way through this? I didn't have any ice-skating moves. I'd have been happy if I managed to go this whole afternoon without falling on my tush!

As Charlie zoomed away, graceful as a ballerina, I took a deep breath and tried to channel my twin sister. I tried to *feel* the ice. The skates were an extension of my body.

Looking around, I saw some young kids just learning to skate, holding on to frames that looked like walkers I'd seen some of the seniors use at Rowena Village. I wished I could borrow one, but there was no way I could explain that to Charlie.

All right, I've got this. I pushed away and began to skate. Short glides at first, but a few strides later, I picked up some speed. Lifted my arms. Felt the cool wind on my face, the flush of exhilaration in my chest. So graceful—it felt even better than dancing. I was doing it! I was incredible! I was flying!

I was—urk! I was tripping! Falling! Crashing!

"Ow," I said, rubbing my side as skaters flew by me.

A pair of hockey skates screeched to a halt, cutting into the ice a couple of feet away.

"You okay?" said a voice.

A familiar voice. But not Charlie's voice.

My heart jumped into my throat as I looked up into the worried expression of . . . my older brother!

Benny stretched his hand out to help me up, chuckling. "Typical Vivvy," he said. "Told you someday you'd regret not letting me teach you how to skate."

My first thought was: *I have missed my brother so much!*

My second thought was: *What is he doing here?*

My third thought? *Oh. No.*

"Hey, Davis, who's this?"

I looked over to see a kid about Benny's age standing there with a smile on his face.

When I swiveled to glance at Benny, I almost lost my balance. He gripped me tighter, holding me up as he turned to the guy. "This is my kid sister, Aviva. Vivvy, this is Mike Parsons. Goalie on my team."

"Your sister?" The guy frowned and looked from me to Benny. I was plenty familiar with that look—the confused one that couldn't comprehend how siblings could look so different from each other.

"I'm adopted," I said proudly, helping him out before he gave himself a headache with the mental gymnastics.

"Oh. Cool," he said in a weird voice. "C'mon, Benny, the guys are waiting for us. Merry Christmas, Aviva. Nice meeting you."

Benny and I exchanged a look, and for a second, I expected my brother to not say anything about the Christmas comment.

It certainly wasn't the first time someone had wished us a Merry Christmas, and it wasn't *that* big of a deal.

But then Benny was squaring his shoulders and turning back to his friend. "Happy Hanukkah, actually."

Mike, who was already starting to skate away, paused and faced Benny again. His brow furrowed. "What?"

"Happy Hanukkah," said Benny. "My sister and I are Jewish."

Mike did a double take at me but then looked back at Benny disbelievingly. "You're *Jewish*? Since when?"

"Since forever," said Benny, seeming to gain confidence with every word.

"How come you never said?"

Benny rolled his eyes. "Gee, I dunno. Maybe so I wouldn't have to have awkward conversations like this?" But the way he was looking at his friend told me everything. He was worried this Mike kid would be judgy. Even though being Jewish was a part of who he was, just like his skin color and that he was a great hockey player and that he hated eating fish. In that moment, I completely understood why Benny felt it was easier sometimes to not say anything.

Which was why my heart was filling with pride to see him claiming his Jewishness, right there in front of me.

In the end, Mike wasn't judgy at all. He just shrugged. "Hey, it's cool. Mazel tov!"

Benny chuckled, and I could tell he was relieved. So was I.

Mike skated away, and I was about to tell Benny what it meant to me that he'd said all that, when something grabbed my attention over Benny's shoulder.

"Oh no" fell out of my mouth.

Benny frowned at me, then tried to follow my gaze. "What is it?"

"Nothing!" I said, moving to block his view. Because the *nothing* I'd seen was totally my twin sister. "I thought I saw someone from school. But, uh . . . you should hurry up and join your friends! Don't want to keep anyone waiting."

Benny gave me a strange look, but then shrugged in that Aviva-being-Aviva way that everyone in my family had mastered. "All right. Try not to break any bones while we're here, okay? Mom would kill me!" Then he turned and skated away as I glanced over to see Holly lacing up a pair of rental skates.

Oy vey. Things were about to get complicated.

CHAPTER 36

Holly

BENNY HAD DISAPPEARED THE SECOND WE ARRIVED AT THE rink, leaving me to get Aaron sorted, although *he* didn't need anything, since both boys had their own hockey skates and knew what they were doing. By the time I got my rental skates, Aaron had already laced his up and was on the ice, zooming around like a pro, weaving in between other skaters.

Now that I had a moment to myself, I pulled out my phone and opened up the text thread with Aviva, rereading from this morning's bombshell:

> **I FOUND THE LETTER FROM OUR BIRTH MOM!!!!**

Wait, what?

> **Was in ur filing cabinet this whole time!**

!!! What does it say?

> **Dunno. Didn't have a chance to open it yet.**

> **I will soon tho!**

I'd paused then, because I didn't know if I wanted her to open it. Did I want to know what it said? Finally, I'd typed back:

How do you know it's from her?

> **It said on the envelope. Ur mom almost caught me so I had to hide it.**

Don't open it!!

Srsly?? Y not?

I hesitated again. Why not? I didn't have a good answer, only this tightness in the pit of my stomach. Mom had kept this letter from me, and Aviva's parents had kept hers hidden away, too. Our birth mom had specifically asked us to wait until we were thirteen. What if I wasn't ready to hear whatever was inside?

We should wait and open it together.

Sigh. Fine. GTG BYEEEE

I hoped she wouldn't open the letter. I knew she wanted to, and I understood why, but I wasn't sure . . . What could be in there? What if what it said was bad? Was that why Mom had kept it from me? What did she know?

One more thing to add to my list of fears: opening a letter from my birth mom. Maybe it was silly to be afraid of a letter, but it felt important, and I wanted to make sure I was ready for whatever was in there. If Mom had hidden it from me, she had to have a reason. Wouldn't it be best to ask her about it?

Aaron whizzed by. "What are you doing? Come on!"

"Coming," I yelled back, happy for the distraction as I toed off my shoes and slid my feet into the ugly brown rental skates. I had just gotten them on and stood up when I glanced over at the rink in time to catch Benny helping someone up off the ice.

A girl. Hmm. That was interesting! When he'd said he was meeting friends, I'd assumed he meant a bunch of guys. *He must really like her*, I thought. He was smiling at her as he pulled her to her feet.

I wasn't close enough to see her face, but she had a coat that looked a lot like *my* favorite coat.

Wait. That *was* my favorite coat!

Benny was helping *Aviva* up off the ice.

I gasped loudly. Suddenly unsure what to do, I dropped back down onto the bench and pulled my hood up over my head.

"I don't understand it, Sylvia. Last year she was so good, and now . . ." There was a pause. "You're right, maybe she's just rusty. This is the first time we've been skating this year. She really loves skating—I'm sure it will come back to her."

I squeaked, then clamped my hand over my mouth. Because of course it was Gramps, sitting just two feet away from me on the bench! He was on his phone and looking out at Aviva, but if he glanced over, he would see me!

I adjusted my scarf, wrapping it around as much of my face as I could, until only my eyes were exposed.

After a brief moment of silent panicking, I stood and hurried out onto the ice, heading toward Aviva. In my haste, I nearly cut off another skater. Which, on second glance, turned out to be *my mom*. "Sorry!" I barked in a low voice as I continued on my trajectory toward my sister.

Benny was holding her arm as she wobbled, and I realized that skating wasn't something we had in common after all—she was obviously a beginner.

I got close to her and did a slow glide by, looking right at her as I angled away from Benny. When her eyes widened, I knew she recognized me. *Bathroom*, I mouthed, and the second she nodded, I skated away from her, doing my best to avoid Benny, Aaron, my mother, and Gramps. It felt like skating through an obstacle course!

Two minutes later, I was in the accessible stall, still in my skates, when the outside door squeaked open. "Holly?" Aviva whispered.

"In here," I said, opening the stall door for her. She lumbered in, her (my!) skates clicking on the rubber mats on the floor.

"Hi!" she said, giving me a quick hug. "I had no idea you'd be here! This is bonkers, right?"

"So bonkers," I said. "Tell me what happened."

"Uh, I fell," she said. "Because I'm terrible at skating, and my brother saw and helped me up."

"He recognized you, even though you're wearing all my clothes?"

"I guess," she said. "I didn't think he was that observant, honestly, but . . ." She looked at me funny.

"What? Do I have something on my face?"

She grinned at me. "No. In fact, you really don't—your freckle has worn off. But I'm smiling at you because you're my sister, and I'm really happy to see you."

"Me too," I said, "but we need to figure out what to do."

"Right," she agreed. "So, Aaron and Benny are out there, but not my parents, right?"

"No. They went to work," I said. "Oh, and Aaron knows I'm not you. He figured it out."

"Whoa!" Aviva's eyes widened. "So clever, that kid. And he hasn't blabbed?"

"He almost did." I laughed, thinking about breakfast. "But no. I explained to him that we were just doing it for a few days. He was worried I was an alien or that you were dead or something."

"Aliens!" She barked out a laugh. "He sounds like you!"

"Anyway . . ." I continued. "He knows, but Benny doesn't. Obviously my mom and Gramps are here."

"Your mom can't figure out why I—*you*—are so clumsy on skates."

"Which makes sense because I'm a great skater. I was so excited when your mom suggested Aaron and I come here with Benny."

"How about this?" Aviva said. "We switch clothes, then you go out there and skate your heart out with your mom and drink hot cocoa with Gramps. It won't matter if Aaron notices you, and I doubt Benny will after he meets up with his friends. When he's with his hockey buddies, he wouldn't notice if the sky started falling!"

The idea sounded good, except . . . "Won't you feel like you're missing out?"

Aviva shrugged. "I already fell down once. That's probably enough for one trip—pun intended—to the rink. I'll just bundle up and go sit far away from your grandpa. Maybe get some kettle corn or something. I'll be fine." She began to unzip her (my!) coat. "But you: Go! Skate. Be a superstar!"

I didn't need to be told twice.

CHAPTER 37
Aviva

MY SISTER REALLY WAS A SKATING SUPERSTAR! AS I SAT ON the bench off the side of the rink, munching on kettle corn, I watched as Holly spun and jumped, looking graceful and confident and totally in the moment.

She was a natural. I knew she had those performer genes somewhere inside her!

I was so focused on Holly that I didn't notice someone was beside me until the bench rattled under me.

"Hey, Holly," Aaron said, grabbing a handful of my kettle corn. "How come you're not out there skating?"

I looked over at my brother. He was smiling at me, and I felt a surge of sisterly love and pride. "It's me, goofball."

His eyes widened, and then before I knew it, he was hugging me, kettle corn scattering everywhere. "Vivvy!" he said into my shoulder. "You're here!"

"Yes, I'm here." I laughed. "Shhh. It's a secret."

He pulled back and looked out at the ice, finally pinpointing Holly where she'd staked out her spot amid the crowd of skaters.

"This is so funny!" he said. "I had no idea you had a twin!"

"Neither did we! Ridiculous, isn't it?"

"Totally ridiculous," he agreed as he took some more kettle corn. "So are you coming home now? Is that why you met here? So you could swap back?"

I shook my head. "This was a total coincidence. See that man over there on the other side by the rental counter? That's Holly's grandpa. And her mom is on the ice somewhere ..." I scanned the crowd of skaters. "There. In the blue-and-green coat. We all decided to come ice-skating today as a fun family outing, because obviously, they think I'm Holly."

"This is the best prank ever," Aaron announced, spitting out popcorn bits. "Like something on TV!"

"So, Holly's being nice to you?" I asked.

He nodded enthusiastically. "She's really great. She tells me stories. Everyone loves her. Although everyone else thinks she's you. I'm not sure why no one else has guessed. You two aren't very much alike, other than your looks." He made a face. "Is she my sister, too? She said she didn't know, but if *you're* my sister ..."

I shrugged. "I'm not sure. But maybe?"

"I want her to be my sister. Even if it's not official. She said she'd like that, too."

I looked over at where Holly was gliding around the ice, looking so happy. She fit right in with my family. Maybe better than I did? *Everyone loves her*, Aaron had said.

"I'm going to go skate now," Aaron announced, jumping up off the bench. "Oh hey, there's Mom and Dad. And Bubbe, too! We're all here!"

We're all *here.*

I followed his gesture, and sure enough, there were my parents with Bubbe. There was Gramps, still on the same bench as before. There was Benny, goofing off with his pals out on the ice, breezing right past Holly and her mom.

We really were all here.

Great. Now what?

Before my brother could skate off, I grabbed his arm. "Wait! I need your help."

"My help? For what?"

"You need to go and head off Mom and Dad to make sure they don't sit near Holly's grandpa. We have to keep the families apart, or we're going to be found out. See if you can get them to come sit over here to put on their skates."

He frowned. "Why don't you and Holly just tell everyone now? Then we could all be like one big happy family."

I shook my head. "We're planning a big reveal."

"What kind of reveal?"

I groaned. Why did this kid have to ask so many questions? "Aaron! It's supposed to be our big holiday surprise!"

He frowned at me a second longer, then understanding brightened his expression. "*Oh*. Right. That's even better. Okay, I'm on it."

He broke away from my grasp and jumped onto the ice, zooming toward my family: Mom. Dad. Even my beloved Bubbe. It had only been a few days, but I already missed them so much I felt my heart ache.

Maybe now *was* a good time to tell everyone the truth. Or at least switch back so I could spend the rest of Hanukkah with my family. Getting ready for Christmas at Holly's had been really fun, but I felt like I was a Christmas tourist. Hanukkah was *my* holiday.

Except if we switched back now, would Holly want to put the letter back unread? She liked to follow rules, and without me there to convince her, would she say we would have to wait until we turned thirteen? There was no way I was going to wait a whole year to see what was in that letter!

I looked over at Holly. She smiled back at me and waved. I nodded my head meaningfully at the new arrivals. She glanced over, and I could see the exact moment when panic set in.

Her head snapped back to me and she mouthed, *Bathroom!*

She skated off to the restrooms, but I couldn't follow her. Aaron was leading my family straight toward me. It took everything in me to not throw my arms around my parents and grandmother, because as far as they knew, I'd just seen them a few hours ago.

But on second thought . . . I had no problem being a little weird. They were used to it.

"Mom!" I shouted, flinging myself into her arms.

Mom laughed, surprised, but not *that* surprised. "I hope you kids always greet me this way," she said as we both sat back down on the bench. "Having fun?"

"Yes, but what are you doing here?" I blurted out, my voice a lot screechier than I'd intended.

"We had a cancellation that led into our lunch hour," said Dad, "so we thought we'd come out and meet you kids for a quick skate."

"I'm going to skate now!" Aaron said. "Maybe I'll make a new . . . *friend*, right, Vivvy?"

Then he gave me an actual stage wink. Sheesh. Obvious, much?

"Have fun!" I said, turning to Bubbe, who had sat on my other side. "Are you skating?" I asked, surprised that she was even there.

She snorted. "What, so I can trip over everything and everyone

I can't see?" She shook her head as she reached for my arm and gave me a squeeze. "No, bubbeleh, I'm here to meet a friend. I just wanted to say hello to you first before I go meet him. He's here with his granddaughter."

The kettle corn in my belly churned into a ball of dread. "Oh? Who's that?"

"His name's Ed. I met him when he was touring the center last week. Turns out he's a famous author."

Mom froze and looked at Bubbe. "Not Ed *Martin*? The mystery writer?"

"Yes," Bubbe said, surprised. "That's him."

"No kidding," Mom said as she returned to her laces. "I've been devouring his books. I'd love to meet him!"

Whoa, whoa, whoa! This was going sideways, fast!

"Okay, good, well . . . I have to pee!" I announced, probably way too loudly, as I pulled the scarf up to my eyes, secured the hood in place over my hat, and started toward the ice, hoping I'd make it to the other side without either (A) falling on my face or (B) having that face get recognized by Holly's mom or grandpa. I honestly wasn't sure which would be worse.

CHAPTER 38
Holly

"MAYDAY, MAYDAY!" AVIVA ANNOUNCED AS SHE CAME clacking into the bathroom, still wearing the skates. "Holly?"

I swung open the door so she could join me back in what I was now thinking of as our secret rendezvous spot: the accessible stall.

"Oh good! I was worried you'd been caught!" I said.

Aviva shook her head. "No, but it was close. Everyone is here, even Bubbe, who is supposedly on a date. With *Gramps*! Can you believe it?" She gasped for air. "Anyway. Hi again."

"Do you have the letter with you?"

Her shoulders slumped in defeat. "No. I had to hide it. But it's safe."

"You won't open it without me, will you?"

She made a face, and I thought she was going to argue, but finally she said, "No. I promise."

"Thanks," I said. "So what are we going to do?"

We stared at each other for a long, silent moment, thinking.

"Okay, how about this!" said Aviva. "First, we find two kids to trade hats and coats with us. We bundle our hair up under the hats, then sneak into our moms' purses and put on their sunglasses and some lipstick, then we skate around in disguise and have a great time while everyone thinks two other random kids are us, until it's time to go home!"

Seriously? "Okay, so I applaud your imagination, but what is with you and disguises?"

She shrugged. "I really like costumes."

"Fair enough. But I highly doubt we'll find two kids to trade clothes with both of us on such short notice."

"Yeah . . . it's a stretch."

"We could pretend to be sick and hang out here until it's time to leave?" I suggested.

Aviva wrinkled her nose. "And miss all the fun?"

"It's either that or blow our cover, isn't it? We've come this far, and we've managed to trick everyone! Well, everyone except Aaron. I was really beginning to think we might make it all the way to the pageant."

Aviva's eyes widened. "The pageant? The plan was to switch back at the dress rehearsal. And you didn't even want to switch in the first place!"

"That's not true! I was curious. About your family, and Hanukkah, and the song . . ."

I could tell that Aviva wasn't buying it, so I sighed. "Okay, here's the truth. At school, my teacher gave us this writing assignment. We're supposed to write about a time when we were brave and faced our fears. And, well . . . I'm not really great at that. Facing my fears, I mean. And after she gave us this assignment, I started to worry that maybe I'm a big wimp. It's not only the stage fright, either. I don't like meeting strangers, or being alone after dark. Up until this week, I'd never done anything remotely scary. But since I met you? I've been doing all kinds of frightening things. And it feels . . . I don't know. Like I'm becoming a different person. A braver person."

Aviva did a double take. "What are you talking about? You're already an amazing person! I just saw you skating like a pro and doing a whole bunch of awesome moves. Jumps even! That's *really* scary!"

"I guess," I said. "I love it, though, and I've been skating my whole life, so it doesn't seem scary."

"You could be in a real ice-skating show!"

I shook my head. "I don't like being in front of crowds, you know that."

"But you're really good," Aviva said encouragingly. "Maybe you could even try out for the Olympics someday. And you should definitely be in the pageant with me."

I grimaced. "I *still* don't want to be in the pageant. And I don't want to be a professional skater, either."

She frowned. "Why wouldn't you want to show people how good you are?"

"Aren't you listening? I'm not like you, Aviva!" I bit out, crossing my arms. "We may be identical on the outside, but we're not the same on the inside. I don't want to be the center of attention. I don't want people to stare at me. I don't want to perform. Skating, singing, or . . . whatever! Can you please get that?"

She lurched backward like I'd hit her. Which I kind of had with my words, but why wasn't she listening?

"Okay, fine," she muttered. "You don't want to perform. I get it. I just thought . . . I mean, you were the one talking about facing your fears."

I flinched. She had a point. But pretending to be Aviva while I spent time with her family was one thing. Singing and dancing onstage? That was fear on a whole other level! "Anyway," I went on, "I'm writing my assignment about us—this adventure we're having—and how brave we are to switch lives and families, and how I'm immersing myself in another culture and learning all the customs. *That's* new and scary, and I'm doing it. But it's getting so complicated. Maybe we *should* switch back."

Determination glinted in Aviva's eyes. "No. Not if we don't have to. You're getting to experience Hanukkah while facing your fears, and I'm getting to experience Christmas, and it's been going really well so far. We can still do our big reveal at the pageant! But we definitely have some serious problems to deal with right now." She nodded toward the door. "Not only are Bubbe and your grandfather on a date, but my mom wants to meet Gramps, the famous author."

Oh no. Before we could get any further, we heard the bathroom door open.

"Holly? Are you in here?"

We both froze, our eyes going wide.

Then—"Yeah?" Aviva and I said in unison.

I shot her a look, and she cringed apologetically.

My mom's ice skates clicked on the mats outside the stalls. "Are you okay? You've been in here for a long time."

"Yeah," I said, hoping she wouldn't look under the stall. Seeing two pairs of feet would definitely give us away, and it wasn't like one of us could jump up to stand on the toilet in ice skates. "I had a bit of a stomachache, but I'm feeling better now. I'll be out in a minute."

"Okay, honey. Do you want me to see if they have any tea?"

"Sure, that would be—"

But Aviva was shaking her head vigorously.

"Er . . . um. Never mind. No, thanks. I'm good."

"You sure?" said my mom.

"Yeah. I'm feeling much better already."

"All right. Well, when you come out, find us over on the bench. The lady your grandpa met at the senior center is here, and he wants to introduce you to her and her family. I think her grand-daughter might be here, too."

Our eyes turned panicky, but . . . what was I supposed to say? *No, thanks, I'd rather not meet my grandpa's new girlfriend and her granddaughter who is my twin sister right now? Try again later?*

"Okay, sure," I said. "Sounds good. I'll be right there."

Mom's skates clomped back toward the exit. I hardly breathed until I was sure she was gone.

"Why no tea?" I asked Aviva.

"Because I hate tea!" she said, sticking out her nose in disgust.

"It wasn't for you, silly. It was for me! Clearly, the jig is up anyway."

"Maybe not," said Aviva, her eyes sparkling. "I have an idea. But first—we need to change our clothes back. Then we need to find Aaron."

CHAPTER 39
Aviva

"DO YOU UNDERSTAND WHAT YOU NEED TO DO?" I ASKED.

"Um. I think so?" Aaron stood in front of me and Holly, looking back and forth between us with his eyes wide and his mouth hanging open. "It's just . . . this is *so weird*."

"Aaron, focus!" I said, nudging him in the shoulder.

He frowned. "Yeah, yeah. I get it. I need to pretend you've been hurt," he said, pointing at me. "Well, I mean, I'll pretend *you've* been hurt." He pointed at Holly. "But you're pretending to be *her*, so . . ." He stopped pointing and rubbed his head like he was getting a headache.

"Just tell everyone that your sister, *Aviva*"—I put a hand on Holly's shoulder—"might be hurt and they need to come right away. We have to get our family away from Holly's family, that's it."

"What about Benny?" he said.

"He's still skating with his friends, isn't he?" I said.

"Yeah . . ."

"He won't notice anything. He didn't even notice I was wearing a different coat when he saw me before. It's Mom and Dad we need to worry about."

Aaron nodded, but he still looked uncertain.

Holly gave him an encouraging thumbs-up. "You've got this, Aaron."

Swallowing, he turned and pushed his way onto the skating

rink. Rather than skate in a circle with most of the crowd, he took off straight across the ice, toward the exit on the opposite side.

Holly and I bent down so we could watch over the wall of the rink while staying out of sight. On the far side of the ice, near the refreshments stand, Bubbe and Gramps were sitting side by side on a bench, while my parents and Holly's mom stood over them. All five adults were chatting like they were old friends.

I hoped this worked. This really was our last chance.

Aaron got off the ice, and we watched him clomp his way over to the group. I wished we could hear what he was saying as he started flinging his arms around—very dramatically. Then he pointed at the rink, and everyone followed the gesture.

Holly and I ducked back down.

"Vivvy? What are you doing?"

I tensed. Holly and I shared a sideways look.

I was about to turn around when Holly grabbed my wrist and I paused. Next thing I knew, Holly was standing up and spinning around to face Benny.

"Nothing! This is a friend from school. We just ran into each other."

I lifted my hand to wave, without facing him.

"Actually, this is perfect timing!" said Holly. "I was coming to find you. To see if you could, um . . . show me how to skate backward?"

I dared to glance out of the corner of my eye, keeping my scarf wrapped securely around my face, enough to see Holly grab Benny's arm and drag him onto the ice.

"Backward?" said Benny. "You haven't even mastered going forward yet!"

"Oh, come on! Show me, please? Or maybe introduce me to your friends."

Benny gave her a look. "You don't have a crush on Parsons or something, do you?"

"What?" Holly blurted, her cheeks getting instantly pink, and not from the cold. "No! I just thought you could teach me!"

Benny hesitated, probably eager to get back to his friends rather than hang out with his little sister. But it didn't matter, because after he sighed and took her hand, they hadn't gone more than a few feet out onto the ice when Holly kicked one foot out, threw her hands up in a dramatic show of losing her balance, and fell down onto the ice. I cringed because no matter how good an actress she was, that had to hurt.

"Ow!" she cried.

"Whoa! You okay?" said Benny, crouching down next to her.

"No, I don't think so," said Holly. "I think I twisted my ankle!"

She was so convincing that for a second even I felt a jolt of concern for her. But then she sent me a look over Benny's shoulder, raised her eyebrows, and jerked her head in the direction of the adults.

I gasped and looked across the ice in time to see my parents following Aaron . . . straight in our direction!

Ack! Right!

I darted around the edges of the rink, not daring to go out on the ice again. In Holly's coat, with my face turned away, I had to trust that they wouldn't recognize me even if they did see me.

It wasn't until I'd rounded to the other side and was hurrying over to Holly's mom and grandpa that I saw another flaw in our plan.

Bubbe was still sitting there on the bench! Why hadn't she gone with Aaron, too?

I froze. *What do I do? What do I—*

"Holly!" shouted Charlie, waving me over. "Finally! Come meet your grandfather's friend."

I swallowed hard.

Bubbe was looking *right at me*. She had a pleasant, friendly smile on her face—not looking shocked to see me at all.

"H-hi," I said, walking closer.

"Sylvia, this is my granddaughter, Holly," said Gramps. "Holly, Sylvia."

Bubbe beamed. "Goodness gracious, you look so much like my granddaughter! I'm told you're the same age," she said.

"Aviva, right?" said Charlie. She looked at me. "She's here, too, but it sounds like she might have fallen. Her parents just went to check on her."

"Oh. I'm . . . sorry to hear that," I said, a little breathless.

"You even sound like my Vivvy," said Bubbe.

I peered at her. *Look like? Sound like?*

Finally, my shoulders started to relax. Bubbe's eyesight hadn't been great for a long time. I guessed she couldn't tell that it was me. Maybe this would work out after all. "I hope your grand-daughter isn't hurt too badly," I said. "I'd like to meet her someday."

"Well, funny you mention it," said Bubbe. "Ed was just telling me that you're working on the pageant at the senior center. My Vivvy's in it! Maybe you two have met already."

"Oh wow, really?" I said. "Maybe we have. But I'm not sure. There are a lot of kids in the show. I'll ask around for her at the dress rehearsal tomorrow."

"Is that tomorrow already?" said Bubbe. "This month is going by so fast."

"Yeah. So, um . . . it's been nice to meet you, but . . . I'm actually not feeling great." I held my stomach. "Mom, do you think we could head home now?"

"Oh, of course, sweetheart. I'm sorry you're not feeling well." She started packing up our things.

"Are you okay here, Sylvia?" asked Gramps, putting a hand on her arm. "I'm sure we can wait until your family returns."

I glanced over at the rink in time to see Holly being led off the ice by my dad on one side and Benny on the other. Aaron was standing behind them, waving his arms at me in a *go!* motion.

I let out a groan, grabbing on to a bench and holding my stomach. Charlie gasped and put a hand on my back. "Holly?"

"I'm okay," I said, even as I twisted my face into a grimace of pain. "But I . . . I think I might puke."

"You all go, go," said Bubbe, nudging Gramps. "I'm fine. You need to get your granddaughter some ginger candies and lemon tea. We can't have her feeling sick right before the big show!"

"It was nice meeting you," I moaned, feigning weakness as Charlie and Gramps led me away.

I barely smothered a grin. Another award-winning performance from Aviva!

CHAPTER 40
Holly

I HOBBLED ALONG, LETTING BENNY AND AVIVA'S DAD SUP-
port me as they led me off the ice rink. Aviva's mom helped me
untie my skate and took it off, gentle as could be, while I hissed
and grimaced in fake pain. Aviva wasn't the only one with acting
skills.

"Is she dying?" Aaron hollered, pressing his palms against his
face in over-the-top distress. "Do we need to go to the emergency
room?"

"Aaron, chill," said Benny. "It's just a twisted ankle."

"Hmm," said Aviva's mom, pressing her fingers tenderly
around my foot. "It doesn't look swollen. Can you move it
around?"

She guided me through a series of movements.

"It's starting to feel better now," I said. "But I don't think I
should skate anymore."

"That's probably for the best," said Aviva's dad. "Dee, why
don't you head back to the office, and I'll drive the kids home
and get Sylvia back to the center?"

"Good idea. Why don't we say goodbye to the Martins before
we go? Vivvy, do you think you can walk on your own?"

"Um . . ." I gulped and looked over to where Aviva, Gramps,
Mom, and Bubbe were still talking. What was taking so long?
Aviva, get out of here! I shot Aaron an anxious look. "Yeah, I
think so."

I stood up on my socked feet. Took a slow, unsteady step. Then collapsed to my knees. "Maybe not!"

"Think it could be broken?" muttered Aviva's dad. "Maybe we should take her in for X-rays . . ."

"No, no," I said. "It doesn't hurt *that* bad."

Aviva's parents exchanged a look. Behind them, I saw Aaron trying to signal Aviva to get the heck out of here!

I took in a deep breath. "I'll try again."

I hissed as I stood up, keeping weight off my foot.

Aviva's dad frowned, tilting his head as he looked down at my feet. "I thought it was the other one that was hurt."

I looked down. Oops! I stumbled forward, switching my weight to the other side. "No wonder that hurt so much!"

Everyone gave me suspicious looks.

"Oh no!" cried Aaron. "She broke *both* of her ankles! What if they have to amputate?"

"I can see your melodrama is starting to wear off on your little brother," Aviva's mom said. "Come on, everyone. Let's go return Vivvy's skates and get Bubbe back to the center."

Aviva's dad gave me an amused look. "I suppose you're hoping for a piggyback ride?"

I shrugged innocently. "I wouldn't say no?"

With a good-natured eye roll, he crouched so I could climb up onto his back. I nervously glanced over toward the benches and breathed a sigh of relief to see Aviva, Mom, and Gramps walking away.

Yes! Crisis averted!

We did it! I can't believe we didn't get found out!

IKR? Scary enuf 4 you?

Totally terrifying! Aaron did a great job, too.

Don't tell him! He'll be impossible.

Ha! Too late.

We need to wrk on song. FaceTime?

Can't. We're doing Hanukkah Mad Libs. Who knew they were a thing?

U get all the fun!

Sorry! Work on the song tomorrow?

For sure! We're going caroling 2nite anywy.

Caroling?

You know, door 2 door singing?

I know what caroling is. But . . . whose idea was that?

Mine!

And Gramps and Mom are into it?

Haven't asked yet but why wouldn't they be?

Ummm. No idea! Never mind! Have fun!

🎵 🎄 👩 🎁

223

CHAPTER 41
Aviva

"SO. HANUKKAH MAD LIBS, HUH?" I SAID, TRYING TO KEEP my voice light and not let on that I would have loved to have done Hanukkah Mad Libs with my family.

"It was really fun!" said Holly, not even realizing she was rubbing it in. Her face was taking up most of my phone screen. Behind her, I could see a bit of my headboard and a corner of my prized *Hamilton* poster. "Aaron kept trying to make everything about aliens, so we ended up with one story where these polka-dotted monsters from outer space were trying to cook latkes with chili peppers instead of potatoes! It was pretty great."

She laughed, and I laughed along, too, but even I could hear that it sounded pretty forced.

We were talking over FaceTime on Thursday afternoon, the dress rehearsal only hours away. Charlie had been gone at work all day, and Gramps was taking his afternoon nap after we'd played a game of Scrabble, at which I did awful. I told Gramps that I had just drawn really bad letters, but I think he was suspicious. It didn't help that I was a terrible speller. One more thing that my sister was better at than me . . .

Mad Libs, though? I was great at Mad Libs. I always had Aaron rolling with laughter as I tried to come up with the most bizarre nouns and adjectives I could.

But . . . of course, my writer sister would be better at *that*, too.

Holly frowned, tilting her head at me. "Is everything okay? How was caroling?"

I made a face. "We didn't go. I guess your mom was tired after ice-skating." When I'd brought it up, Charlie had laughed and asked what my obsession with caroling was about this year, then walked away to start dinner. I guess it wasn't Holly's thing, but . . . wasn't it, like, one of the biggest Christmas traditions? We had to do it at some point, right? "Will you listen to me practice the song?"

"Oh. Sure, of course," said Holly, smiling at me. "I can't wait to hear you sing it."

I leaned the phone against Holly's pillow and pulled her notebook into my lap. I cleared my throat and sang, keeping my voice low so I wouldn't wake up Gramps.

When I finished, I looked up to see my sister beaming at me. She clapped her hands. "Aviva, that was amazing. Perfect except for one part, where you need to adjust your phrasing."

I looked down at the lyrics. "Where?"

Instead of telling me, Holly—my super-shy sister with stage fright—broke into song. Only for one line, but—

"Holly! You have such a great singing voice!"

She smiled at me, her cheeks pink.

I couldn't believe she'd been holding out on me when she had such a wonderful voice—almost as good as mine! "Are you sure you don't want to do the number with me? We could change the lyrics to be about Christmas *and* Hanukkah."

Holly's smile fizzled away. "Yes, Aviva, I'm sure. And I wish you would stop bringing it up."

I sighed. "Fine, fine. It's . . . after seeing you on the ice yesterday, I could picture how incredible you'd be onstage. You're a natural performer!"

Holly scoffed. "Sure, until my breakfast spews all over the stage."

"That's just your stage fright talking. And the only way to get over that is to be brave and face your fears—like that essay you're writing!"

Her jaw tensed, her gaze hardening.

I grimaced and held up my hands apologetically. "Right! Sorry. No more talk of the pageant, I promise."

"Thank you," she said, still sounding annoyed.

Maybe it was time to change the subject. "Hey, speaking of facing our fears . . ." I sat down on Holly's bed and picked up the phone so I could hold it at eye level. "Tonight is the night."

I fished the letter from our birth mom from beneath Holly's pillow. I'd managed to sneak it out from beneath the filing cabinet as soon as Gramps fell asleep that afternoon, and it had taken every ounce of willpower not to tear into it immediately. The right thing was to wait and open it with Holly, but the suspense was killing me! "Let's open this when we see each other tonight. I'm dying to know what's in it!"

Holly's eyes went wide. "The infamous letter! Hold it closer so I can see."

I did, angling the phone camera down toward the handwritten words on the envelope.

To my daughter,
To be opened on her 13th birthday.

"Wow," breathed Holly. "She had nice handwriting."

"Right? I thought that, too."

I held the phone up to me again. "I was thinking I'd bring it to dress rehearsal tonight, but . . . I could open it right now?"

"No!"

Holly's response was so loud and abrupt I nearly dropped the phone.

"I mean . . ." Holly started again, biting her lower lip. "Aviva, I don't know. Maybe we shouldn't open it. We're not thirteen yet. It says 'to be opened on our thirteenth birthday.'"

Exactly what I'd been afraid of.

"You're not seriously going to make me wait almost a year to know, are you?"

"Well . . . we don't even know it's for sure meant for us. It doesn't have our names on it."

I rolled my eyes. "She gave us up for adoption when we were newborns. She probably didn't know what our names were going to be."

"Yeah, good point," said Holly before she let out a big sigh. "It's just . . . Aviva, I'm not sure I want to know what's in it."

"Holly! What if she talks about me? About us?"

"I already know about you. What else could she possibly have to say that would matter to me?"

"I don't know. But aren't you curious? I mean . . . what if we're *triplets*?"

"Triplets! Now you're starting to sound like me, with that big imagination."

"You never know. Two weeks ago I would have said it was impossible that I had an identical twin. At this point, who knows? And the only way to find out"—I waved the letter at her—"is to see what she wrote to us!"

Holly's face contorted, like she was actually in pain. "I just don't think I'm ready. I don't know if I want to know about my birth mom . . . *our* birth mom. I'd never really thought about my biological family before, and now everything seems to be happening really fast."

I frowned. "I'm your biological family, Holly. If we hadn't met, would you be happy going on without me? Without knowing that I even existed?"

"That's not fair, Aviva. This is totally different."

"You can't know that, because you don't know what's in the letter!"

"I said I want to wait! Give it more thought. Once we read it, there's no going back."

I groaned and tossed the letter onto the floor. "First you won't be in the pageant, and now you won't even read a stupid letter! Why are you being such a wimp about all this?"

I regretted the words the second they were out of my mouth.

Holly gasped, and I met her gaze, instantly feeling awful. Her words at the skating rink came back to me, how honest and vulnerable she'd been to tell me about her writing assignment. How she was trying to be brave, to face her fears.

"I'm sorry," I said. "Holly, I didn't mean—"

I stopped midsentence.

My sister had already hung up.

CHAPTER 42

Holly

UNBEKNOWNST TO SANTA, HIS SECOND-IN-COMMAND, *Barnabus the elf, was up to no good. But this wasn't new, for Barnabus had been on the Naughty list his entire life. One year he'd led the very impressionable Prancer to cheat at the reindeer games. Another time, he'd swapped out the sugar for salt on the humbug candy production line. He never should have gotten a job at Santa Inc., but those folks at the North Pole were a trusting lot, and were always willing to give an elf a second chance. And a third chance. And a ninety-seventh chance . . .*

And now that he'd climbed the candy cane ladder to the top, the ruination of Christmas was within his grasp. [Insert maniacal laughter and gleeful rubbing of hands here.] But first, he—

"You almost ready to go to the center for your dress rehearsal?"

I looked up to see Aviva's mom leaning against the doorframe. I was on my sister's bed, working on my story for Gramps, which had proven to be just the distraction I needed to take my mind off the Letter and my big argument with Aviva.

"Oh, yeah, sure," I said with a smile that I hoped didn't look fake. Even though it was. Totally and completely. The last thing I wanted to do was go to the pageant dress rehearsal.

But of course, Aviva would need to be there to practice her number, so that meant I had to go. I might have been angry with her, but that didn't mean I was going to sabotage her performance. I wasn't a Barnabus.

"What are you wearing?" her mom asked. "For the pageant, I mean."

Good question. "It's a surprise. You'll have to wait and see."

She rolled her eyes, but good-naturedly. "I'm looking forward to it. I know you're excited. Your grandmother is over the moon."

"It'll be great," I said. I didn't particularly want to talk to Aviva tonight, but I still knew that she would be amazing in the pageant.

"All right," her mom said, pushing away from the doorframe. "Be ready in five. We can light the menorah later when we get home. And I'm sorry to say that your dad is tired of cooking and I'm frankly latke'd out, so we'll stop at KFC to get some very on-brand fried chicken. Then we can watch that *Love, Lights, Hanukkah!* Hallmark movie. Sound good?"

"Sounds great!" I said, because that part of the evening sounded absolutely perfect.

But first, I had to figure out my disguise.

And how to face my sister.

I'D DUG OUT THE BLUE WIG AND CAT-EYE READER GLASSES from the box of costumes in Aviva's room, and no one in her family batted an eye when I showed up wearing them, proclaiming that I was ready to head to the dress rehearsal. Aaron was staying home this time, muttering something about a special Hanukkah project, so it was just me and Aviva's mom on the drive to the center.

I was desperate to ask her if she was enjoying Gramps's books, but I was afraid it was a very un-Aviva-like thing to talk about, so

I busied myself by looking out the window. The town looked so pretty with all the lights strung across rooftops and a Christmas tree in almost every window. The sight gave me a pang of homesickness, and for a minute, I couldn't even remember why I'd agreed to this swap in the first place. Aviva's family was great. Hanukkah was great. I'd definitely faced a lot of fears.

But now? I kind of wanted to go home.

"I'm going to visit with Bubbe while you do your rehearsal," said Aviva's mom, waving me off at the door to the social hall. "Have fun!"

I waved back and made my way into the chaos. Despite all of Director Doris's efforts, the pageant did not seem to be getting any more organized as the big night approached. Well—maybe that wasn't entirely true. I spotted a bunch of kids in shepherd and wise man costumes by the windows, one of them holding a baby doll, so that had to be the nativity scene group. And as I walked through the crowd, I heard various carols being sung from every direction. A trio of girls were wearing sugar plum ballerina outfits in one corner, and the kids trying to make the human pyramid while singing "O Tannenbaum" were . . . Well, they were still pretty much falling over every time I saw them. But I really hoped they'd have it figured out before the show. Unless, maybe it was supposed to be a comedy number?

I noticed Gramps sitting on a chair in the back, and my heart jolted. I'd been so focused on trying to maintain my cover during ice-skating that I hadn't realized how much I missed him. A part of me wanted to throw off the itchy wig and give him a big hug.

Soon . . . I told myself.

After the pageant, Aviva and I would switch back. I'd be with my family again, celebrating my holiday, and so would she. Although, after our fight, maybe Aviva would want to switch back tonight. That had been the original plan, after all. And I wouldn't argue. I'd tried something new, and in the end I'd managed to get in a big fight with my brand-new sister. This whole swap was starting to feel like a big mistake.

"Holly Aviva!"

I jumped and spun around. Doris was approaching me, fanning herself with her clipboard, looking like she'd just run a marathon. Being in charge of so many kids and trying to put on a show looked like a workout.

"I need to know about the music for your Hanukkah performance," she said.

"Right. Um." I looked around, but Aviva was nowhere to be seen. "So, we—er, *I* wrote the lyrics based on some instrumental music that I found. I can send you a link to the file. Will that work?"

Doris made a note on her clipboard. "Fine. I'll mention it to the sound guy." Then she pulled her glasses to the end of her nose, giving me a sharp look. "Is that what you'll be wearing?"

I looked down at the jeans and sweater I'd grabbed from Aviva's closet, before realizing Doris was probably asking about the wig and glasses.

"No?" I said uncertainly. Aviva had mentioned a costume a while back, but I wasn't sure what she'd decided.

Doris raised an eyebrow. "So you don't have a costume yet? This is the *dress* rehearsal."

I swallowed. I wished Aviva was here to answer Doris's questions. She was the one who would be performing, not me!

"I'll have something. I want it to be a surprise!" I gave her my most Avivacious smile. "It will be epic!"

Doris's lips twisted to one side, and she hummed suspiciously. "Well, are you at least ready to rehearse your song tonight? Or is that going to be a surprise, too?"

I bit my lower lip, smiling sheepishly. "Everyone likes surprises . . . right?"

"Not when they are trying to pull off a holiday pageant with dozens of children and they've had less than three weeks to prepare," she snapped. Then gave an aggrieved sigh. "But fine. I have too many other kids who need to rehearse tonight, anyway. Just . . . please send the music."

I nodded. "Yes, ma'am."

She huffed and walked away, shouting, "Jimmy! Stop playing with the lights!"

I let my shoulders drop in relief, so glad that was over. I was not good at confrontation.

Then I felt a tap on my shoulder. I spun around and found myself face-to-face with Aviva.

Speaking of confrontation . . .

CHAPTER 43
Aviva

HOLLY WAS STARING AT ME, HESITANT AND UNCERTAIN. I guess I was feeling the same way. I'd said some awful things, but I was also still frustrated with her. Why couldn't she just get over her fears and be in the pageant with me? Why couldn't she be as eager to open the letter as I was? We were supposed to be identical twins, so why did we have to be so *different*?

"Hi, Aviva," she said, her tone strained.

Then, suddenly, I clued in. The wig! The glasses!

Had Holly changed her mind about being in the show? Was this her way of showing me that all was forgiven?

"You look so cute!" I said. "I'm so glad you came to your senses, sis. I shouldn't have pushed you about the letter, but as long as you're in the pageant with me, we don't even have to think about that tonight! This is going to be epic, you'll see. But we'll have to hurry to change the words to the—"

Holly stepped back, shaking her head. "I'm not. I mean, I didn't come to my . . ." She huffed. "I didn't change my mind. I'm here because your mom knew *you* had to be here for the dress rehearsal. She's visiting Bubbe."

"So, wait." I crossed my arms. "You're seriously not going to do the pageant with me?"

She crossed *her* arms and shook her head. "No. And I've made up my mind about the letter, too. I want to wait until we're thirteen, like it says."

I gaped at her, irritated and appalled and a million other emotions all swirling around inside me. "Well, it isn't just your letter, is it? If you aren't ready, then I'll just open it without you."

Her jaw fell. "You wouldn't! You promised!"

"I promised because I thought we were going to open it together, like, *soon*! Not a year from now."

Holly's cheeks were turning red, the same way mine did when I was really ticked off. "Well, the letter you found is *mine*, so I expect you to give it back to me, unopened! You want yours? You'll just have to find a way to get it from your parents, then."

"Are you serious? You know, you're supposed to be the one facing your fears, but you're being such a chicken about this. All of this!"

"And you're being such a bully about this."

A bully! I was just trying to get her out of her shell and help her with her project! Not to mention learning about *our* birth mom, our history, our family! I opened my mouth to say as much, when her eyes darted over my shoulder.

And then they went very wide.

"Gramps!" she yelled as she pushed past me.

My instinct was to hide—*Gramps can't see us together!*—but Holly's cry hadn't been a warning.

I spun around, scanning the room. There was Gramps, barely visible through the crowd of bodies. And . . . *oh no.*

He was lying on the floor, his cane several feet away.

The room spun. For a second, I couldn't breathe and all I could see was Gramps. Hurt. *Unmoving.*

Thoughts of maintaining our cover fled from my mind as I stumbled after Holly and dropped to my knees beside her.

"Gramps?" Holly asked, her voice hitching. "Are you okay?"

But obviously he wasn't. He was bleeding from a gash on his forehead. He must have hit his head on the nearby table when he'd fallen. Lying there, he hardly looked like the same person I'd come to know these past few days. He looked so frail and vulnerable. So weak. So . . . *old*.

I pulled out my phone and called 911 as Holly started to sob beside me.

"Gramps? *Please*," said Holly, her voice trembling.

Then Gramps moaned and rolled onto his side, his eyes squeezed shut.

"Don't move," I said. "I'm calling for help."

As I talked to the dispatcher and asked them to send an ambulance, a crowd formed around us, including some staffers from the center, wearing scrubs and barking at the kids to move back.

"Not her," I said, pointing at Holly. "She's his granddaughter. And there's an ambulance on the way." I held up my phone.

"Thank you," one of the staffers said to me. She turned her attention to Gramps. "Don't move, but can you open your eyes, sir? I'm Barb, one of the nurses here. Can you tell us what happened?"

Gramps's lids fluttered open, and he looked up at us, his eyes darting back and forth between me and Holly.

"Sir?" the nurse said, trying to get his attention. "Can you tell us what happened?"

"Obviously, he fell," I said impatiently.

The nurse glanced over at me. "I need to assess his cognition. Can you give us some space?"

"Sorry," I muttered, standing. I gently tugged Holly up and pulled her a few feet away.

She was still sobbing, her eyes red behind my costume glasses. "He'll be okay," I said as I put my arm around her.

She looked over at me. "How can you know? Maybe he broke something. Maybe he's going to be paralyzed now. Or he could have a concussion. Why isn't he getting up?"

"Holly," I said, giving her a squeeze before turning to look her in the eyes. "They'll take care of him. They're probably making sure he doesn't hurt himself more."

"How are you so calm?" she asked, swiping at her tears.

"Because you're my sister and you need me to be." Even though on the inside I was bawling for her and for Gramps.

She nodded, turning her eyes back to her grandfather. "Is my mom here?" she asked.

"No. Gramps drove. So you're going to have to drive his car to the hospital."

That got her to look at me in horror.

"I'm kidding, sis."

She glared at me. "Not funny." But the corner of her mouth had twisted up into a bit of a smile.

"If you're going in the ambulance, we should swap clothes," I suggested.

"I don't want to leave him," Holly said, fresh tears running down her cheeks. "I have to call my mom."

"The nurses are with him. He'll be fine for two minutes. The ambulance isn't here yet, so we can go change. Give me your phone—I'll call your mom."

WE SOON LEARNED THAT GRAMPS WASN'T PARALYZED. HE was able to get up, with help, once the paramedics arrived, though they still secured him on the stretcher. Holly went with him into the back of the ambulance. The big doors closed with an ominous-sounding *kerchunk* and then they were off.

I turned back toward the center and joined the rest of the performers in the social hall. Our . . . No, *my* number was after the "O Tannenbaum" tree pyramid and before the nativity play, but as I watched the kids all dressed in green (except the star, who was dressed in yellow) up onstage trying to sing while they built a cheer-style pyramid, my heart just wasn't in it. How was I supposed to even care when Gramps was on his way to the hospital?

"Holly Aviva?"

I turned toward Doris. "Yes?"

She frowned at her clipboard. "You're up next. We managed to download your music, so you're good to go."

"Oh. Um . . ."

"Vivvy?"

I turned again, this time toward Mom and Bubbe.

"What happened?" Bubbe asked.

I stared at her, not sure how to respond. So much had happened this past week that it was hard to know what she was asking about.

"We saw you helping that man when the paramedics came," Mom clarified. "Was that . . . ?"

"It was Gramps," I said, then flinched. "I mean, Ed. He's my . . . friend's grandpa. You've met him, too, right?" My head was spinning. Weighed down by sadness, it was getting harder to keep this story straight. But did it even matter at this point?

"Do they know what happened?" Bubbe asked, her voice full of concern. "Will he be all right?"

"He fell and hit his head. I don't think there were any broken bones, though."

Bubbe's hand came up to her mouth. "Oh no."

"He'll be okay, Ma," my mom said, putting an arm around her.

Bubbe looked at her. "I think we should go to the hospital, too. If they're allowing visitors, I'd like to see him."

Mom looked at me and then nodded toward the stage. "I can come back for you after the rehearsal, Vivvy."

My eyes pricked with the tears that I'd barely managed to hold back as I tried to be strong for Holly. But now that I'd had a second to process what had happened, I was desperate to go to the hospital, too. There was no way for Mom or Bubbe to know what Gramps meant to me. How in the last few days I'd spent as Holly, he'd become like my own grandfather. I couldn't tell them now without it getting really complicated. We just needed to get to the hospital. Pronto.

So I just shrugged and said, "I'm done here. I'll come with you."

Mom nodded and dug her keys out of her purse. "Okay, let's go."

I was such a good actress that I was able to act like I didn't even hear Doris calling out a desperate "Holly Aviva! You're on next! Er . . . Holly Aviva? Where are you going?"

CHAPTER 44
Holly

I SAT IN THE HOSPITAL WAITING ROOM, KNEES PULLED UP tight against my chest. It was noisy and busy and full of people: patients waiting for care and medical professionals bustling about, doing their best to help and comfort them. It was the kind of place that Gramps always said was full of stories and ideas. But I didn't care about any of that right now.

My tears had more or less stopped once the nurse came out to tell me that Gramps was going to be okay and they only had a few more tests to run before I could see him, but my whole body felt hollowed out. I was exhausted and sad, and I just wanted to go home and have some hot cocoa by the Christmas tree. The Christmas tree that I hadn't even seen in real life yet.

What had I been thinking, trading places with Aviva all week? What if something truly bad had happened to Gramps and I hadn't been there for him? Feeling the start of tears again, I buried my face in my arms.

"Holly?"

I jerked my head up.

Aviva!

She was walking toward me, holding Bubbe's arm. She had taken off the wig and glasses that I'd last seen her wearing when we changed outfits at the center. "Are you . . . Is he . . . ?"

Sniffling, I jumped to my feet and threw my arms around my sister. "I'm so glad you're here."

"Me too," she said, squeezing me tight. "Mom's parking the car and then she'll be in. So . . . is Gramps . . . er, your grandpa . . . is he . . . ?"

"They say he's going to be okay. I'm hoping they let me see him soon."

I rubbed the tears from my eyes and looked at Bubbe, biting my lip. I braced myself for a moment of recognition.

But Bubbe just smiled and pulled me in for a hug, too.

"I'm Sylvia, Aviva's grandmother," she said. "We met at the ice-skating rink, remember?"

"Y-yes, of course I remember," I said, glancing with confusion at Aviva. My sister pointed a finger at her eyes. *Oh*, right. I guessed she couldn't tell that we were twins.

"I'm so relieved to hear that Ed is going to be all right," Bubbe said. "How are you holding up? Is there anything we can do for you?"

"I don't think so, thank you," I said. "My mom should be here soon."

"Holly?" called a nurse. "Holly Martin?"

I spun to face her. "That's me."

Her smile was soft and kind. "You can go see him now."

I squeaked out a thank-you as my whole body lightened. But as soon as I'd taken a few steps forward, I paused and looked back just as Aviva was helping Bubbe into a chair. My sister gave me an encouraging nod, and feigned pushing me forward with her hands.

Taking in a deep breath, I turned back to the nurse. "She can come, too, right?"

The nurse's expression turned sympathetic. "I'm afraid only

fami . . ." She hesitated, looking from me to Aviva. "Oh! I didn't realize. Yes, of course."

Aviva looked at me, her eyebrow raised as if to say, *If we do this, the jig is up.*

I nodded back, because all that mattered now was seeing Gramps.

Aviva took Bubbe's hand. "I'll be back soon, all right, Bubbe?"

"Well, I suppose . . ." she said, clearly confused, but Aviva and I didn't wait for her to start asking questions. We left Bubbe in the waiting room and followed the nurse through a set of swinging doors and down a hallway filled with machines and carts and wheelchairs. The whole place smelled like sharp antiseptic and reminded me of when my grandma died years ago. I was so young that I didn't remember a whole lot about it, but I definitely remembered the smell. It sent a chill up my spine and filled me with dread.

We reached a room with a chart hung on the wall outside with *Edward Martin* printed at the top. The nurse held the door for us. I grabbed Aviva's hand as we tiptoed inside.

Gramps was sitting up in the hospital bed. A pale green blanket was draped over his legs, and a tray with a half-eaten sandwich and unopened pudding sat next to him. A small TV hung in the corner of the room, showing a gingerbread house baking competition on mute.

Gramps turned his head to look at me. And even though he had a bandage on his forehead, his hair was a mess, and his eyes looked so tired there were actual purple spots beneath them, the smile he gave me was filled with so much love I could feel it taking up the entire hospital room.

Then he looked at Aviva, and his smile faltered. His eyebrows furrowed together. He brought one hand to his face and rubbed his eyes, then blinked at us again.

"Seven stitches in my head, but I didn't think I'd hit it *that* hard," he said. "Holly, could you call the nurse back in? It would seem that I'm seeing double."

"You're not seeing double, Gramps," I said, tugging Aviva forward until we were both standing at the foot of the bed. I took a deep breath. "This is Aviva. She's Bubbe—*Sylvia's* granddaughter. And . . ." Aviva and I looked at each other. "And we're pretty sure—no—*absolutely* sure—she's my twin sister. We were both adopted, and we share the same birthday, and—"

"Holly, please, slow down," said Gramps, holding up a hand. For a moment, he looked between us, studying our faces with disbelief. Finally he let out a slow breath. "Well, I'll be. You are identical, no doubt about it. That's . . . astounding." Understanding brightened his eyes. "That's why you were asking all those questions about twins being separated at birth."

I nodded.

He chuckled wryly. "Well. That is some plot twist indeed." His gaze scanned Aviva's face again. "It is a fine pleasure to meet you, Aviva. I'm sorry it has to be like this." He gestured at the hospital bed.

Aviva and I exchanged looks again, and she cleared her throat. "Actually . . . we have met before."

"Oh, I think I'd remember if I'd met my granddaughter's doppelgänger."

"Are you *sure*?" I said, scratching the back of my neck.

His frown deepened. "I beg your pardon?"

243

We told him everything. How it had been Aviva who had cut down the tree and posed for portraits. How Aviva had faked the stomachache at ice-skating to try to get Gramps and Mom away from her own family, so no one would figure us out. How Aviva had been living with them for days.

"Are you mad at us?" I asked once we'd told the whole story.

Gramps looked a little dazed, like he was replaying the last few days over in his head. His silence made me nervous.

But then . . . he started to laugh.

A big, boisterous, joyful guffaw. One I hadn't heard in a long time.

"Well—that certainly clears some things up!" he said. "Not the least of which is why Sherlock has been so cantankerous this week!"

Aviva made a face. "Cats usually like me, I swear!"

He looked from Aviva to me. Me to Aviva. "What a miracle this is," he said, suddenly serious, though happy tears were glinting in the corners of his eyes. "Two granddaughters, each one as kind and clever and talented as could be. I don't think I've ever felt so lucky in my life."

He stretched his arms out, and Aviva and I both ran around the sides of the bed and leaned in for a hug.

"I'm not mad," he said. "Though if either of you ever decide to go spend a week in the home of complete strangers again, I will feel strongly compelled to ground you until you're thirty."

"Duly noted," I said.

Aviva pulled away. "We were hoping to tell our families after the pageant. I thought it could be this fun, big reveal for the holidays." Her gaze flickered up to me, and I knew she was once again wishing that I was going to be in the pageant with her, but when I shook my head, she gave me a tiny nod of understanding.

"I won't tell a soul," Gramps promised. "Though I suspect Charlie will be here soon, so if you don't want her to see you together yet . . ."

"Right, I should go check on Bubbe anyway," said Aviva. "And let her know you're okay. Maybe she can visit you later? I think she has a crush," she added in a stage whisper.

Gramps coughed in surprise, though his eyes were twinkling. "Let *my friend* know she can visit anytime."

With a smile, Aviva turned to go.

"Aviva, wait," I said. She paused halfway to the door.

I smiled and went over to give her another big hug. Pageant or no pageant, letter or no letter. All I knew was that I didn't want to be fighting with my sister anymore.

"Thanks for coming," I said. "I love you. No matter what."

Aviva's hug was almost crushing, in the best way. "I'm sorry about that letter stuff, okay? I love you, too, sis. No matter what."

CHAPTER 45
Aviva

IT FELT SO STRANGE WAKING UP IN MY OWN BED, EVEN after just a few days away. I'd been on longer vacations, but I'd started to feel at home in Holly's room. And as I opened my eyes and looked around my own, I had to admit that it had been nice being in her clean and organized one.

Well, clean and organized until I got through with it. I cringed and laughed at the same time while I reached for my phone, looking over the texts between me and Holly from the night before.

She'd let me know that Gramps was doing better but the doctors wanted to keep him under observation for a while because of the head injury and they weren't sure when he'd get sent home. He might not be able to make it to the pageant.

But ur coming, right?

I'll try.

Something about her tone in those two little words told me we hadn't resolved everything. But it was the most I could hope for. I was about to text her now to get a status update but remembered that she wasn't exactly a morning person and might still be sleeping, so I'd have to be patient and text her later.

And also, we still had the letter to talk about.

I hadn't even put my phone down when a flash of blue pajamas came running into my room and jumped on my bed.

"I'm glad you're back," Aaron said, grinning at me. "Although Holly's pretty cool, too."

"Shhhh!" I hissed at him, glancing at the open door. Of course I'd told him everything when we got home from the hospital.

"Why is it still a secret?" Aaron asked.

Good question. "Because . . ." I sighed. "Even if we aren't going to do a big fancy pageant reveal like I'd hoped, I still want Holly to be here with me when we tell the family. It's her secret, too."

"But she isn't going to the pageant? Because of her grandpa?"

"Yes, that. But also, she never wanted to be in the pageant to begin with. She wrote my song for me, though, and a part of me kept hoping that maybe she'd want to perform onstage with me, too."

"Why doesn't she want to do it?"

I shrugged. "She gets stage fright."

Aaron nodded knowingly. "Me too. Being in front of crowds is scary."

I ruffled his hair. "For you. And I guess for Holly, too. But performing is life."

He frowned. "Not for everyone."

"Maybe not," I said. "But I think she *wants* to do it. And she has a great voice. That's what's so frustrating. I wish her fear wasn't holding her back from doing something amazing."

"So . . . you think that even if she's scared of doing something, she should do it anyway?"

I nodded. "That's what it means to be brave. But I can't force her. She has to decide for herself."

"Hey, kids," Mom said from the doorway. "Your grand-mother just called and wants to go to the mall. On the day before Christmas Eve, for some inexplicable reason. You want to go with her?"

"No, thanks!" Aaron jumped off my bed and zipped toward the door. "Benny said I could go skating with him again."

Mom looked at me, her eyebrows up.

"Sure. Why not?" What else did I have to do? And anyway, with our regular Sunday date falling on Christmas, we wouldn't be able to go to the mall since it would be closed.

"All right," Mom said. "I'll drop you off, but I'm not dealing with those holiday crowds. Bubbe'll need to Uber the two of you home."

THE MALL WAS BONKERS. IT MADE TOTAL SENSE THAT MOM would want no part of it. A zillion people weaving in and out of the crowds, arms filled with packages, on phones, frantic, the roar of so many people nearly drowning out the Christmas music being piped in from every corner.

"And why did you want to come to the mall on the busiest day of the year?" I asked Bubbe as we walked down the aisle, trying not to get jostled.

"I'd like to pick up something for Ed as a get-well gift," she said. "But also, I have to admit, I love the energy. Everyone is des-perate to finish shopping, but most people are in a good mood.

They have the gracious spirit of the season in them, and I just like to sit back and watch."

"Spirit of the season, I like that," I said. Then I looked at her sideways. "Wait a minute, do you want a picture with Santa? You might be a bit old to give him your list."

"Funny girl." She nudged me with her elbow. "Although there was maybe a time when I had Christmas envy. It's hard, I know, with so much focus on Christmas this time of year. It's easy for us to feel left out. The gifts, the music, the television—even at Rowena Village, which doesn't have a religious affiliation, they have a tree in the lobby and serve Christmas cookies for dessert. They may be delicious, but still . . ."

"It's everywhere," I agreed, looking around at the decorations that were strung all over the mall and in every store window. "So . . . why are we here again?"

"You're going to think this is meshuggeneh," she said.

If she was bringing out the Yiddish word for *foolish*, this was serious. "Maybe?" I admitted. "But tell me anyway."

She grabbed my hand. "When I'm here, amid all the Christmas, I feel very Jewish."

"Okay, Bubbe, that makes zero sense. It *is* meshuggeneh."

"I told you!" she laughed. "What I mean is, the decorations, the music, the hustle and bustle, the running around to get gifts, it's all lovely. But I can just sit back and enjoy it. Like a tourist. It's not my holiday."

A tourist. I'd thought the very same thing. She was so right. The more I'd learned about Christmas, as fun as it was, the more I felt my own Jewishness. Not because it was better, but because it fit me better. It was part of what made me . . . *me.*

"Since I started to lose my eyesight, I've come to appreciate this time of year even more. The Christmas lights on the houses, they are beautiful, even to these old eyes. I don't see them clearly anymore, but the way the colors blur together is special, too. And yet . . ." She grinned cheekily at me. ". . . they are never as beautiful to me as a menorah glowing in a window. I can see those, too. And it reminds me how much I love our customs. The menorah, the dreidel . . . the latkes! Don't you?"

I nodded. "Very much, Bubbe, very much."

"Good. Now come, let's go to the food court and see if we can get some candy cane lattes. Just because we don't celebrate Christmas doesn't mean we can't enjoy some Christmas treats."

"I like how you think," I said, putting an arm around her. "Although I'd like my latte to be eggnog."

We were halfway to the food court when I stopped in my tracks. "Bubbe, just a second."

Forget the wigs! Because there, in the window of the party store, were the most perfect pageant outfits I ever could have imagined.

I turned toward my grandmother. "Bubbe, I know it's almost a year away, but I'm going to need an advance on my bat mitzvah money."

CHAPTER 46
Holly

AT SOME POINT BETWEEN ME GOING OFF WITH THE DAVIS family and me coming home from the hospital, a bomb had gone off in my bedroom.

A bomb named Aviva, evidently.

When I first got home, mentally drained from the hospital and everything that had happened, I was annoyed. I'd barely had the energy to straighten out my bed covers before crashing into my pillows. Mom let me sleep in, and it was almost eleven by the time I finally woke up.

I wasn't ready to face the day yet, so I busied myself cleaning up the chaos in my bedroom. Soon I stopped being annoyed, and was actually grateful that I had something to do with my mind and hands. Putting clothes on hangers. Tossing out granola bar wrappers and empty juice boxes. Neatly pairing up my shoes on the rack in my closet. It was calming, in a way. Just going through the motions of putting my life back in order.

When the room was finished, I finally made my way out into the apartment. Mom was sitting at the table. She smiled when I came in.

"There's my sleep-in girl," she said. "For a minute there, I thought you might be evolving into a morning person."

"Nope," I said. "Everything is back to normal now."

Well . . . not everything.

"Have you heard from Gramps?"

"Yes, I called him while you were sleeping. He's doing well, but still tired. The doctors want to keep an eye on him for another day or two. But they're optimistic that he's going to be okay."

I sighed. "Is he going to miss Christmas?"

Mom took my hand. "I don't know, sweetheart. But we can always celebrate once he does get home."

"Okay," I said. "Can we go see him today?"

"Of course. Why don't you go get dressed? We can pick up donuts on the way. You know if there's one thing he's going to complain about, it's going to be the hospital food."

"Good idea," I said.

Mom probably didn't need to know that I'd already eaten my bodyweight in jelly donuts this past week.

"THE DOCTORS WILL TRY TO TAKE ALL THE CREDIT FOR saving my life," said Gramps, licking glaze from his fingers, "but I'm telling you now, it was this bear claw that really did the trick."

"A good appetite and a good sense of humor," said Mom. "You must be feeling better." She gathered up our napkins. "I'm going to go get a coffee. Can I bring you anything else?"

"I'm fine. Thank you, Charlie."

As soon as Mom left, I scooted my chair closer to Gramps so my knees were pressing into the mattress. "You're really feeling better? No headaches or blurry vision?" I'd done some panic-googling on concussions during our drive this morning.

"I'm feeling fine," he said. "I've got some bruising from where I fell, and I'll need to come back to have my stitches taken out once the cut on my head is healed. But all things considered, I got lucky. No broken bones. Nothing that's going to keep me down for long."

I took his hand. "I was really scared when you fell."

"I know. I know. But it's all okay now." He gave my hand a comforting squeeze.

I looked down, guilt tightening my throat at what I was about to say. I tried to swallow it back down, but it just kept creeping up again. "Gramps . . ." I said. "I hope you won't be angry with me for saying this, but after what happened, I've been thinking, and . . ." I cleared my throat and dared to meet his eye. "I wonder if maybe it does make sense for you to live at Rowena Village, instead of with us?"

His eyebrows ticked upward, but otherwise his expression remained neutral. "Your mother put you up to this, did she?"

"No!" I gave a hasty shake to my head. "I swear, she hasn't said anything. But I just keep thinking about how you looked when you fell. You seemed so confused and shaky, and the blood, and I thought . . . if it happened at home . . . I don't know that I could have helped you. I was so scared already, just think how scared I would have been if I was trying to help you all by myself. But because there were nurses there, they were able to step in and—"

"Holly, Holly." Gramps reached forward with his other hand too, so that both of mine were enclosed in his. "It's okay, my little Holly Tree." He smiled softly. "I'll admit, I've been having some of these same thoughts myself. And being here in the hospital, eating this awful food, it's certainly proven one thing." He scowled at the tray of meat loaf beside him. "That food at Rowena Village was far superior to this rubbish."

I laughed. "I didn't want to say it around Mom, but I thought that fettuccine was actually pretty good."

"Dare I say, more than decent, even." Gramps winked at me, then sighed and leaned back into his pillow. I could tell he was starting to get tired. "But you're right. If this had happened while I was at home, alone or even with just you there . . . things could have been a lot worse. It would be good for me to have more assistance. On top of all those 'perks' your mom's been hammering on about. Bingo nights, ice cream socials, blah blah blah." He rolled his eyes, resigned. "Your mother will be insufferable once I tell her that maybe she was right all along."

I grinned, even as tears were pricking my eyes. "But, Gramps . . . I really am so sorry. I shouldn't have gone off with Aviva's family. I shouldn't have lied to you. You could have needed me, and now . . . what if . . ." I nearly choked on a sob. "What if this was our last Christmas together? What if I wasted it? I just ran off and abandoned you and—"

"Now, now," said Gramps, pulling me against him again. I buried my face into his shoulder. "It's all right, my Holly Tree. Everything is all right."

He let me cry until I was all cried out, rubbing my back. Finally, when I had nothing left but sniffles, he took my face into his hands and rubbed away what was left of the tears. "This wasn't our last Christmas together. Maybe I won't be at the apartment next year, but I won't be far, and we'll visit each other all the time. And maybe you can help out with the pageant again next year."

I nodded, but I was still feeling sad about the idea of Gramps not being home during the holidays next year, and upset with myself for spending so much of this Christmas season with Aviva's family. I was definitely not thinking about the pageant. "I'm really going to miss you."

"Not half as much as I'm going to miss you." The wrinkles around his eyes deepened as he let go of my hand so he could brush some of my new bangs away from my eyes. "We have a couple of weeks, though. Nothing will happen until after New Year's. I need my holiday with my Holly Tree, don't I?"

I smiled at him, though my vision was still watery.

"Besides, let's look at the bright side," Gramps went on. "Rowena Village does have that library . . ."

My smile became a little less forced. "I haven't seen it, but I can't wait to. And you know I'll come visit you all the time! For Scrabble nights, and fettuccine! Plus, *Sylvia* will be there . . ." I said, not even bothering to hide the teasing in my voice.

He narrowed suspicious eyes at me. "Don't tell me that you and your sister were playing matchmaker all this time."

"What? No! I swear, we had nothing to do with that. You and Sylvia found each other all on your own." I beamed. "But I can tell she really likes you."

"Yes, well. For a long time, I never thought I'd feel like I'd want to spend time with a special someone again. Not since your grandma passed. But . . . I enjoy Sylvia's company. And you're right. Having a friend there won't hurt."

"A *friend*. Sure." I gave him a big Avivacious wink.

He grunted. "Enough of that, young lady. How is your sister? I woke up this morning wondering if I'd dreamed it all."

"She's good, I think. I've been texting her with updates. But . . ." I picked at a thread on my sleeve. "Actually, before your fall, we kind of had a fight. And we haven't talked about it, with everything going on, and I'm not really sure where we stand now."

"Now that you have a sibling, I think you'll come to find that this is par for the course. Siblings fight sometimes. It doesn't mean you don't love each other."

I nodded. I knew Aviva loved me, and I loved her, but that didn't make this hollow feeling in the pit of my stomach go away.

"What was the fight about?" Gramps asked.

I was about to mention the letter, but I couldn't talk to Gramps about it while he was still in the hospital. I didn't want to risk making him upset.

"She wants me to be in the pageant with her," I said. "I wrote her an original song for it, and she keeps saying how much fun it would be to perform it together. But, Gramps, you know I get scared. You remember the *Charlotte's Web* debacle in third grade, right? I'm not made for the stage. I feel sick just thinking about being in front of all those people. But Aviva *loves* performing, and she's really good at it and she's a natural and wants me to do it with her." I had to stop for a breath. "But I'm . . . well, I *wouldn't* be good."

"And you have no interest in performing in the pageant with your sister? As in," he paused to stare right into my eyes, "if you weren't afraid, you still wouldn't want to do it?"

I looked down at my hands, and tried to really think about the question. Normally my immediate fear of performing made it impossible to even think about what it would be like if I wasn't afraid.

"I mean, it would be fun to do the big reveal for our families," I said. "That was Aviva's dream all along. That the two of us would walk out onstage together and surprise everybody. But . . ." I shrugged. "I'd probably puke or faint or worse. She doesn't understand how terrible it would be."

Gramps steepled his fingers together, the same way he did when he was trying to help me through a tricky writing problem. "Would you like my advice?"

A lot of adults would just give advice, regardless of whether or not you asked for it, and I liked that Gramps wasn't one of them. I took a deep breath and then nodded.

"I think it's important for us all to find our own path. It's a sign of maturity, figuring out what we enjoy and what makes us happy, rather than going with the crowd only because that's what's expected of us. If you truly don't want to be in the pageant, you shouldn't feel forced into it. And even though Aviva doesn't see your side of it right now, I think she'll come to understand why you made this decision."

I looked down at the blankets. In a way, he was saying what I wanted to hear. He was right. I shouldn't be forced to do something I didn't want to do. I was justified in my choice to not do the pageant, and Aviva should respect that. But for some reason, it didn't make me feel better at all.

"That said," Gramps went on, "I have to wonder . . . do you really not *want* to be in the pageant? Or is this choice being guided by fear?"

I swallowed hard and met his gaze. I *was* afraid. There was no doubt about that. And being afraid made it hard to figure out what my feelings were underneath.

Pressing my lips together, I tried to picture what it would be like if I did do the pageant. I tried to picture being onstage in the social hall. The crowd of people. The stage lights. The familiar music swelling around me. My heart started to pound and my palms began to sweat, just imagining it.

But then I thought of Aviva standing next to me. Grinning at me as we took each other's hands, right in front of everyone.

And yeah ... I did want that. It would be hard to step out from the curtains. It would be absolutely terrifying.

But with my sister at my side, I had a feeling I could do it. And it would be worth it.

"Gramps, will you excuse me? There's something I need to do."

Aviva?

Hi, sis! How's Gramps?

Much better.

♥ ♥ ♥

. . .

. . .

Ok.

. . .

. . .

I'll do the pageant.

. . .

. . .

Is this a joke?

No. Unless I puke. Then it will be a bad joke.

Really? U will do it? Really REALLY?

Yes, really.

OMG SISTER I LOVE YOU SO MUCH AND IT WILL BE EPIC
AND OMG!!!

Ha ha. So you're excited?

OH AND ALSO:

Where did those come from?

I saw them @ the mall and hoped u'd change ur mind!

YOU ARE RELENTLESS. But they are beautiful and perfect. Thank you!

Thank Bubbe, she bought them!

What about song? It's only about Hanukkah! Won't have time 2 change & memorize!

I have an idea. But we'll have to enlist your brothers and I'm going to have to raid my mom's craft supplies.

Glitter? I'm in!

😳 You'd better call me.

CHAPTER 47
Aviva

WHERE IS HOLLY? WHERE IS HOLLY? THE WORDS KEPT whirling around and around in my head. But seriously, where was she? The pageant had already started, and my sister hadn't arrived. The several texts I'd sent remained unanswered—I knew because I was checking approximately every four seconds from my spot in the wings.

The pageant had opened with the Rowena Village Choir—made up of residents—singing "Silent Night," which was nice but I couldn't focus on it because *where was my sister?*

Of course, I hoped Gramps was okay, but what I was really worried about was that Holly had let her nerves get the better of her and she wasn't going to come after all.

Please, Holly, if you can pick up my twin telepathy, don't bail! I sent out into the universe. It was a long shot, but I was desperate!

"Sorry, sorry! I'm here! I'm sorry!"

I pivoted to see Holly standing in the darkness of backstage, out of breath and looking frazzled.

Twin telepathy was a thing!

I gave her a hug, partly because she looked like she needed it and partly out of my own relief.

"I'm so glad you're here!" I whispered into her ear, not wanting to disturb the performers. "I was worried you might not show."

She pulled back, looking sheepish. "Don't think I didn't con-sider it, but no. I'm committed to it. To you. No, I'm committed to *us.* Love your Hanukkah sweater, by the way. Blue looks great on you. Please tell me you brought mine."

"Of course I did!" I dug out the mass of red knitted fabric from the bag at my feet and thrust it at her. "Quick, put this on over your tee."

Holly didn't hesitate, and—presto chango!—she was ready for the pageant.

"It's perfect," I said. "I have such great taste in ugly holiday sweaters!"

She looked down at herself, then up at me, and grinned. "Agree."

"So, where were you?"

"Mom was running late. She had to drop me off on her way to the hospital." Her smile faltered. "Gramps won't be able to make it."

We'd been worried that might happen but had learned the center was livestreaming the pageant. "She has the link, though, right? So they can watch?"

Holly bobbed her head. "It won't be the same but . . ."

"No, but at least he'll be able to see you."

"Us," Holly corrected me.

"Holly Aviva?" Doris whispered, coming up beside us, her eyes down on her clipboard that was lit up by the lamp strapped around her forehead. "We've got your music queued—"

Her sentence broke off as she looked at me. And then Holly. And then back to me.

Her mouth fell open. "Oh my word. There are *two* of you?"

Holly and I exchanged a glance and then turned back to her and nodded.

"Aviva," I said, pointing at myself.

"Holly," she said, doing the same.

"We're twins," I explained unnecessarily.

Doris blinked several times and then shook her head. "Okay, fine. I haven't got time to even think. Just tell me you're going on after the pyramid and that you're still using that song file you sent over."

"Yes. And we're doing the number together."

Doris nodded. "Remember to smile!" she said, then disappeared further backstage.

Holly beamed at me. "Poor Doris."

"I know," I said, leaning into her. "I feel bad that we didn't tell her sooner, but . . ." I shrugged.

Her smile dissolved as she blew out a breath. "I'm freaking out, Aviva. That's normal, right?"

I laughed. "Totally normal. When I start to get nervous, I tell myself it's just my body getting ready to perform. That adrenaline is a good thing." I took her hand. "Do you want to peek at the audience?"

Her eyes widened. "No, I do not! Adrenaline might be a good thing for you, but I really might throw up. Can we just watch the performances from the wings? Maybe that will distract me."

I wrapped my arms around her. "We've totally got this. And I'm going to be with you every step of the way, sending you my best calming vibes."

She nodded, like maybe I'd helped. Although the truth was, I was pretty nervous, too.

CHAPTER 48
Holly

THE PAGEANT WAS GOING WELL. THERE WERE SO MANY fun skits and songs and dances, that for brief moments I forgot to be afraid! But then Doris appeared again, still looking put out by the discovery that Aviva and I were two different people. "All right, Holly Avi—er . . . Holly *and* Aviva. You're up next. Your song is already queued up, so be ready!"

She walked off without waiting for our response.

"Well," said Aviva. "I guess I better go get in position. Are you ready?"

"No," I said with a nervous laugh. "But I'm doing this anyway."

Aviva grinned. "I'm proud of you, sis. You're going to be great, I promise." Then she gave a little squeal and hurried off behind the back curtain so she could take her spot on the other side of the stage—*stage left*, she'd told me, in theater terms.

I inched closer to the stage, taking care to stay behind the curtains so the audience couldn't see me. The kids onstage were just about done with their "O Tannenbaum" skit. The human pyramid was complete, except for the star. I was nervous for them, because I had yet to witness this going well in rehearsals. But I was also distracted by my own nerves. My stomach was churning, and I was having bad flashbacks to third grade. I'd barely been able to eat anything all day, which I might have been grateful for if it all started to come up . . . which felt like it could happen at any minute.

Onstage, the little boy in his bright-yellow outfit playing the star started climbing up on the backs of the kids on their hands and knees, making up the center of the tree. It was a nice momentary distraction. I held my breath, squeezing my fingers tight in hopes he would actually—

Yes! He was up! For one blissful moment, O Tannenbaum had its star!

And then one of the kids in the bottom row whooped in giddy surprise, and they all started laughing, and the tree collapsed right there in the middle of the song.

Luckily, no one seemed to be hurt, and everyone was laughing so hard they forgot about singing. The audience was loving it—making it an even harder act to follow.

The song finished, and the kids took their bows, then scurried off the stage, pouring around me in the wings.

And . . . *This is it.* Aviva and I were next.

My heart pounded and I felt suddenly dizzy and hot. I wiped my hands down the front of my sweater.

I looked out at the audience, and there was Benny in the front row with his cue cards. I nodded at him that it was time. He stood up and came closer to the stage so we could see the new, revised lyrics to the song that Aviva and I had written.

We'd barely had time to write it, let alone memorize it, so we'd had to bring in help. We'd asked Aaron first, since he already knew about us, but he'd refused, so, without the time to convince him, we'd had no choice but to ask Benny.

Thankfully, he'd been on board after we'd explained everything and answered his gazillion questions.

The first notes of the song began to play over the speakers. I glanced up to see Aviva emerge into the lights. Her smile was at full wattage as she strode boldly across the stage. She started to sing, her voice so strong and beautiful, I could sense the entire audience leaning forward in their seats, like moths to her flame.

Light the menorah in the window,
Burning bright for all to see.
Now that Hanukkah has arrived,
In the kitchen we will be . . .

My nerves started to fade as I watched her, amazed and filled with pride that this absolute superstar was my sister! I only wished in that moment that Gramps could be here to see it live. He would have loved this.

Frying latkes while the dreidel whirls,
But it's not the only holiday for these girls . . .

Aviva turned toward me and swept out her hand in my direction.

My heart leaped. I took a deep breath.

That was my cue.

CHAPTER 49
Aviva

HOLLY HESITATED.

Oh no. I was sure she was either going to vomit or run away. But then, as I held the note on *girls* and extended my hand toward where she stood at stage right, she took a deep breath and began to walk dramatically out of the wings to join me onstage.

Focused on her as I was, I still heard the loud gasps from my parents in the front row. It took all I had to stay focused on the song and my sister. My amazing, brave sister, who turned toward the audience (or at least to where Benny stood with the cue cards) and began to sing.

Deck the halls and pour eggnog,
Put the star up on the tree.
Light a fire with the yuletide log,
A burning symbol of warmth and family.
The radio might be playing "Let It Snow" . . .
But it's everyone's season to make it glow!

We looked at each other for half a second before we both turned toward the audience and sang the chorus together.

Lights and candles they are twinkling,
Shining brighter than the stars.
The menorah and the tree

Are both a part of who we are.
It's time for us to celebrate—
Hurry, sis! Let's not be late!
With warmth and love and lots of snow—
It's time for us to let it glow.

We'd barely gotten through the first line of the chorus when the audience began cheering. Holly still looked terrified, but she was doing it. My sister was doing her scariest thing, and I'd never been so proud. I looked out at the crowd again, and there was my family: Mom and Dad and Bubbe right up front, and Benny off to the side with the cards. But wait . . . where was Aaron?

Just then, the applause got even louder. Something grabbed my attention to my left. Still singing, I glanced over, and to my surprise, there was Aaron. My shy little kid brother, wearing a dreidel costume made out of a cardboard box. And he was spinning and spinning around the stage, arms out, *being* the dreidel.

I nearly sputtered in proud laughter, but somehow managed to keep singing, leading Holly to her next verse.

CHAPTER 50
Holly

IT TOOK ALL MY FOCUS AND WILLPOWER TO KEEP SING-ing when I really wanted to laugh at how absolutely adorable Aaron was in his homemade dreidel costume! Something about being onstage with him and Aviva together made my shoulders relax, and the tight knot in my stomach finally began to unwind.

Our traditions might be different—
We wouldn't change them if we could.
Jelly donuts and gingerbread,
They both taste oh so good!

My body was on autopilot as I mirrored Aviva's sweeping hand gestures. Benny turned to the next card, and Aviva launched into her next verse.

So let's gather, me and you,
To share our customs old and new.
On every present tie a bow,
Break out the dreidels and mistletoe——
It's time to let it glow!

I sang with everything inside me as Aviva and I launched into the second chorus and Aaron spun and twirled around the stage.

The menorah is oh so bright,
And the tree lights up the night.

Aviva and I walked toward each other, meeting in the middle of the stage and taking each other's hands. Aviva was effervescent, entirely in her element, and I had a sudden moment of understanding. *This.* This *is why she loves performing.*

I pulled my gaze away from her, glanced at the card, and then looked out into the audience as I sang the next part.

On both Hanukkah and Christmas Day,
It's time for us to celebrate
With warmth and love and lots of snow—
You and me, we'll let it glow.

My attention landed on Aviva's family. They felt like my family now, too.

And right now—their faces. *Their faces!*

Confusion. Disbelief. Utter shock. And that was only the beginning.

'Tis the season to honor both our pasts
And shout it to the world, together at long last.
Now we've found each other, we'll never be apart.
We're so much more together, let the celebration start!

As Aviva sang the words, so powerfully it sent a magical chill down my spine, I noticed the two people sitting next to Bubbe.

My heart leaped. Mom . . . and Gramps! They were here!

Mom looking every bit as stunned as Aviva's family did, and Gramps . . . well, he just looked amazingly proud.

I started to get choked up and worried for a second that I wouldn't be able to make it through the final chorus. But then I looked at my sister, and somehow I found my voice.

CHAPTER 51
Aviva

It's time to let it glow—
This is who we are,
Together we will glow.
Shining brighter than the stars.
On both Hanukkah and Christmas Day,
It's time for us to celebrate
With warmth and love and lots of snow—

WE SANG THE FINAL WORDS TOGETHER, AND I WAS ALREADY sad that it was almost over. This had been the best performance of my life. Even Broadway would pale in comparison to singing with my sister. But I hardly had time to think about that because then it was my turn to belt out the very last line:

You and me, we'll let it glow.

I held the final note as long as I could as the audience erupted into applause and many people even got to their feet. A STANDING OVATION!

Holly and I smiled at each other as she gave my hand a tight squeeze. We turned back to the audience (that was STILL applauding and whistling) and took our bows.

But wait. "Benny!" I called, waving him up onto the stage. Then I looked into the wings, and there was Aaron. "You too! Get over here!" I yelled, gesturing until he shyly came out onto stage to more applause.

The four of us took a bow. Well, three of us did. Aaron tried, but it didn't quite work because he was wearing a giant cardboard box. Instead, he did a little squat-curtsey, making the crowd laugh, even while they were still clapping.

"Holly! Aviva!" I heard from the wings. I glanced over to see Doris trying to shoo us off the stage. She was surrounded by all the kids who were waiting to put on the nativity play.

I looked out at the crowd—the rest of our families—and I couldn't wait one more second. I led Holly, Benny, and Aaron down the front steps and right over to the front row.

Bubbe came toward me first, pulling me so tightly into her arms that I was legit worried she was going to crush a rib. "Bubbeleh, bubbeleh," she said into my ear, her voice cracking. "I am so proud of you."

I couldn't have said anything if I'd wanted to, because she wasn't the only one choked up with emotion.

"But," she whispered, not letting me go, "what is going on with this other girl? Isn't that Ed's granddaughter? Why is everyone so upset?"

I pulled back out of the hug and looked at her. She had no idea. She'd seen the two of us up on the stage and couldn't see that we were identical. I glanced over at Holly who was hugging Gramps.

A throat cleared, drawing my attention to my parents.

Who were staring at me. Some might say *glaring*.

In all our planning and practicing for the pageant, Holly and I hadn't discussed what we would do or say at this point.

I glanced over at my sister. *Now what?*

"So, thank you, Holly and Aviva for that lovely number," Doris announced into the microphone. "If we could all please take our seats so we can continue on with the evening's program."

For a second it looked like my mom was going to march Holly and me out into the hall for explanations, but instead she just glowered and took her seat so we could watch the rest of the show.

With no available seats in the front row, Holly and I shrugged at each other and sat down on the floor in front of our families.

"That was amazing!" she whispered. "You are amazing."

"*We* are amazing," I corrected her.

The huge smile on her face told me she agreed.

AFTER THE NATIVITY PLAY, THE CHOIR RETURNED TO END the pageant with their beautiful rendition of "Have Yourself a Merry Little Christmas." Once it was over, everyone was invited to the back of the social hall for refreshments. Our families: the Davises and the Martins—had all moved as a pack to a quiet(er) corner of the social hall to sort out everything that had been revealed, first taking the time to explain to Bubbe what all the fuss was about.

"Twins?" she said, bewildered. "Identical twins? I could tell there was a resemblance, but . . ." Trailing off, she took Holly by both shoulders and squinted, peering intently into her face and smoothing the bangs from her forehead. "Unbelievable."

Then she turned to me and took hold of my hand. I tried

to imagine what she saw when she looked at us. How much of her vision was lights and shadows, or colors all blurred together? I knew a lot of details were lost on her, but maybe the details weren't important in that moment. She was seeing me and my sister, together, for the first time. Maybe that was enough.

"My gramps called it a miracle," Holly whispered.

Bubbe sniffled and nodded. "Indeed. A Hanukkah and Christmas miracle, all in one. The best kind."

Holly and I grinned at each other.

"So wait a minute," Dad said. "You two swapped places and slept in each other's beds and fooled us all for—"

"Not me!" Aaron blurted out, spraying bits of shortbread cookie everywhere. "I knew it all along!"

That wasn't totally true, but he *had* figured it out when no one else had. Mom, Dad, and Charlie were already on the edge of freaking out about the whole thing, so I figured the less I spoke, the better.

"Aaron, please," Mom said, pinching the bridge of her nose, which was the face she made right before she delivered a grounding sentence. "We'll deal with the *swap*"—she said *swap* as though it was another kind of four-letter word—"later. What I'm really interested in right now is—" Her voice caught, suddenly full of emotion.

"How did we not know?" Dad finished for her, shaking his head. "We never would have kept this from you if we'd known."

"Same here," Charlie said, wiping tears from her eyes. "I'm so sorry you never knew about each other."

Holly and I traded looks. "It's okay," I said. "We know about each other now."

I was about to mention that there was probably an explanation in the letter from our birth mom, but Holly and I hadn't had a chance to discuss the letter since our fight, and it didn't seem like the right time to bring it up.

"Also . . ." Holly said, getting everyone's attention. She cleared her throat. "To make up for lost time, I was wondering if maybe Aviva could come sleep over tonight?"

I bounced eagerly on my toes. I *loved* slumber parties! But also . . . "Are you sure? It's Christmas Eve."

Holly nodded. "I know. This way, you can be there for Christmas morning!"

I made a face. "But . . . I'm Jewish. I don't really celebrate Christmas. I was just being a Christmas tourist before."

She shrugged. "So you can Airbnb Christmas. You don't have to move in, just have a little Yuletide getaway. But mostly I just want to spend time with you. As much time as I've been with your family this week, you and I haven't seen each other hardly at all. You want to, don't you?"

I smiled. "I would love to! If we aren't grounded until Groundhog Day . . ."

We both looked hopefully at our parents.

Charlie seemed to think about it for a moment, then shrugged. "It's fine with me if it's fine with Aviva's parents."

My parents did not look like they wanted to let me off the hook for our switch and, oh, also that whole not-telling-them-I-had-discovered-that-I-had-an-identical-twin thing. But before they could say no, I said, "Please? Can I spend an evening with my identical biological sister that I never even knew I had until very recently so we can, as Holly says, make up for lost time?

It has been a whole twelve years we've been separated, after all. Practically an eternity!"

Mom rolled her eyes. "Laying it on a bit thick, Aviva, don't you think?"

"I am an actress!" I said, even adding some jazz hands. "So, can I?"

She shared a look with Dad and then he nodded and said, "Yes, you may go. Under one condition."

I resisted the urge to do a fist pump because I'd learned it's always best to hear conditions before celebrating.

But Dad looked at Charlie instead of me and said, "The condition is that tomorrow evening, assuming you don't have plans, you all join us for the final night of Hanukkah."

Charlie laughed. "Sold."

That's when I did the fist pump.

CHAPTER 52
Holly

I'D ALWAYS FELT LIKE THERE WAS SOMETHING EXTRA enchanting about Christmas morning. Waking up to find all the sparkly presents with colorful bows and curly ribbons that magically appeared beneath the tree while I was sleeping. Me and Mom in our coziest pajamas and Gramps in his ratty old robe and slippers, sipping coffee and hot cocoa with extra dollops of whipped cream. Oohing and aahing over every little gift in our stockings. The sweet smells wafting through the apartment while cinnamon rolls baked in the oven. I looked forward to these traditions every year.

But there was nothing quite so magical as waking up Christmas morning to find my twin sister sitting cross-legged on the bed, beaming down at me.

And . . . okay, it might have been a *little* creepy.

"Don't move," Aviva said when she noticed me stirring.

I stilled. Aviva's smile was a little bewildered and I realized that she, too, was sitting as motionless as a statue.

"What's going on?" I whispered. "You're not taking unflattering pictures of me sleeping, are you?"

She rolled her eyes. "Sherlock is letting me pet him," she whispered back.

I heard it then—Sherlock's telltale purr coming from the foot of the bed.

I slowly sat up. The cat was curled up between me and Aviva, gamely allowing her to rub his belly.

"Wow, belly rubs," I said. "That is a true sign of trust."

"I knew I'd win him over eventually."

I watched my sister getting her fill of kitty love for a while, but the anticipation for the start of Christmas grew stronger with every moment until I just couldn't wait any longer.

"So?" I finally asked. "Are you ready for Christmas?"

"So ready!" she said, scratching Sherlock under his neck. But then her expression seemed to grow solemn and she pulled her hand away from the cat. "But first . . . I have something for you. Not a gift . . . That will come later. But . . . here."

Aviva went to her overnight bag and pulled out a familiar envelope. It was looking more wrinkled around the edges than when I'd seen it over FaceTime before, but I knew immediately what it was.

I swallowed hard, eyeing our birth mother's handwriting.

"This is yours," said Aviva, sitting next to me and setting the letter in my lap. She smiled softly at me. "Whenever you're ready to see what she wrote to us, I'll be ready too. Whether that's tomorrow or on our thirteenth birthday, or even if it's never! I can wait. All I ask is that when you are ready to see what she had to tell us, we'll read it together."

I held the envelope between my hands. Felt the all-too-real crunch of twelve-year-old paper that smelled a bit musty.

"What do you think it says?" I asked.

Aviva shrugged. "Probably it talks about us—tells us that we have an identical twin."

"Maybe it explains how we were separated," I said.

"And why she gave us up for adoption to begin with."

"It probably talks a lot about how much it hurt for her to give us up. How much she loves us."

"And hopes our adoptive families will provide us with the wonderful life that she couldn't. Or something like that."

I met my sister's eyes and took in a slow breath. "It might say all of that . . . or none of that. But all that really matters to me is that I found you. We have each other now. Everything else in this letter can wait. Right?"

I was worried she would get upset again, but Aviva just leaned closer, giving me a tight hug. "Of course it can wait, sis. We have each other now. And I'm not going anywhere."

Pulling away, she held her hand out for the letter. "Want me to put it back in the filing cabinet?"

"Let's do it together."

We climbed out of bed and poked our heads out into the hallway. No sign of Mom or Gramps so far, but that was normal. Christmas was probably the only day of the year when even *I* became a morning person and was up before anyone else.

"Come on," I said, grabbing Aviva's arm and tugging her into the living room.

And there was the tree, gorgeously decorated and all lit up, its boughs stretching out over the mountain of presents that . . . yep, had magically appeared. We both paused to stare at it, but I couldn't help sneaking a look at Aviva, pleased to see her wide-eyed expression.

"Wow," she breathed. "That's . . . *a lot*."

I tried to see my holiday through Aviva's eyes. Though most of the gifts were gorgeously wrapped, a few were left open and visible around the tree. I saw a new pair of beautiful white ice skates leaning against one wall; a brand-new scratching post for

Sherlock; and for Gramps, a framed photo sitting on the table beside his chair. It showed the Christmas portrait they'd taken with Aviva, but now a picture of me had been photoshopped in! I wondered when Mom had time to do that and thought I should probably give her credit for being more tech-savvy than I realized. Plus, I could already picture that photo front and center in Gramps's new apartment at Rowena Village.

I heard Aviva gasp, but when I glanced at her, she wasn't looking at the tree or presents. She was looking at the stockings on the fireplace mantel. I followed her gaze. The stockings had our names hot-glued onto them in shiny green fabric, because Mom sure loved her crafts: Charlie, Ed, Holly, and . . . *Aviva* (with extra glitter).

It was a lot. And yeah, I definitely looked forward to the presents and the stockings every year, both giving *and* receiving them. But Christmas was more than that. It was about being with the people I loved the most—Mom, Gramps, and now Aviva. It was about making memories together and sharing our favorite traditions. It was about kindness and generosity and spreading good tidings to everyone we met.

I was lost in thoughts about how much I loved my holiday when I heard rustling down the hall.

"Quick! The letter!" I whispered.

Aviva hurried over to the filing cabinet and pulled open a drawer. Lickety-split, she'd tucked the letter away and shut the drawer, just as Mom appeared, grinning brightly. "Merry Christmas," she said, completely oblivious to Aviva's snooping. She gave us each a hug. "And Happy Hanukkah! I know stockings aren't a Hanukkah thing, but I couldn't not put something out for you."

"I love it!" said Aviva. "Thank you!"

We beamed at each other, then helped Mom prepare our traditional cinnamon rolls. Once they were in the oven, Aviva and I made some hot cocoa while Mom brewed the coffee. By the time we were ready, Gramps had gotten up, too. He had taken the bandage off his head. There was still a bruise around the visible stitches in his brow, but even though it looked bad, I was grateful that it hadn't been much worse. And when he'd joked that he looked like Frankenstein's monster, I knew that meant he was feeling better.

We opened our stockings, finding matching cozy socks, candy canes and jelly beans, yummy smelling soaps, and a big juicy orange buried deep in the toe of each one.

We all laughed when Aviva pulled out her net bag full of foil-wrapped coins and yelled, "Hanukkah gelt!"

I had no idea how Mom had managed to fill a stocking for Aviva on such short notice, but it made the morning extra magical to share this tradition with her. Although, who knows? Maybe it had been Santa himself. I wasn't about to ask.

"By the way, Aviva," said Gramps, when Mom went to check on breakfast, "one of the nurses at the hospital mentioned to me that the local children's theater is going to be holding auditions for a performance of *Cats* next month."

Aviva's eyes got as wide as the cinnamon rolls Mom was currently pulling from the oven. "Really? I'm so there!"

Gramps chuckled. "It would be a *cat*astrophe if they didn't cast you in a leading role."

Okay, terrible puns? Gramps was definitely feeling better.

"I was born to be Grizabella!" Aviva singsonged and then turned to me. "Will you try out too?"

I recoiled. "No way! That pageant was a one-time deal. I'm just going to be a spectator from here on out."

Aviva's nose wrinkled. "I thought you had fun!"

"I did. And I'm glad I did it with you." And that I'd be able to finish that assignment about facing my biggest fear and being brave. "You know I'm happier writing than performing. But I'll be in the audience for every single one of your shows."

"I guess I can accept that. And speaking of writing . . ." She waggled her eyebrows at me.

"Oh yeah! I'll be right back!"

I rushed to my bedroom, returning a minute later with a package wrapped in white craft paper and covered in stickers.

"This is from me and Aviva," I said, handing it to Gramps.

"For me?" He tore off the paper, revealing the little handmade book inside. The cover, decorated with an illustration of a train in the snow, read *The Christmas Caper* by Holly Martin and Aviva Davis.

We had worked on it until late the previous night, long after Mom and Gramps thought we'd gone to bed. Aviva had helped me finish the story and had given me a great idea for the final climactic face-off between Santa and Barnabus. Once it was done, we typed it up and printed it out, turning the pages into this little booklet that, I thought, actually looked a lot like a real book. Given how little time we'd had, I was pretty impressed. We made a great team.

"A book!" said Gramps as he flipped it open. "And look! It's even been signed by the authors!"

Aviva nudged her shoulder into mine. "I told you he'd appreciate that."

Gramps grinned at us both. "Thank you. I can't wait to read it, and you know I will treasure it for all time."

"It will be collectible someday," said Aviva. "Once Holly becomes a famous author like you."

I blushed, but also sort of hoped that maybe she was right.

"Are we about ready to eat?" said Mom. "The cinnamon rolls are still warm, and if we wait too much longer, we risk spoiling our appetite for what I hear is a spectacular feast happening at your house tonight, Aviva."

Aviva preened. "It'll be the best! Holly might be burned-out on latkes, but I can't wait!"

"We're all really looking forward to it," said Gramps. "It was very thoughtful of your parents to invite us."

"We're family now," I said. "Maybe this will start a new tradition?"

"Yes! I love that idea! Martin-Davis family celebrations forever!" Aviva raised her hands in the air, and we gave each other high fives. But then her expression became confused. "Speaking of traditions . . . one thing has been bothering me."

"What's that?" I asked.

"This is the last day of the Christmas season." She gestured toward the window. "So when on earth are we going to go caroling?"

I blinked at her, then traded looks with Mom and Gramps, before looking back at Aviva. "Oh. Well . . . we don't really go caroling."

Aviva stepped back, stunned. "*What?* Why not?"

"I don't know. It's just not something we've ever done. Gramps?"

He shook his head. "I, for one, have never gone caroling. Charlie?"

"Nope." She shrugged. "And I don't think I know anyone who has."

"Sorry, sis," I said. "I guess there might be people who still go caroling as one of their traditions, but . . . I think it's more a Hallmark Christmas thing than a *real* Christmas thing."

"No caroling?" Aviva slumped dejectedly onto the sofa. "All this time I thought I'd get to go door to door, spreading my joy through song, only to find . . . it was nothing but *lies*!" She wailed melodramatically.

We all laughed, though to be honest, I wasn't entirely sure that she was acting.

CHAPTER 53
Aviva

AFTER WE SANG THE BLESSINGS AND LIT ALL EIGHT CANdles with the helper shamash candle, the final night of Hanukkah was filled with Mad Libs, playing dreidel, more latkes than anyone should ever consume, the telling of the story of the Maccabees, and laughter.

So. Much. Laughter.

And the most important thing the evening was filled with? Family. Both my immediate family and my new extended one.

It was perfect.

During dessert, Holly was telling her family the meaning of the jelly donuts, when Aaron appeared in his slightly beat-up cardboard dreidel costume and twirled around and around the room, singing the dreidel song and banging into furniture until Dad laugh-yelled at him to stop before he knocked over a lamp.

And somehow, in that moment, the night became even more perfect: when I looked through the doorway into the next room and saw Bubbe up on her tiptoes, giving Gramps a kiss.

I nudged Holly. "Look," I whispered as I jutted my chin toward the happy couple.

"Aw," she said, leaning into me. "And no mistletoe in sight. I'm calling that another holiday miracle." Then Holly actually *winked* at me, and I could tell I'd been rubbing off on her. "I'm so glad to be a Hanukkah tourist."

"You think this is awesome?" I said. "Wait until you're a Passover tourist!"

Her eyes widened. "Oh! Is Passover fun?"

"Uh . . ." I cringed. "I'm not really sure, to be honest. I don't think we've ever celebrated it."

"Oh," Holly said. "Okay. Well, I'm sure it will be great!"

"Plus," I went on, "Bubbe said she was going to pay for me to go to Jewish Sunday school. I'm going to sign up in the new year for that and bat mitzvah lessons because that's less than a year away. I can't wait! Another epic performance courtesy of Aviva Davis."

But it was going to be about more than just a performance. I was excited for that part of it, of course, but I couldn't wait to learn about the meaning of it all and more about what it meant to be Jewish.

"Oh, that's so wonderful! You're going to rock your bat mitzvah."

I did a shimmy. "Obviously."

My sister chuckled, and we looked around the table. Everyone was chatting, except for Benny and Aaron, who were sneaking more donuts while no one was paying attention. Not that anyone would have stopped them.

Aaron looked ridiculous with jelly and sugar all over his face. But what made my heart swell with love and pride was the memory of his dreidel dance during the pageant. He'd admitted to me after that it was seeing how brave Holly and I were to switch places that had inspired him to do it.

My sister had been brave, too, and I couldn't have been prouder.

I smiled at her, beaming love her way. "I adore our family. Not mine and yours, but *ours.*"

"Me too," she said, beaming that love right back at me. "Can I steal you away for a second?"

"Of course." I slid off my chair and gave her a sideways look. "What for?"

"I have something for you."

I glanced over at Mom and Dad. "We're going to do family presents after we clean up from dessert. Spoiler alert—they got you a bookstore gift card. But I have something for you too. It's in my bedroom, come on."

She stopped by the front hall to pick up a shopping bag and then followed me into my room. "I see you're still just as slobby here as you were in my room. Thanks for that, by the way."

I gave her a sheepish grin. "Sorry, but you have to take me as I am. I mean," I waved toward her, "I accept all your flannel."

Holly crossed her arms. "Oh really. Says the girl who is right now wearing one of my favorite flannel shirts. I didn't hear you complaining when you put it on at my house this morning."

"Pfft," I said, trying not to smile and mostly failing. "Do you want your present or what?"

"Yes, please," she said, sitting on my bed.

I reached into my bottom dresser drawer and pulled out the paper bag. "I didn't have time to wrap it, sorry."

She shrugged and took the bag. She slid out the notebook I'd bought at the mall, what felt like ages ago, right after I'd found out I had a twin sister.

Holly gasped when she saw it.

"Every writer needs lots of notebooks, right?" I said. "It's your favorite color. Well, close to your favorite color—they didn't have aquamarine exactly, but hopefully that works." I suddenly felt flustered, hoping I'd gotten her the right gift. "Merry Christmas, sis."

"I love it," Holly squeaked, smoothing her hand across the cover. "Thank you."

She stared at the notebook for another second and then put it down on my bed to hand me the bag she'd brought.

Now it was my turn to gasp when I pulled the shadow box frame out and saw that it was a collage. "Holly! When did you make this?"

"I've been thinking about doing it for a while and had a lot of the stuff already, but I did most of it yesterday before the pageant. It was a good distraction from Gramps being in the hospital ... and how nervous I was about performing. I put the finishing touches on it last night after you fell asleep."

I stared at the frame, taking it all in: the pictures of our sweaters from the pageant, a lock of hair taped on a piece of paper that had to be from her bangs, the lyrics to the song we'd performed together, and, right in the middle, the selfie we'd taken the first day we met.

I couldn't help it. I started bawling. It was perfect. It was everything I never knew I wanted. I jumped up off my bed and hung it on the wall, replacing the *Superstar* word cutout that I'd find a new home for later.

"Happy Hanukkah, Aviva," Holly said behind me.

I stared at the collage for a minute and then pulled Holly in for a hug. "I love it so much. But you know, the best gift I've gotten this year ... is you."

"Well, I should certainly hope so!" she said. Then her voice turned more serious. "Of course, I feel the exact same way."

Together, we headed back out to join our families in the living room. The menorah's candles flickered in the window, and the snow outside glistened from the colorful lights on the neighboring houses. It seemed in that moment that the whole world was glowing just for us . . . because this was our holiday.

Let It Glow

Light the menorah in the window,
Burning bright for all to see.
Now that Hanukkah has arrived,
In the kitchen we will be . . .
Frying latkes while the dreidel whirls,
But it's not the only holiday for these girls . . .

Deck the halls and pour eggnog,
Put the star up on the tree.
Light a fire with the yuletide log,
A burning symbol of warmth and family.
The radio might be playing "Let It Snow" . . .
But it's everyone's season to make it glow!

Lights and candles they are twinkling,
Shining brighter than the stars.
The menorah and the tree
Are both a part of who we are.
It's time for us to celebrate—
Hurry, sis! Let's not be late!
With warmth and love and lots of snow—
It's time for us to let it glow.

Our traditions might be different—
We wouldn't change them if we could.
Jelly donuts and gingerbread,
They both taste oh so good!

So let's gather, me and you,
To share our customs old and new.
On every present tie a bow,
Break out the dreidels and mistletoe——
It's time to let it glow!

The menorah is oh so bright,
And the tree lights up the night.
On both Hanukkah and Christmas Day,
It's time for us to celebrate
With warmth and love and lots of snow—
You and me, we'll let it glow.

'Tis the season to honor both our pasts
And shout it to the world, together at long last.

Now we've found each other, we'll never be apart.
We're so much more together, let the celebration start!

It's time to let it glow—
This is who we are.
Together we will glow,
Shining brighter than the stars.
On both Hanukkah and Christmas Day,
It's time for us to celebrate
With warmth and love and lots of snow—

You and me, we'll let it glow.

Acknowledgments

Writing this book turned out to be a period of pure joy for both of us, filled with wonderful bouts of laughter, merriment, and quite a lot of learning about each other's holidays right along with Aviva and Holly! We are so grateful for each other (!) and also for the incredible people who helped us bring the book to life and get it into the hands of readers.

Thank you to Liz Szabla for championing this book, seeing our vision, and taking it to the next level. And more big thanks to the rest of the Macmillan Children's team: Johanna Allen, Robby Brown, Mariel Dawson, Rich Deas, Sara Elroubi, Jean Feiwel, Carlee Maurier, Megan McDonald, Katie Quinn, Morgan Rath, Katy Robitzski, Dawn Ryan, Helen Seachrist, Naheid Shahsamand, Jordin Streeter, Mary Van Akin, and Kim Waymer.

Thank you to Celia Krampien for the most beautiful and heartwarming cover we could have hoped for, and to our incredible narrators, Rebecca Soler and Gabi Epstein, for bringing Holly and Aviva to life in audio.

Much gratitude to Danielle Joseph and Liza Wiemer for their very thoughtful reads to bring accuracy and authenticity to the entire Davis family.

Many thanks to Ana Deboo and Esther Reisberg for your keen eyes and much-appreciated fixing of our errors.

Thank you to Hilary McMahon, Joanne's agent and friend, for the ongoing support and especially for that phone call that turned into an idea that turned into this book.

Thank you to Jill Grinberg and her agency team for championing this book and helping to get it into the hands of readers the world over.

To our spouses and staunchest supporters:

Deke, Team Snow co-captain, chauffeur extraordinaire, fellow pet wrangler, best ever pitmaster, and the most supportive partner anyone could ever ask for. Thanks for embarking on this wild journey with me.

Jesse, fan club president, skilled carpenter, fellow child wrangler, not sure what a pitmaster is, and the second most supportive partner anyone could ever ask for. Thanks for embarking on this wild journey with me.

And lastly, thanks to *you*, Reader. We are so happy you chose to join us for this holiday.

Thank you for reading this Feiwel & Friends book.
The friends who made *Let It Glow* possible are:

Jean Feiwel, Publisher
Liz Szabla, VP, Associate Publisher
Rich Deas, Senior Creative Director
Anna Roberto, Executive Editor
Holly West, Senior Editor
Kat Brzozowski, Senior Editor
Dawn Ryan, Executive Managing Editor
Kim Waymer, Senior Production Manager
Foyinsi Adegbonmire, Editor
Rachel Diebel, Editor
Emily Settle, Editor
Brittany Groves, Assistant Editor
Maria W. Jenson, Designer
Helen Seachrist, Senior Production Editor

Follow us on Facebook or visit us online at mackids.com.
Our books are friends for life.